LAST DAYS IN PLAKA

Henriette Lazaridis

PEGASUS BOOKS

NEW YORK LONDON

LAST DAYS IN PLAKA

Pegasus Books, Ltd.
148 West 37th Street, 13th Floor
New York, NY 10018

First Pegasus Books cloth edition April 2024

Interior design by Maria Fernandez

Library of Congress Cataloging-in-Publication Data is available.

ISBN: 978-1-63936-561-6

10 9 8 7 6 5 4 3 2 1

Printed in the United States of America
Distributed by Simon & Schuster
www.pegasusbooks.com

For my parents

PART ONE

T his is not her story. She stole it from the young woman who did not realize until the end that it was hers.

She lived in a small apartment in the oldest quarter of an ancient city, the rent having been paid for in an act of charity. She had made a friend of the priest thanks to her frequent visitations to his little church, and he had come to learn of her financial straits and had managed to offer for free the small space with one bedroom and a window overlooking the square without making her feel shame. He needn't have worried. She was not a person much inclined to shame. On her daily walks down the neighborhood's ancient streets, she boasted to each shopkeeper or waiter of the enthusiastic reception she had received from the one before. She sometimes told these men of her good fortune to be taken in by the church, and even then she arranged the story to convince her listeners it was the church and not she herself who should be grateful of the arrangement. Her listeners were almost always men, for even in her advanced years she was possessed of classic Hellenic beauty—the same beauty of the statues in the new museum just a few streets from the little square. It was said in the neighborhood that on the day a giant crane had lifted the ancient statues from the old museum over the rooftops to deposit them into the new, the men had joined the old woman in the square to watch, looking from the marble forms aloft, to her, and back up again, remarking on the likeness.

When the young woman stopped at the old woman's apartment to deliver a basket of fresh figs from the priest's family while he was still at weekday service, no one would have expected her to stay for conversation, especially not the young woman herself who had something else to do. But our story thief, our beauty—Irini is what we will call her—invited the young woman up for tea and encouraged her to eat two figs from the basket and poured a glass of lukewarm water for her to drink, and she did not send the young woman down the stairs into the square until the rooftop cinema across the way had begun its early show and bats were swooping through the mulberry trees.

This is not the old woman's story. It is the story of the young woman who arrived that day with the first figs of the season to drop off and left to find her mobile alive with messages she had not even thought to listen for. *Where are U, Anna? Anna. Can't stay longer. C U later heading home.* Anna: we will give her this name as simple and symmetrical as that of the old woman. She put the mobile in the back pocket of her jeans and swung her leg over the motorbike she had locked to the lamppost many hours before and drove away.

Her friends did not in fact go home to the apartments where they lived still or again with their parents, crammed into the formerly gracious spaces with high ceilings and tall cupboards that had once held gowns and suits. They went instead from the square where they had messaged Anna to another square in another part of the city and forgot about Anna until she arrived on her bike, knowing she would find someone there to have a drink with. This was a run-down quarter of the city, once the location of silk mills where worms had munched on mulberry leaves in broad trays beneath glass ceiling panes. Now the streets were lined with decrepit houses that gave space to buzzing galleries and bars. Anna's friends sat at one of these, the one with the caged parakeet by the espresso machine, and looked up at her with mixed surprise and indignation. What happened to her? They'd given up. No, they hadn't gone home after all because what were they thinking, it was Friday. Not that it mattered to them what day of the week it was since none of them had jobs that adhered to any sort of weekday schedule. They were artists, musicians, actors. They were, like so many of their generation in the aftermath of the great economic crisis, unemployed.

Anna chained her motorbike to a railing and dragged a chair across the cement into place at her friends' table. She drew out cigarettes and her lighter from her jeans, lit one, sat back, and said, "Hey."

"We waited for you."

"I know. Sorry."

"You never picked up."

She said all this in its Greek equivalent, having learned the language early and quite thoroughly from her immigrant parents in the United States. She knew, for instance, that the Greek version of the casual *hey* of an American was to say, upon arriving, *come*.

Anna's friends didn't know how frequently she went to church, and she preferred to keep them in ignorance. It was not cool to be twenty-seven years old and attending the liturgy. It was not cool to like not only the scent of incense and the refreshing air of the tiny stone building with the plush red carpet down its stubby nave, but also the serene eyes of the icons and the priest's words promising of something exalted. So, she said only that she had had an errand and let the friends think she had been engaged in one of the many regular tussles with bureaucracy they all engaged in on their own behalf or for their parents. Perhaps she had been paying her parents' phone bill. Perhaps she had been registering her motorbike, or perhaps she had been in a pharmacy line for contraception. All of these could have taken long enough to have made her ignore her messages and meet her friends by accident and late.

When the waiter came, she ordered beer and listened to the conversation among her friends, but finally could not resist.

"I met this cool old lady. In Plaka," she said, naming the ancient city quarter with the little square and the rooftop cinema.

"OK."

The friends went back to their conversation.

"No, guys. She was really cool. Not what you're thinking."

"What are we thinking?" They laughed. "You met a Yia-Yiá."

They shrugged and went on talking. Their lives were populated with old women in the figures of their grandmothers and great-aunts, and Anna's news of meeting yet one more struck them as neither rare nor particularly desirable.

"No. I don't know," Anna said. "I wasn't going to stay. But she invited me in. She told me stories about Plaka. She's lived there her whole life."

"A snob, then."

"An aristocrat."

"No," Anna said. "I don't think so." She realized she did not know this to be true. The old woman's social class was muddled by her dependence on the church. But she must have been well-to-do once. In the apartment there were silver picture frames arrayed on a walnut sideboard and leather-covered books in a case. Her clothes were nothing fancy—a twill skirt and a blouse with buttons down the front and a man's collar—but she wore them with a sort of flair that had made Anna reconsider her own high-tops with the tongues pulled out and the tight ruching of her black tank top.

"Maybe a snob," she said. "Or maybe upper class. But not a snob."

Anna's beer came, and in the time she took to drink a few big gulps of the lager, the conversation moved on to other stories, tales of other parties, jokes someone had said, moments of comical failure at a club or on the beach. Anna pretended to listen while she thought back to Irini and her little apartment and how, when Anna had licked her fingers from the figs, Irini had jumped up, spry for a woman that age—an age Anna couldn't quite place—and returned from her kitchen with an embroidered napkin. The initials on the napkin were ΕΣ. Irini S. The priest had not told Anna the last name of the woman to whom she was to bring the figs. Miss Irini, he had said, and told her to ring the second bell from the bottom. The label had come off.

⁂

And what had occupied their time, hers and Irini's, while Anna ate the figs? The woman had told her how Plaka had been before the war, when all the houses were still old and neo-classical, tall structures with French doors and balconies that seemed to Anna more Parisian than Greek when she passed one of the few remaining. The building in which Irini lived was new and ugly, with concrete mottled on purpose in panels across the front to create a sense of decoration. Anna had not noticed this when she had arrived, but had stood in the twilit square looking up at it before she had unlocked the motorbike to leave. She had caught a glimpse of Irini moving across her window. Irini had told her of her own family home, damaged nineteen years ago in the great earthquake of 1999 and too expensive to repair. Irini said no more about either that house or the parents she had inherited it from or the husband she had lived with in it. When Anna finally stood to go, she drew close to the picture frames and saw in one a man with blue eyes and slicked-back hair, and in another a child—a daughter—and then a young woman, and then the same young woman older and with a little boy. My grandson, Irini had said.

The boy had what Anna assumed were his grandfather's blue eyes, and in the photo he held up to the camera a piece of wrapping paper in one hand and in the other a tambourine. He seemed to be sitting in the lap of his mother, who looked to be a bit older than Anna. Just a bit older than Anna and already the mother of a little boy. As Anna had woven through the narrow streets from Irini's apartment and through the traffic at the roundabout by Omonia to reach Metaxourgeio and her friends, she had thought about what it would be like to have a child now instead of this life of snatching up jobs and internships as they drifted by, lingering in the old warehouses where the new bars set up their spots, and taking spray cans to the sides of apartment blocks to paint the street art pieces and murals her new friends had encouraged her to paint. She couldn't really think of it.

Her mind went to her own childhood, not in Athens, not in Greece, but in America where her parents had dropped the suffix from their name and never cooked a lamb or octopus and sent her almost grudgingly to visit with cousins she barely knew in an Athens suburb the year she turned fourteen. That summer she had fallen off a Vespa driven by the boy cousin with little regard for his obligatory passenger. The boy's mother had daubed her leg with Mercurochrome and slapped her hand later when she tried to pick at the long scab. She wondered what it would be like now to have a little girl like the child Anna herself had been—in skirts and dresses and always wanting bows in her hair. Anna couldn't imagine it. Your grandson's cute, she had told Irini as she moved into the hall toward the front door to the apartment. He is in high school now, the old woman had replied.

⁂

Once the young woman Anna was gone, Irini double-locked the door to the apartment and crossed back to the living room to clean up after her visitor. As she bent toward the coffee table, Irini noticed the girl standing in the square and looking up at her windows. She considered waving to the girl but pretended not to have seen. She took up the bowl of figs and the glasses with a finger in each one so that they clinked together the way they did for the waiter at her most frequented taverna, and she drifted back into her tiny kitchen. The girl had left behind a fug of sweat and cigarette smoke, and Irini returned to the living room with an atomizer of perfume—a decades-old Fracas she used so sparingly that it had lasted—to clear the smell away. Irini had never taken up smoking, though she understood the fascination. For a brief period during the summer when she had been courted by the man who would become her husband, she had attempted to adopt the habit. But the smoke had made her eyes sting and their watering had in turn smudged her mascara on those nights sitting at the rooftop bars of elegant hotels or in the planted terraces inside the Royal garden. So, she had relinquished cigarettes and had foregone this opportunity for glamour. Her husband smoked a pipe.

She examined the living room and set to straightening the picture frames that Anna had picked up to look at. She smoothed the fabric on the couch and on the chair that she herself had sat in and looked once more at the photographs of her daughter and grandson and of her husband when he was young. Not your type, she said to his image. She said nothing to the photos of her daughter—as a girl and as a mother with her boy—but pressed her lips together in concern. She had told Anna she did not see her daughter, and had allowed for the likely inference about a mother with a teen-aged son that these two members of younger generations were too busy for the older woman. She did not see her daughter or her grandson, and she was in fact quite busy on her own. She had two pinochle games and a book club and the need for time in which to read each month's selection—which was currently the first volume of Proust translated into Greek and which Irini was attempting in the original. She prided herself on her French accent and often earned delighted praise from tourists who wandered through the little square and sought help from her in French-inflected English. In their own tongue, she would then tell them how to get to the Acropolis—this was the only question she was ever asked. Turn left at the far corner of the square, she would tell the tourists, pass the fruit seller on the left, and then turn right onto the pedestrian boulevard. Sometimes, if the tourists seemed especially attentive, she might tell them how the traffic had once surged in chaos where they were about to walk, or how the art deco mansions along the boulevard were slated for demolition. Or she might even tell them of the statues that had been moved from the old museum to the new. She did not overdo this. She was careful, sensitive to her audiences. She would not risk being seen as a doddering old fool who had so few people to speak to that she broke into conversation at the slightest opportunity.

She was busy most days, and this did not even take into account her time spent in the church or speaking with the priest or, every now and then, joining him and his family for lunch at one of the tavernas. He was a young priest. Irini knew he was thought of as a hip priest. His children—two boys—played soccer with him between courses at lunch, passing a red mini-ball back and forth while Irini thought of things to say to their mother. She generally enjoyed these meals and made a show of offering to pay for a pastry tarte at meal's end. The priest never accepted, having already gone into the kitchen to ensure that the waiter would bring the bill only to him. He assumed that Irini wanted the pastry for herself and so ordered it for the table to share, and this was added to the bill at the priest's expense. Irini preferred ice cream to pastry, and so she took only the smallest bites and trusted the boys to eat the rest. Their father never noticed this when their lunches ended and Irini said goodbye and thank you and turned the corner for the kiosk and not home. She would buy herself a Magnum ice cream and eat almost all of it there under the kiosk's awning before it melted and she lost the chocolate coating to the cobblestones.

On cooler days she sometimes bought two Magnums, if she could trust the second one to survive the walk home. She pulled one Magnum now from the small collection in her freezer and returned with it and a china plate to the living room. The sun had gone down and the Acropolis was lit, and she sat in her chair and watched the walls of the ancient palisade and the illuminated columns of the Parthenon as if they were her television.

And what did she think of as she gazed on the stone and marble? She thought first of the Sound and Light shows on the Acropolis, donated to Greece by the French nation, and how she used to take her daughter to the shows at the end of every school year. She thought of the lights moving up an ancient path to match the prerecorded sound of sandals on gravel as the runner Pheidippides came from Marathon to announce Greek victory in battle and then collapsed into death. She thought of the Proust and how the man had made a career from illness and how she could do the same herself, if she stayed inside her tiny apartment. Except she was not ill. Old, but not ill. High blood pressure that was common even for those much younger than her eighty-two years, and a cataract that had clouded her vision. But that had been taken care of and she could see even better out of that once-cloudy eye and needed no correction. She had popped the left lens out of the glasses she used at home where no one would comment on her frugality.

She was not ill as Proust had been—if he had been. Irini considered always the possibility—though in her view it was far more than possible—that people told themselves as many lies as they told others. Proust's illness might have been the tale he told himself, the ancient marathoner's health the lie he told to his commanders who sent him on the errand that killed him. She thought then of the girl, Anna, whom she realized she should call a woman and not a girl since at Anna's age Irini had already lived through two wars. The girl—the word had already become a habit—had not even lived through the military junta. She had not even seen the roundups of political prisoners and after seven years the arrival of new freedoms and the gathering up of all the junta flags and hiding them away in favor of the new flags of the republic. She was born after all that. The girl had come to Greece knowing none of it.

Not that they had spoken of all this, but Irini could tell. There was a certain bright-eyed nature to this girl and there was her hopefulness about the church—rare in someone of her generation, though likely the hip priest had something to do with that. But here she was, this child so young she was born after everything, arriving into a country to take up a job when there were hardly any to be had, thanks to the crisis, working in a gallery, she had said, for little money. Yes, that was the important detail, the tendency of young people to call a job something they did for free for someone else. Irini would call this charity. This was a strange thing about the young. They gave so much away even as they were always looking for what someone else could give them. Irini was neither fool nor hypocrite. She relied on the munificence of the kind priest and his church, and about that, she claimed few falsehoods.

So, Anna had come here for this job at an art gallery and when every Greek her age wanted to leave the country, she had stayed. Thanks to a passport from her parents' Greek birth, she could stay as long as she liked. When Anna said the word for passport, Irini heard the accent. It was not strong, but it was there. The girl could almost pass for native, but if you really listened you could hear that she was something else instead.

The buzz of noise from the square grew suddenly louder, and Irini checked her watch. The Timex had been her husband's and the black band was cracked and far too loose on her wrist, and yet she wore it with the large face that knocked against her wristbone. Just after eleven. Over at the rooftop cinema, the credits were scrolling against the screen, which was in actuality the blank wall of the adjacent building. The audience members were spilling out of the lobby and into the square, and she could hear people making plans for dinner or drinks. Irini rose—something she still did easily and without pressing up on the arms of the chair—and fetched the Proust from the bedroom and took the book to the kitchen and began to read while she waited for her kettle to boil. She would drink a chamomile and read for one hour before bed.

※

This was all happening in a city that had its way of keeping people apart and then thrusting them together as if by some heaving of tectonic plates, in a gentler version of the heaving that had seriously damaged Irini's family home and that several times a year rattled the china and the flat-screen televisions inside its millions of apartments. Not long after Anna had first arrived to work for no pay in the gallery, one such earthquake had knocked to the polished marble floor several artworks fortunately fashioned from canvas and unglazed. Alone in the space, she had hunched in a doorway while plaster drifted from the walls of the high transoms and a car alarm wailed outside the door. The day after Anna took the figs to Irini's house, a Saturday, she went to the gallery to work, and Irini went out for her walk around the neighborhood, and though they were only a few hundred meters apart, they did not cross paths until the Sunday.

Sunday, Irini went for morning mass to the church with the stubby nave and took her customary seat beside a column where she rested her head against the stone. In the summer the column was cooler than the rest of the church, which was almost cool enough. She closed her eyes to listen better to the liturgical singing of the young priest and to rid her mind of the image of him with his priestly bun resembling too much the sort of hairstyle sported by the secular young men of the city. The last time she had seen him, her grandson had affected such a style, with a portion of his hair bound up on top of his head as if he had forgotten to form a complete ponytail out of it. This priest was so young that sometimes she mistook him for her grandson's age. He must have been not much older when he had married and had the first of his two boys.

Because her eyes were closed, Irini did not see Anna arrive and take up a seat across the aisle from her, though she did sense an alteration in the scent of the space, a shift in the incense toward something even darker and richer. This was a scent Irini recognized from tourists who sat in the little square sometimes with small dogs at their feet and thick leashes of rope they draped over their wrists. She knew from the waiters that these tourists spent even less money than the Greek young people who sat for hours over a single inexpensive coffee. The waiters complained to her and did not seem to mind that Irini herself spent even less than all of them, for most of the time she paid only in a greeting as she passed the cafés and earned in exchange another round of praise for her agility. The waiters did not use this word—they exhorted imaginary listeners to *look at her*—but Irini knew that this was what they meant. They knew from her talk of the war how old she must be—she did nothing to conceal her age—and she knew they expected her to be barely able to put one foot before the other, and not to tramp to the Acropolis on the days of free admission or to carry her shopping in her string bag instead of pushing it in a little cart over the cobbles like the other women of her generation.

Irini opened her eyes to see the source of the offending scent that reminded her of the broke tourists and saw it was the young girl Anna. Irini recognized the odor of stale cigarettes and sweat that had lingered in her apartment after the girl had brought the figs, mixed now with the scent—it was patchouli—that she found particularly odious. Anna sat with her eyes closed and her head leaning like Irini's against the answering column on the other side. Anna did this not to cool the back of her head but to sense the priest's words—though she did not always understand the ecclesiastical Greek—as coming to her from somewhere beyond this touristed corner of the ancient city where she was still subject to the calls of gift-shop owners.

When Anna had first arrived in the city, she had brought with her a wardrobe she thought fitting for a gallery assistant but had soon learned that the black of her clothing was too hot for all but the deepest winter days and, in the spring, had stood out far too starkly against the bright stones and the brighter light that surrounded her. Her shoes had proved dangerously slippery on the sidewalks of cement that had been polished to a shine as if they were as ancient as the steps to the Acropolis, where she had seen a woman fall and break her hip. So, she had converted to the high-top sneakers with the pulled-out tongue and the skinny jeans and tight-fitting tops she had seen at the cafés of Metaxourgeio. On days when a new exhibit opened, she threw a blazer over the tight tops and this was enough. The gallery owner was almost never there except in winter, preferring to spend the warm weather on an island in the Aegean, and the artists who did come in seemed to see a kinship between themselves and her.

Though she did not always understand the formal language of the liturgy, Anna expected by now to seem like a native. And still whenever she walked a few blocks into the Plaka, the shopkeepers addressed her in English, a language she used now only on her weekly Skype calls with her parents, who drifted into the tongue of their daughter's American upbringing. They spoke English with the faint accents of Greek America, while Anna was beginning to bring a delicate Hellenic cadence to her English speech. It seemed to her that for the first time in her life she and her parents spoke the same language: Greek-accented English. She tried once to hold the weekly Skype call in her parents' native tongue and found she had outstripped them. She quickly turned to English to spare them all the embarrassment of this strange linguistic exile.

She was to call her parents that night, as she did each Sunday. This had been her request, not theirs. They had seen it as nothing or almost nothing to be in a land not your own, having embarked for the United States in their twenties without knowing anyone at their destination. And they reminded Anna that Greece was not really foreign to her. Her parents had been disappointed to discover that Astoria was the strange, hyphenated hybrid that was wholly neither of its two terms. The residents of Astoria were neither truly Greek, like Anna's parents, nor quite American, and so Anna and her parents had become an island unto themselves within that enclave of Queens. They did not send Anna to Greek school at the local church, insisting quite correctly that, even for the faithful, churchgoing was not a custom of their country. They did not socialize with their neighbors, preferring instead to make American friends—they stressed the word with the weight of fantasy—but struggling to find them. Anna's parents pointed to the summer visit when she was fourteen as if it had cemented her identity as someone of the place. All it had given her had been a scar on her knee and a few cotton shirts she had worn in America only once before realizing the garments were made solely for the tourist trade and also quite decidedly out of place outside of Greece.

What would she tell her parents in today's call? She had not yet told them about her church attendance and would not do so today either. Anna knew that hardly any Greeks attended liturgy on Sundays, even among the most devout. Most Greeks required the special occasion of a holiday or a milestone event in their own lives—an important journey or a rite of passage—before they would go to church, and then mostly as a kind of good-luck superstition. She would perhaps find another way to tell her parents about the old lady Irini, concocting a different story for how they had met. Or perhaps she would say nothing of her at all. The woman had come into her life one afternoon and had already passed out of it. An idea had formed in Anna's mind that her meeting with the woman, with its conversation and cup of tea, carried about it something illicit, despite having been arranged by Father Emmanouil.

She listened to him now, realizing he had shifted from the melodic chanting of the service to his spoken homily. She opened her eyes and saw that his attention was focused across the aisle. She shifted her gaze just enough to conceal her focus on anything besides the holy setting and saw the old lady herself in the seat that was counterpart to Anna's own. She made to tuck her hair behind her ear and looked again more closely. Yes, it was Irini, with white hair cropped in what would have seemed a pixie cut on a woman of Anna's generation, in a collared blouse and trim skirt like those she had worn before. Irini was a widow but Anna took note of the fact that unlike others she did not wear only black. Her blouse today was a pale but electric blue and her skirt a charcoal gray.

The priest smiled, at Irini it seemed, and then signaled with his eyes toward Anna. Anna caught a movement from across the aisle and turned fully, feigning new surprise at the acquaintance. Irini dipped her head in Anna's direction and smiled. The smile was yielded rather than offered, as if the woman shared Anna's sense of the illicit nature of their connection. In fact, Irini was annoyed to be drawn out from the conversation she was conducting with her God and with which she felt the priest at least should be trusted not to interfere.

Seeing Irini's smile, the priest looked out upon the congregation, his introductions now complete. The congregation that day numbered six. Besides Anna and Irini, there were two old women in black, clearly widows. Irini knew the women and tried to avoid all association with them as she knew them to be her age. She considered them living reminders of how close they all were to death. She should have embraced these memento mori as license for her own electric blues and oranges and greens. But Irini did not like even to approach the widows lest their nearness to death become contagious and lest she somehow be compelled to trade her colors for their somber and penitent attire. A few rows behind the old women were two young men Anna's age from Ethiopia who had arrived in Athens two years ago from Addis Ababa. Oumer had worked as a barista there and Tamrat as a journalist, and they had met in the Ethiopian Orthodox church in another part of Athens. They had left Ethiopia not out of desperation—and in fact were fed up with the assumption made by so many Athenians that they were economic refugees. Tamrat had, at least, had cause for a quick departure, since his reporting often put him on the wrong side of the leading party. But Oumer had come to Greece because of Santorini. In a film he had seen a man free-running through a north African city, and this had led him to take up the sport of parkour. It was on the terraced buildings of Santorini that the world's best ran and leapt and swung and twirled. And more than

Oumer was a barista, he was, now, a member of a team of free-runners with their own matching tracksuits and their routes around the city's parks and construction sites, and sometimes he arrived in church with smears of red dust along a tracksuited knee or hip.

Oumer and Tamrat had left the Ethiopian church in Nea Kypseli and arrived at this church in Plaka with the stubby nave because they shared a frustration with the ethnic politics of the priest. They had become apostates of their own home Orthodoxy and chosen this of all of Athens' churches. Father Emmanouil's welcome of them had been fueled in part by his enthusiasm to share his experiences of Lalibela where Oumer's and Tamrat's Christian ancestors had carved cruciform churches down into the living rock. The priest had traveled there just before attending seminary, before his marriage, before his own country had become an accidental destination for those hoping to reach greater European prosperity farther north. So, when Anna had first arrived, he had delighted in introducing her to Oumer and Tamrat and in telling this new-comer from America his story of his travels and his backpack and the churches in the rock. Her arrival at Father Emmanouil's little church, and her regular return for Sunday liturgies, was a small miracle the priest greeted with excitement and relief, though he quickly gave up hope that the girl would lead her young friends to join her and swell his congregation.

*

When the service finished, the priest accompanied his congre-gants toward the entrance, where the heat of the city was as solid as a wall. The two widows left quickly, not wishing to be seen to socialize with the Ethiopians who, in their eyes, were marked as undesirable by their nationality and by the color of their skin.

Nothing Father Emmanouil had said to them could convince the women otherwise, and they determined that their attendance at church most Sundays more than made up for their opinions. Irini lingered, for she wished to thank the priest for the figs, and it pleased her to ask the Ethiopians about their week within earshot of the widows who would purse their lips together at the untoward behavior of someone who should have been like them. Irini could not afford to venture to the coffee shop where Oumer currently worked, and Oumer was not yet in a position to serve her coffees on the house, but she had promised him that when he did open his own shop, as was his stated plan, she would be among his first customers for coffee served in the gracious way of his homeland. When she had said this, she had cautioned that, of course, she might not still be alive by then, and she had made her customary tip forward of the head to accept Oumer's compliment for how ageless she both seemed and was. She did not mention that she would be the kind of customer whose business comes at a cost to the barista.

The girl Anna was there by the entrance too, and the truth was that Irini realized she had been seeing the girl at Sunday liturgy for weeks now but had never paid attention to her until she had appeared in the foyer of the apartment building and Irini had buzzed her in not knowing who it was. This was a practice that the priest's wife disapproved of and scolded Irini for, but Irini did not see the trouble as, at her age, she had little to lose and less to be stolen and sometimes those who came into the building offered coupons and free samples. In this way, she had over the years obtained a very nice lavender soap and a free ice cream and a set of plastic cups. So, when the girl had stood at the base of the steps in the foyer that led up to the old cage-style elevator and Irini had peered over the railing from the second floor, she had vaguely recognized her but without knowing from where. She would have let the girl in even without that hint of recognition, for the girl said Father Emmanouil had sent her and she had held a basket of figs with both hands on the handle. She had made Irini think of Little Red Riding Hood and, in that case, if the fairy tale were to serve, Irini would have been either dead already or a wolf in disguise. Again, and always, she had nothing to lose and the potential of reward from extending an invitation to the girl to come on up.

Today she had come to the church to show her appreciation and respect for the priest, her landlord, as if the service were a play or a recital he performed for which he would require an audience. And she had come also to complain to God, to scold him for his uncooperative nature of late. Listen, she had told him before she had seen the priest making meaningful gestures with his eyes to the young girl across the aisle. Listen, God, I know you think you needn't bother with me at my age of eighty-two, but I'm still here and I show no sign of disappearing, unless you have some rash and frankly unfair plans for me. So, give me, please, a little peace in the hip joints. Is that too much to ask? Because I don't fancy switching to flat shoes, and I have spent a lifetime negotiating these cobbled streets in heels and don't intend to change my habits now. And didn't we speak already about the cost of electricity? You're going to have to find me something to do to make more money—which I think could be difficult because, again, let me remind you, I am eighty-two and you and I both know I have not lost my looks, but there is little I can do with them now. And what would I do? Join Oumer at his espresso bar? She had chuckled to herself then and that must have been what had set the priest to his meaningful glances. But this was not funny, she had gone on, and if her God found this amusing then he was not the sort of God she could place her faith in after all. He had better get to work and either bring the government to its senses so they could lower the taxes on electricity so she could keep her fan running when it was very hot, or convince Father Emmanouil, who worked for him, after all, to include utilities with the free rent he was already providing.

Now that the service was over, she told the priest how much she had enjoyed it and said her hellos to Oumer and Tamrat and said a polite hello to the girl Anna. Before she could depart—her irritated prayer had made her more eager than usual for solitude—the priest asked her to another Sunday lunch. Join us, he said to Irini, meaning his family, and yet the girl Anna assumed that it was she who was indicated by the plural.

"Oh, yes, do," she said to Irini, and then she thanked the priest for the opportunity, which, Irini could see from the discomfiture he tried to hide, he had not intended. It would be rude of him to pay for Irini's lunch and not Anna's and so, with the girl joining them, he would have to justify the expense of two lunch guests as church business, and though the Greek Orthodox church had lots of money, the priest's particular establishment depended on a small budget and the infrequent benefactions of a Plaka-born shipping magnate.

"Of course," he said and then repeated his invitation. "Please come today, Irini. Though the boys will be sad to hear they missed you." The boys were spending the day with his wife's parents. The boys, Irini was sure, would miss not her but the pastry of which she would have let them eat the lion's share. But thinking of the pastry made her think of the ice cream she could have instead—since her lunch would be paid for and she would thus have less spending on the day's food and she would require only a yogurt and a boiled egg for her supper before bed, following so large a meal at midday. So, she agreed and tried not to notice the great enthusiasm of the girl. Didn't this Anna have better places to go? Shouldn't she be on the back of a motorbike headed to a beach, instead of having lunch in Plaka with a priest's family and an old woman? Irini said exactly this to her and watched the girl's face turn a deep crimson as she searched for a reply.

"Don't mind Irini," the priest said. And Irini snapped a frowning face toward him. "She says what she thinks, but she never means you harm."

The priest knew nothing about Irini's intentions to create harm. She doubted he had the kind of access to such information his employer was supposed to have, and today she doubted that that kind of insight was available even to her God.

"Yes," she said, with a smile to Anna and a reminder to herself that she had in fact passed several pleasant hours in the girl's company just two days prior. "Don't mind me. I speak my mind, but I know when to ease up."

The lunch was not an altogether unpleasant affair in the beginning. The priest led them to the usual taverna after sending a text message to his wife, a message that employed a liberal use of emojis to indicate—as she and only she would understand—that he was making the best of the situation and that the lovemaking they had been looking forward to would have to wait. His wife's reply with the image of a clock and a dancing lady could easily have been construed as something innocent, were the priest's phone to fall into someone else's hands. When he told her this concern that evening as he stepped out of his briefs in their dark bedroom, she burst into muffled laughter and teased him for thinking like a spy. As they made love, her laughter bubbled up periodically and she agreed he would not want the phone to fall into enemy hands. Now as the group arrived at the taverna, he stuffed the phone deep into the pocket of his cassock to be certain no exposure would occur, and he resisted every impulse to retrieve the phone each time it buzzed with a notification until his wife arrived in person to join the meal.

Without the boys there, the conversation among the four adults took some time to become established. Freed from the interruptions of the boys' chatter and their comings and goings from the table, the discussion faltered where it had room to flow. It was not until they had all completed the long process of ordering and not until the dishes had been described to Anna, who wished she knew the cost of each one so that she could order with modesty in case the priest was paying and with slightly less frugality in case she would be paying for herself—not until then did the priest's wife, whose name was Nefeli, ask how Anna and Irini had become friends. Nefeli saw her choice of words had been a poor one as the older woman sat up in surprise and the younger reddened.

"Young Anna here brought me your figs," Irini said. "She was the fig-bearer." Anna smiled agreement, not certain whether this title came from an ancient statue she should know.

"The basket you wanted me to take to Irini," the priest said to his wife. "I had an appointment to get to and Anna offered to help, so I sent her to Irini. And the rest is history."

His final comment was unfortunate, for no one at the table, not even Father Emmanouil himself, knew what he meant by it. Who was he, Irini wondered, to make such a claim on her life and on her time? Who was he to make such assumptions of her personality, that he could introduce this girl who knew nothing and who worked for no money to Irini, who had attended the finest school for girls in all of Athens and who had been introduced to royalty, meeting Queen Friederiki not once but many times before the war? And besides, to say the rest was history was to imply a future and Irini's future was already spoken for, no matter what she told her God in her defiance. Anna was no less bewildered by the priest's statement but she was not displeased. To think of herself as already connected to this woman with the pixie cut and the trim skirt and the men's watch that dangled from her wrist like jewelry was to consider herself one step closer to something important. She could not say what, exactly, but it was a corpus of understanding, of wisdom, that she knew she did not possess. She knew that she knew nothing. She knew that when she sat down beneath the birdcage by the espresso machine and laughed at slang she was only beginning to understand, she was approaching a life from which she was still off-center, peripheral. Her friends she met at the bar with the birdcage were no closer to that center than she was. They were all born after everything, and they complained of being reminded so by their grandmothers and great-aunts who lived with them in their parents' houses. But because they were from here, even in their ignorance they had access to something Anna could not reach.

The only thing to do with a comment like the priest's was to repeat it.

"Yes," Irini said. "And the rest is history."

Father Emmanouil tore a piece of bread from one of the pyramidal chunks in a plastic basket on the table and chewed energetically while he thought of what next to say.

"Irini, as you know," he said, when he was finished, "has been a congregant since long before I arrived."

"You are my fourth priest," she said, "and the youngest by a great deal."

"It's good," said Nefeli, "to have youth in the priesthood. I'm sure it's part of what appealed to you, Anna, isn't it?"

Irini did not think Nefeli should be asking Anna or any woman Anna's age what about her husband was appealing. The man did not simply kick the soccer ball with his two boys. He played on Wednesday evenings in a clearing by the ancient Agora and, as she returned from her book club meetings past the broken columns and the open field beyond, Irini had seen the muscle definition of his chest and hips beneath his uniform. Anna had seen him too, Irini was certain, for once again the girl reddened, and this time the blush was not of delight but of embarrassment.

"What *did* bring you to the church, Anna," Irini said. "I must know what brought you into our little world."

The waiter arrived then with an arm cantilevered out to support the dishes: stuffed tomatoes for Nefeli and thus for Anna who had matched her order to that of the priest's wife, pork chops for Irini, and giant beans in red sauce for the priest. A teenaged boy with his hair cut into a mohawk handed the waiter the rest of the order from a respectful distance: fried potatoes and a platter of dandelion greens dressed with oil and lemon, which the waiter added to the table. Without having to ask, he brought a large beer for Father Emmanouil and a small one for Irini, and a Coca Light for Nefeli. Anna contented herself with water, which she poured from a sweating glass pitcher. She could have answered Irini's question by saying it was Oumer who had brought her to the church with the stubby nave. She had gone into a coffee shop near Monastiraki months ago and the barista, Oumer, had seen the cross on her necklace and struck up a conversation. Come on Sunday, he had said. The priest is good. And because Oumer was handsome and soft-spoken, she had gone. But Anna knew Irini was not concerned with the logistics of her arrival but with the very fact of her devotion.

"Why the church?" Irini said again, the interruption sharpening her question. "The young—pardon, Father—do not favor the church."

It would have made for an interesting conversation had Anna known what to say in answer to the older woman, or rather had she been willing to say what she knew she felt. But she did not have the words. It was not a question of language, for she had

had to defend against this accusation—what was it if not an accusation—one night at the birdcage bar, insisting to her friends that she was neither conservative nor boring. It was that she could not say it in front of the priest, could not tell him that she came to his church every week to make up for lost time. She came as a way of living like a woman of an older generation, or two, or three, a woman who knew what it was like to have been in the country all those years and seen things Anna could not even name for she was utterly ignorant of history. Irini had her four priests. Anna wanted at least this one priest as a guide to and through a life she should have known about, a life her grandparents might have lived in their village in Thrace, a life her parents would have lived had they not both departed Athens at the age of twenty-five.

There were no real events in the church, she knew that, not the way an election or a protest or a general strike were events—and she had witnessed all of those since coming to the city. But there were moments and actions that happened over and over, year after year, unchanging and endlessly repeating over centuries. These moments she prayed with and to. She told herself it didn't really even matter that Father Emmanouil was Greek Orthodox. She would have gone to a synagogue or mosque had they been easier to find in Athens. Instead, she had come to this little church when she had first arrived in the city and had not yet learned that Plaka was where all tourists go, and she had followed the directions the barista Oumer had given her and crossed the little square to reach the church with the stubby nave. It had been January then and the tourists had been few, and she had glimpsed the version of the city that lay beneath all that, the city of heat lamps at the cafe and fireplace smoke hanging in the narrow streets and the rain-slicked squares where people stooped beneath the awnings of the kiosks to buy newspapers and magazines even though everybody had a smartphone.

If Anna was being honest, it did matter that Father Emmanouil was Greek Orthodox and not a rabbi or an imam, not a Buddhist or a Copt. It was her parents' and her ancestors' time she wished to connect to and if she was to find the timelessness through her religious activity, that activity would do well to be in the tradition in which her ancestors had existed. She liked to think of herself as advanced, as more open-minded than the Greeks of the city. When she met her friends beneath the birdcage, she sometimes challenged their proclamations about the Syrians. To them all refugees and immigrants, regardless whether they came from Iraq or Afghanistan or Syria itself, were Syrians, except the Albanians who were always Albanians and the Georgians who were always Georgians and who were frequently employed by their parents to care night and day for their grandparents. Everyone else, everyone who had dark skin—though what this meant was complicated, since most Greeks tanned very dark in summer—was Syrian. So, when Anna's friends said something derogatory about all Syrians or expressed a condescending frustration in the guise of unbiased frankness, she challenged them to consider what they really meant. She offered her Ethiopian friends—she called them friends though they would in fact not call her the same—as examples of whatever point she needed to convey. They worked very hard, she said, without knowing if this was true, if she wished to counter an assertion of laziness. They were well-educated, if she wished to counter an alleged ignorance on the part of all refugees. That they were beautiful everyone agreed even without seeing them, though Anna knew that, even though she found Oumer particularly handsome, she should insist on some bit of ugliness in him in freedom from generalization.

"I don't know how to explain it," she said finally, and let her fellow diners think it was her Greek vocabulary that was lacking. "What does the church mean to you, Irini?"

"You can hardly ask me that in front of Father Emmanouil," Irini said. "That's like a new mother asking if her baby is ugly. Of course it is. All infants are. But you can't say so to the mother's face."

"Are you saying you don't like my services, Irini?" said the priest with a smile.

"Your services are fine. It's your God I have problems with."

"He's not my God. He's yours, Irini. He's everyone's."

"Tell that to the Buddhists, Father," Irini said.

"Or the atheists," Anna said, sensing an opening.

But this annoyed Irini, when the young ceded authority only to suddenly claim it once their elders had cleared the path through a complex thicket of ideas. The girl needed to understand that it was easy to make identifications. It was much harder to express dissatisfaction without robbing it of meaning.

"God disappoints me, Father," Irini said, "when he ignores me, even though I claim only an instant of his time. And what is time to him when he is part of eternity? Time matters to me because I have so little of it left. And that, young lady," she said, turning to Anna, "is why I come to the church even though I have become an unsatisfied customer. I come back because I see my time diminishing and I am hoping to learn how to extend it."

The girl leaned forward ever so slightly at this, and Irini feared she was about to opine again in the cocksure way of those whose opinions have been prepared for them. But the girl said nothing and Irini took a moment to consider what she herself had just said and whether she really did mean to extend her life. That was not it, and how, after all, could attendance at this church make any changes in biology, for Irini's life had been mapped when she was born to parents of good health and freedom from ailments of the heart or tumor. She wished to deepen her life, not to extend it. Lately she had allowed herself to understand that what she really wished for her life was to repair it in the time that she had left. And she returned almost every Sunday to the church to see if she could find out how.

❦

Irini cut into her chop and chewed the meat that was, as always, just a hair too cooked for her taste. But she would not complain about the doneness of the meat in a donated meal, and she could rest easy that she was still in possession of all her teeth and was not limited as were others of her generation. Even her husband had had to give up certain cuts of meat in his later years, prolonged malnutrition during the war having resulted in a weakness to his bones and teeth. His family had not been well-to-do like hers, and while she had passed the German occupation supplied with honey and cheeses and legs of lamb from farmers beholden to the family estate, her husband's family had been among those to sell their lamb and honey for the funds with which to purchase firewood and olive oil and grain. In his later years, her husband had taken to risottos and pasta dishes or soft-cooked chicken in tomato sauce, most often cooked by the tavernas in the little square, as Irini was no more than an indifferent cook. When they dined out in the square, the waiters pretended that her husband's were the more delicious choices. Irini never ordered those soft foods, not then, not with the priest's family on Sundays, and not on the rare occasions when she sometimes convinced a friend from the book group to treat her to a meal out. When she paid what was to her an exorbitant amount to go to the cinema on the rooftop, before the cold weather drove the operation to the indoor auditorium, she made the most of the rare expense and bought a paper cone of toasted melon seeds and she could crack them without fear between her teeth.

"Irini," Nefeli said, "I think you already know the secret to extending time. I don't know any other woman like you in all of Plaka."

"All of Plaka," Irini said. Plaka was a tiny area bounded by the Acropolis on one side and by formerly grand boulevards of the nineteenth century on the others. With so many of the old houses now converted to hotels or shops or razed to make way for office buildings, there were hardly many women in Plaka with whom Irini could compete. But she allowed Nefeli her compliment. She had been impressed upon first meeting the priest's wife to see how fashionable she was—dressing in blocks of color and clean lines that reminded Irini of Jean Seberg. Nefeli, long accustomed to the effect she made and adept in detecting the reaction in people's eyes, had told her that just because she'd fallen in love with a priest, that didn't make her stodgy.

"Seems to me," Nefeli went on, "you don't need the church to work your personal miracle."

"Nefeli Bourdzis," Irini said, "that sounds like blasphemy. Watch your wife, Father."

Nefeli shrugged dramatically—she had given up dreams of a stage career—and reached across her husband's plate for a toothpick. The priest and his wife and the young girl Anna continued to look at Irini, Nefeli doing so with one hand covering her mouth while the other held the toothpick with which she tidied her teeth after partaking of the dandelion greens. But Irini had nothing more to say on the subject of her relationship with the church, nor did Anna have any more to add on the subject, as she was, on this topic, too, ignorant.

Irini cut another piece of pork, delicately slicing it away from the bone. She had been taught well as a little girl barely able to grip the handles of her knife and fork, and she adhered to a list of foods one was permitted to touch with one's fingers—among them a fruit such as the figs Anna had brought two days ago—and the list was very short. Even at Piraeus harbor waiting for the boat to cross to the island of Hydra with her husband, she ate the skewered souvlaki meat—this fare of ship embarkations in all Greek ports was on her list—without daubing her chin with grease. She never lost the accompanying napkin to the sea breeze before using it to clean her fingers.

"When was your first priest?" Anna said.

Irini paused in her slicing upon realizing the question was addressed to her.

"Pardon?" she said.

"You said Father Emmanouil was your fourth priest. When did you start?"

If the girl sought a long history of Irini's life in the church with the stubby nave, she would be disappointed. For the priests who came to Plaka never lasted more than four or five years in the posting. The second priest had wanted to be closer to what he felt was a truer Greece, freer from tourists, and the first had fled a Plaka still emerging from its time as the neighborhood for bars specializing in loud music played on old Greek instruments but favored by the nouveau riche. She and her husband would have liked to have fled in those years, but this was well before the earthquake that had so damaged the family home, and they felt they had an unspoiled asset whose value was artificially depressed by the sordid nature of the neighborhood and sure to rise. So, they had waited for Plaka to change—which it had—but the first of Irini's priests had not been interested in waiting and he had accepted a post somewhere in Thessaly. The third priest had had an affair with the wife of the owner of the rooftop cinema and had been so badly beaten by the husband, who had wept pleas for forgiveness with each blow he struck, that he had given up the post before the church authorities had time to kick him out. Now that Irini lived within sight of the cinema, she often saw the husband and the wife, still married, pulling down the grilles over the door and the ticket window at night in twin moods of grim resignation. It was said that because the cuckolder had been a man of the cloth, the cuckold and his wife must not compound the sin by divorcing, and so they remained together while their adult son shook his head in bewilderment. Irini told Anna none of this.

"The year two thousand," she said.

"That's eighteen years ago," Anna said. She looked at Father Emmanouil as if to confirm her calculation.

"Yes, it is," Irini said.

She broke off a small chunk of bread and swiped it over her plate to catch the juices from her chop. It was in part because of the coming of the new millennium and in part because of the earthquake of the previous year that she had begun to attend services at the little church. She did not like to admit this, and in a way it was her good fortune that long gone was the priest who had first heard her observations that the turn of a new millennium of Christianity could be a propitious time to assess what the whole church project had to offer. The symbolism of the enterprise had seemed appealing to Irini then, a new millennium beginning merely months after Athens had been cracked open, and a new exploration for her to undertake. It had not been lost on her that the change of the calendar that year would mean something even more. And it was not lost on her—though she wished she could consign this fact to oblivion—that her own life had cracked open with the earthquake that year and that she too could benefit from a new beginning.

She had been sixty-three and her husband sixty-five and their daughter had been already thirty-five and pregnant with many miscarriages behind her. Secretly Irini had made a vow to herself that if she began to attend church services, her daughter would have her child in the new year and Irini's line, her heritage, and her family genes, if not her name, would go on. That had been her first prayer ever, and her God of those years had answered it. Not without exacting payment in return. They had been just getting to know each other then, Irini and her God. If only he were as prompt now. She had begun to go to the church with the first priest in January of that millennium year, and by Lent she was forced to admit to herself that she was at the church to learn about eternity. She had by then accrued a debt that might require eternity to repay.

"We never went to church in the States," Anna said, "with my parents. I'm sorry, Father E." Conveniently, Anna's abbreviation made the same sound as the first syllable of his name.

"Don't be sorry, Anna," the priest said, and he raised his arm in what almost looked like a benediction but was a call to the waiter to come and take his cash. "You're here now."

"Yes, and I'm so glad. It means a lot to me. And now," she set a hand on Irini's arm, "I've met *you*."

Irini tried to conceal her flinch from the girl's touch, but everyone at the table saw it. Even the boy with the mohawk who assisted the main waiter at the restaurant caught the snap of movement at the priest's table. He glanced over his shoulder at the table one more time as he brought soiled dishes to the kitchen and, tripping over an uneven flagstone in the square, sent the dishes smashing. Now it was the priest's table that glanced in the direction of the boy and his commotion.

"There go his tips for the day," Irini said. "Poor boy."

But she was thinking of her good fortune that the boy's stumble gave her and the priest and his wife something else to discuss besides her shock at Anna's excessive enthusiasm for having met her. Not that enthusiasm in itself was to be frowned upon. This was a culture and a country in which speech was accompanied by vivid gestures, sweeping or staccato, and where the tones of even casual conversation were regularly mistaken by tourists for heated arguments. It was not the enthusiasm in itself that posed a problem now. It was Anna's extension of her hand onto Irini's arm in a way that had been ever so slightly condescending, ever so slightly suggesting something of infirmity in the older woman and charity in the younger. They had all seen it—except Anna who had seen only that Irini had twitched away, and whose attitude of condescension or charity had been purely accidental.

"Poor kid is right," Nefeli said. "And that woman who got splashed by it," she went on. "Look."

Anna followed Nefeli's gaze and Irini met the priest's eyes with a silent message. Do not thrust upon me this young woman with her overexcitement at our meeting.

"Anna," the priest said, "you must have waited tables in America. Most young people do, don't they?"

Father Emmanouil liked to maintain his connection to the experiences of youth—his own and others'—which he felt were not so far behind him.

"For summers, a little. But what I mean," Anna said, turning to Irini again but this time refraining from a gesture, "is that I love coming to services, but it's just nice to meet someone from the neighborhood. To make a friend."

"We are your friends, Anna," Nefeli said, and the girl nodded with silent vigor. Irini thought she saw her eyes begin to well up and she caught herself from scolding her. There was a difference, in Irini's mind, between expressing one's emotions and losing control of them.

"Surely you have friends your own age already," she said. "You've been in Athens several months. Isn't that what you told me?"

"I do. No. Of course I do."

Anna picked at the crust of bread beside her plate. Here was a new source of embarrassment for them all at the thought they had exposed the young woman to be friendless and lonely. It occurred to Irini then that for the girl to be attending the liturgy at ten thirty on a Sunday morning, she could not be staying out late on a Saturday night, unless she came to church straight from the clubs. Irini looked at her closely now—yes, those were tears in the girl's eyes—and saw clean hair and a fresh face with only the light makeup of the daytime. No, the girl had come from home.

"Where *is* your neighborhood?" Irini asked. When the girl had brought the figs, she had explained that the little church in Plaka was convenient to an apartment she rented on the north side of the Acropolis hill.

"Well, not exactly Plaka," Anna said. "I couldn't find anything I could afford." Her face reddened with impressive speed. "I mean," she said, but stopped.

"It's all Airbnbs now, isn't it?" Nefeli said.

"I wanted something more—" Anna hesitated. She had already overstepped some boundary with the old woman and now she had raised the possible shame of the charity the woman received from the church, as if Anna were suggesting she too should be eligible, when her own tight finances were the product of her youthful choice and not a final condition.

"Something more authentic," Irini said.

"Yes."

"And where did you find it?"

"Anafiotika."

Irini sputtered a laugh at the name of the latest trendy district of the city.

"Why?" Anna said. "What is it?"

Irini took her in once more. The girl was having a worse morning even than the boy who had destroyed his pile of plates. She was creating embarrassment left and right and nearly drowning beneath the waves of it that crashed back upon her. She had a nice face. Round, with a slightly upturned nose, and dark eyebrows she plucked artfully. She seemed to have no guile and no agenda. She had brought Irini the figs and she had listened to her stories of the war for hours. Irini wondered what more the girl might bring her in future visits, but the overeagerness of Anna's innocence was almost great enough to strip the thought of all potential interest.

"Anafiotika is nice," Irini said. "It is, however, not very authentic. The families from the island of Anafi who first settled there and gave it its name have mostly moved away. It's full of new people now, and most of them run Airbnbs."

"But I'm renting from one of those Anafi families," Anna said.

"Well, good for you. But Anafiotika was never authentic in the first place."

"Irini, that's not fair," Nefeli said.

"Of course, it is. It's true. When the first people came, they made a pretend island village in the middle of Athens. It was never real."

"They missed their home island and they wanted to recreate it. There is nothing wrong with that."

"What they built has nothing to do with the place they came to."

"We all suffer from nostalgia," Father Emmanouil said. "The Anafi islanders simply expressed their sorrow in their buildings."

"Not everyone could have had a grand house like yours, Irini," Nefeli said. "Some of us aren't even from here. And I'm not even talking about Oumer and Tamrat, bless them. Father and I are from Thebes. Surely that doesn't mean we need to go away."

"No. I never said it did," Irini said and sat back from the table. She glanced out for the waiter in hopes that she could signal to him as the priest did, to bring the check for the priest's payment. She was growing frustrated now with this Sunday lunch she had not even wished to attend, except for the economy it would allow her and the additional ice cream she would be able to buy from the kiosk. She was trying to be nice to the girl and now Nefeli was adopting the wise kindness of the priest's wife. Irini had reached a point in her life when certain utterances should drive directly to their meaning and every meaning should be instantly understood. She did not have the time for other people's detours and digressions. When she sat in her little living room with the Proust on her lap and the French-Greek dictionary on the small table beside her, she often cursed the man's unwillingness to come directly to the point. It was as if he were some kind of self-appointed Scheherazade and must unwind his story in the longest possible way lest his life end in time with the telling. Which was not a bad strategy—though Proust had failed at it by dying before his book was finished. But why should Irini have to take the rest of *her* life to read about *his*?

"You are, of course, right, Nefeli," she said, and she looked at each of them in turn. Anna, Father Emmanouil, his wife. "And doesn't the church and our own tradition as Hellenes teach us to welcome the stranger?" She waited a moment. "I just wish the stranger had better taste in architecture."

She smiled to show that she was making a joke and the smile and the laughter of the others released them all from the tight bounds of the conversation, and Father Emmanouil signaled to the waiter who stood ready with the check because he too had sensed their need for freedom and wished also to seat another party in their place. With the boys absent, there would be no dance of pastry offers to extend the meal today. They pushed back their chairs and rose.

"I'd love to see your family home sometime," Anna said, as they paused before departing.

"It's not far from here," the priest said.

"Anyone can see it anytime," Irini said. "You don't need me to take you."

The goodwill of the meal's end vanished beneath Irini's brusqueness. Father Emmanouil could not understand the woman's determination to be unkind today. He prided himself on remembering details about the previous lives of his few parishioners but summoned up no information to explain Irini's mood. Was it a tragic anniversary? Was it the remembrance of an important date in the city's history? The crushing of the student uprising: November. The street battles at the end of one war and the start of the next: December. The German invasion: April. The end of the military junta: July. There was nothing in August to mar the mood of an Athenian save the searing heat to be experienced by those who had not traveled to the islands to escape.

"The good news is that the house isn't going anywhere," he said. But it was clear to everyone this was a foolish assertion, considering the city's and the house's own history of upheaval. "You have all the time in the world to go see it, and I'm sure Irini will be glad to show it to you." He looped his arm through Nefeli's. "I will see you both at service next week," he said, "if not before."

Nefeli kissed Anna on both cheeks and watched the girl step backward to avoid the delicacy of having to kiss Irini the same way as custom would allow. Anna had learned her lesson, though it would be only five days before she touched the old woman again. Now she waved a hand and made her way across the square so that she could skirt the base of the Acropolis. When she had first come to the city, she had raised a gale of laughter at her first departure from the bar with the birdcage over the espresso machine. Her friends had explained that it was rude to show the flattened palm and had taught her to wave in a one-handed clapping gesture bringing her fingers to her palm. Now when she reached the corner by the entrance to the rooftop cinema, she turned to see if the other three were still there. They were and they were watching her. She raised her hand and made the clapping shape, a gesture that reminded Anna of a baby's greeting, hoping they would see her through the branches of the mulberry trees.

"If you want her to see my house so much," Irini said, "you show it to her. I'm busy."

"Always?"

"Always."

"Except when you come to church."

"Whether or not I come to church is my business."

"Actually, it's very much mine. It's my *only* business, Irini."

He laughed, but there was nothing humorous about this situation, in Irini's eyes.

"You're matchmaking, Father." He gave a look of dramatic indignation. "Yes, you are," she continued.

"I'm doing no such thing."

"She's a nice girl," Nefeli said. "She only wants to be helpful."

"Nobody her age just wants to be helpful," Irini said, but this was more true of her own age than of Anna's. Irini moved away as if to leave, but she had more to say. "You two have decided I need watching. That's it, isn't it? And I don't. What about me makes you think I need a young person to check in on me?"

The priest and his wife had not rehearsed this conversation—though Nefeli had played her part in feigning ignorance of how the two women had come together. But they had ample practice in convincing their parents to do what they thought best, the latest success being to cast a weekend with the grandsons as rejuvenating to the older couple. Father Emmanouil stepped forward now while Nefeli receded.

"You've said your hip is bothering you," he said.

"I told you that was what I was hoping God would help me fix. Or help me find the patience for. Or the money. But that doesn't mean *she's* going to do anything about it."

Again, Irini began to walk away.

"But—" Nefeli took Irini's arm, knowing that her touch had been earned and would face no ill consequences. "It will be nice for you to spend time with someone from a younger generation."

"Why? Why do you both think I must spend time in the company of someone younger than myself? I have my friends. I have my chats with you two. If I am to add another person to my social circle, it will be because I chose her."

"Why not spend a little time with the girl?" Nefeli said, as if Irini had not spoken.

It was at this moment that Irini realized it was not for her benefit that the priest had brought her and the girl together, but for the girl's. She felt a flush of satisfaction, to be singled out with this sort of importance, and to see that she could move now by invitation. But Nefeli mistook the resultant smile on Irini's face for the older woman's affection for the girl and she pulled Irini into an embrace.

"I knew you were too kind at heart to resist," she said. "You'll do it, then?"

"Nefeli, no."

"She'll do it, Father," Nefeli said.

With her back turned to Irini she made large eyes at her husband, signaling to him to go along. They would produce enough enthusiasm to sweep Irini up into their idea, and by the time Irini realized she had become fast friends with this girl more than fifty years her junior, it would be too late for her to extricate herself. Nefeli had been on the beach at Kineta one day when a little boy on an inflatable Mickey Mouse had drifted far offshore. Pregnant with their first son, she had been terrified to see the rescued boy, himself terrified and unmoving in the arms of the water-ski boater who had returned him to his wailing mother. The sight of him returned to safety had called up every possibility for how he might have perished. Anna was hardly young enough to be Nefeli's child—twenty-seven years old to Nefeli's thirty-two—but she was someone's child, alone in a large and chaotic city and without the carapace of cool to protect her. The girl wanted so much. This had been clear to Nefeli and to the priest who had seen right away when Anna had lingered in the tiny courtyard before the church that she was charged with yearning. For what had not been clear. Nefeli had maintained to her husband that the girl was not devout, but he had not seemed to mind, preferring any body in the congregation to no congregation at all. Nefeli had felt this was perhaps a kind of cheating, to embrace someone who might want no more from the church than an embrace. This is the whole point, the priest had reminded her. To embrace even those who are unsure.

"Excellent," he said now.

"No," Irini said. "I will not do it." She stepped away from the two of them who stood beaming at her. "I have my life set the way I like it and I am too busy to play babysitter to this girl."

Something changed in Nefeli's face at that moment that Irini could not read but that she hoped meant a casting off of this enthusiasm she found so tiring. She should have simply walked away, having won the argument, but—for all her quarrels with this lazy God—she could not turn her back on a priest.

"What?" Irini said.

"She told me about the figs."

"What figs?" Irini knew exactly what figs, as she had craved more when those were done and had not found any ripe ones in the market on Saturday.

"She told me how she was going to drop them off and leave to meet her friends but you served her tea and made her eat with you."

"I never made her do anything."

"In a good way," Nefeli said. "And she enjoyed your stories so much that she changed all her evening plans, just to stay."

"So, you see, Irini," said the priest. "It seems you might have liked talking to her after all. Just a little bit." He held up two fingers to show her exactly how little. It was an ecclesiastical gesture—to bring the fingers together like a trinity to make the sign of the cross—and it made the priest look slightly awkward now to be using it by habit in his joke. He was not in his element. That was why he had let his wife persist in this social maneuvering. Irini *was* in her element. She stood in the same street she had been pushed down in an infant carriage, or had walked or run or strolled on for eighty-two years. The reason she never stumbled in the streets of Plaka even in her heels was that she had been walking every meter of them since she knew how to walk. She sometimes wondered if she *could* walk outside the confines of the city's oldest quarters, beyond the Plaka and the Acropolis and the footworn marble of the ancient theater. She had not left Athens since her husband's death. Plaka was her element, and Father Emmanouil and his wife were from Thebes and had come to Athens only lately. She had every reason to shape her own life as she wanted and to be unmoved by any pressures coming at her from inside or out.

"I will be at church next Sunday, Father. Nefeli, give my love to the boys when their grandparents return them."

"Irini, wait."

"There's no need to apologize," she said. "I know you mean well." She found this a useful way to remind the unapologetic that they were in your debt. She walked off toward the little square and realized that she was trembling, not with weakness but excitement. If her God would not listen to her, at least she had the priest and his wife in her control.

She waited until they would be gone from the little square before going to the kiosk to purchase her Magnum ice cream. She stood in the shade of the kiosk awning around the back where the owner kept a pink plastic chair for when he had no business. She peeled the wrapper off, racing to eat the ice cream before the chocolate coating melted. This was a far better product than the ice creams of her youth and of her daughter's youth, tangy from goats' milk and coarse with crystals of ice. If she abstained from the rooftop cinema this week, she would purchase another of these ice creams before next Sunday.

In August the city gave itself over to the disconnected, those who, because of a deliberate or unwanted rootlessness, broke off from the customs and patterns of the country and did not flee the city on holiday. These people remained in what felt like an evacuated place in a time of conflict. They rejoiced in the emptiness, but they despaired of it too. There was much that they could not accomplish in these evacuated days—dry cleaning, a shoeshine, the signing of a contract—but there was much they could achieve only with the city in its lassitude. It was possible in August for those with money to spend to find a table at a restaurant even at the coveted time of ten o'clock when most Athenians began to consider dining out. It was possible for those without money to sit in a park and stretch their legs out. It was possible for everyone to cross the boulevards that framed the edges of Syntagma Square without nearly being felled by a speeding motorbike. Nevertheless, in August, Athens was hot. The heat switched on with the first direct strike of sunrise and flattened the city with a blinding white light.

If Anna had told her parents she had offered to keep the art gallery open during August on behalf of her employer, they would have explained. They would have told her the gallery owner surely would not be bothered by closing the place for the month, as most of his clients would be at resorts in the Dodecanese or the Croatian coast. The backpackers and foreign families who toured the Acropolis en route to Mykonos or Santorini were not his clientele. Anna's parents had grown up in an eastern section of the city and had been identically rushed off, as if to safety, to spend the month in beach towns where their grandparents could watch them play in the sand from their hotel balconies. Sometimes the sameness of her parents' lives before they left Greece bothered Anna, for she suspected them of covering over childhood hardship and arriving at identical fictions. They were not siblings, after all, but boyfriend and girlfriend and then husband and wife. How could their upbringings have been so similar? What Anna did not understand was that class determined everything in Greece and that the patterns of behavior were long established within each class. It was as determined that her parents were going to go from childhoods in Chalandri to summers in Kalamata as it was set that they would emigrate specifically to Astoria when they were twenty-five.

But Anna had said nothing to her parents during any of their Sunday Skype calls about her August plans, and when they had asked her in late July where she was going to flee to, she had explained that she was staying. Her parents had expected her back in the States long before this point, as the term of her internship had come to an end in March. Whenever they imagined her in her extended time in the city, they assumed that she had found that loveliest of Greek things that they had never been able to replicate in Astoria: the parea, the group of friends. They assumed their daughter had been held in Athens in the arms of her parea, staying out late on weekends, spending long afternoons at one of the beaches in Glyfada or Lagonisi. They had assumed she would go with her parea to one island or another for the month of August. Anna explained that she did have a parea—and she did; she was not lying about this—but that she wanted to see what the city would be like when all the noise fell away. She knew her parents had left not for a month but forever because they had wanted to be able to afford such comings and goings for the rest of their lives. Her parents would have been deeply saddened and embarrassed too to think of their daughter remaining behind with, as they would have put it, the poor. So, Anna had cast all this as a desire for quiet, letting them picture her strolling easily through Kolonaki and onward to the smaller of Athens' hills that rose up to face the Acropolis. From there, she would relax and catch the breeze drifting toward the Aegean between the twin ranges of Hymettos and Parnitha. As if in demonstration of an allegory, the city was framed by a monastery on one side and a casino on the other.

Anna had a parea. This was true. She was not always sure that her parea had *her*, for she knew that she remained peripheral to them. They got together, for instance, in smaller groups that she was not part of, and they had a history of many years together as teenagers from the same school, meeting others in art school, and adding family friends and cousins over the years. They had swept her up among them a bit as a curiosity, pulling her in as the new assistant in the gallery where another of them had once worked, and who already spoke excellent Greek and had the coloring and eyebrows to look it but who was also clearly foreign. They had encouraged Anna in the change from her all-black outfits to the high-tops and tanks she wore now. But they resisted changing her over completely, as they liked the tiny differences that set her apart when more intimate and personal aspects of the parea were being

discussed. This August, Anna's parea announced they had decided
to go camping, which meant setting up tents beneath sharp-needled
evergreens along the west coast of the country where the beaches
were wild and pebbled and the water of the Ionian was azure and
clear. They would go for the second half of the month, and Anna had
said that she would join for a few days if the gallery owner could be
persuaded to close. She had not asked him yet and was unlikely to
do so, as she was afraid to interrupt his holiday with her phone call
and imagined his displeasure at being pulled away from a cocktail
or a dive off a yacht or worse. Worst of all was the possibility that
the gallery owner would grant permission and she would travel to the
coast to find her parea awkwardly surprised to see her.

&

When Anna had told Father Emmanouil about her intention to
stay in the city all of August, he had insisted that she leave. Nefeli
had nearly pushed her *onto* a boat—go at least to Hydra for a few
days—and professed herself ready to drive her to the campground
on the western coast when the time came. Instead, the priest and
his wife did the next best thing. They brought her together with
Irini. There had been a time in Irini's life when she would have
been shocked, insulted even, to think that *she* would stay in Athens
during August. She had spent her childhood Augusts on the island
of Siros, paddling in rocky pools and dropping sea urchins into a
bucket, and riding her bicycle past neoclassical harbor houses not
unlike the family home in Plaka. Her mother had had a nanny
for her then, so that the little girl Irini could play safely while
her mother and grandmother drank tea or lemonade beneath the
portico that fronted the embankment. Then with her husband,
Irini had brought their daughter for years to the same house on

the same island, venturing to Nafplion one summer only and to Kerkyra another before realizing that no matter where they went, they always stayed in the same kinds of places with the same kinds of house. Not for them, the low, whitewashed structures of the Cyclades where the tourists thought they found something *echt* Greek. They preferred high-ceilinged neoclassical buildings just like their home in Plaka, built on islands by the wealthy to be occupied by the wealthy on vacation.

Then Irini had stopped being wealthy. Not all at once but slowly. First there had been the never-explained cut to her husband's pension, and then there had been his refusal to budget to this new reality, and then there had been the dispute with Irini's brother and sister over the house on Siros, which she lost, and then the earthquake in Athens that had caused so much damage to the house that had been given outright to Irini as her only financial stake. And then their move to a small apartment, and then the husband's sudden death, and drastic reductions to the widow's pension she had inherited, now explained—the economic crisis and austerity. From there it had been onward to various liabilities of the old house—liabilities of more than an economic nature—and Irini was no longer wealthy. She was, if she admitted it, almost a ward of the State—though, as she thought of it, weren't they all. Her medical costs were paid for by the State, her Metro pass, her entrance to museums, all paid for by the State. If that was all she ever wanted to do—not read or eat well or see movies or buy clothes—she might survive. This was another thing Irini liked about the Church, besides the charity of her free rent: the Church had money, lots of it, and being inside even the little church with the stubby nave made them all feel like kings and queens, surrounded by gold and silver. This was probably not a thought Father Emmanouil should ever hear, preferring as he did to emphasize the shared humility of the congregation before God—whose palace, after all, this was—but it afforded Irini some satisfaction.

Now it was August 2 and anyone regularly attending church and even many who did not would begin a mental preparation for the Assumption on the 15th. Some would even fast in the days leading up to the holiday, as the priest had exemplified with his lunch of giant beans in red sauce. To prepare his congregation beyond their dining choices, Father Emmanouil liked to give out small sheets of photocopied paper to his congregants with a list of Bible passages to read in order to bring the mind and soul in line with this great event of Mary's ascension into the heavens. He had made the mistake a few years ago of marking the sheets with the specific date and so every year since then he handed out these photocopied instructions that, though they were supposed to pertain to something eternal, reminded everyone of how much time had passed. Nefeli tried to convince him to recycle these pages and print new ones without a date at all, but he believed the most environmentally friendly practice was not recycling but reusing. So, as Irini sat in her little living room with her morning coffee and the Bible, she consulted a reading list of Biblical passages dated from four years prior. She tried to remember what she had been doing four Augusts ago, and realized it was the same. How could it not have been? Four years ago she was in Plaka, as always, living in this little apartment, and she had had her book club and her cinema to round out her days. They had been reading *Moby Dick* then and it had been a failure, the arcane English words of whaling and seamanship nearly lost to the translator in the Greek. There was a small measure of delight for her then in being newly resident in the little apartment with its grand view of the Acropolis. She had left herself no place else to go then—and still now—and the charity of the apartment had been rescue and relief from mounting rent bills and the need to layer sweaters and blankets on a raw winter day to save the cost of heat.

Now, as soon as Irini took up the photocopy and the Bible, she set them down again. For one thing, the paper was that sort of photocopy that glistens like a dolphin skin and curls and grays slightly at the edges, and something about it this morning made Irini shudder at the touch. For another, she was bored. Or, rather, she was reminded to be bored. Four Augusts in a row had found her doing the same thing, in the middle of a life of the same things, in the same place. If repetition was the hallmark of eternity, it now occurred to her she might want nothing to do with an after-life. Could she not extend her life *itself* in some way that made it interesting? She was struck suddenly with the desire for variation, though she was a woman who shook her head at change whenever she encountered it. She wanted the world unchanged—a time when Plaka's neoclassical houses contained families with servants and when the grandest buildings were schools and concert halls, not electronics stores—but she wanted to move through it. She wanted to *do* things, and something about the slick feel of the priest's old photocopies gave her a sense almost of horror—horror for days wasted, for opportunities missed, for days adding up toward her final limit when instead she should be pushing and stretching them away and apart. More than the electric bill—which was not at all insignificant—she had debts and she could not be wasting time to settle them.

She finished her coffee quickly, with her eyes on the Acropolis to watch the Greek flag hoisted up the flagpole for the day. She vaguely remembered the day the Nazi flag had gone up in its place—she told people she had actually seen it though she had not—and the day a few weeks later when the two teenagers from her neighborhood—the parents of one of the boys were acquaintances of Irini's own—had slipped past the German soldiers to raise the Greek flag once again. This Greek flag the Acropolis was using now replaced an older pennant that had faded with the sun, and it was vivid in that particular blue of a proper Greek flag. Not royal blue and not the turquoise shade that disgusted her when she saw it replicated in the flag images on hundreds of refrigerator magnets and T-shirts for sale along the streets of Plaka. This was a proper deep electric blue, suggestive of the blue of the Aegean, and if they were raising it now, the time must be nine o'clock. When she checked her husband's wristwatch, she saw it was ten past the hour. She rose to fill the day, while wishing not to look too closely at how little she had with which to fill it.

Irini made her usual circuit through the shops in Plaka but then stretched her loop toward the garden of the Zappeio, which required the crossing of one of the major boulevards, already in its August state of near desertion. Little was altered there since Irini's childhood. In its institutional locations, Athens retained a constancy it lacked utterly everywhere else. The essentials of a park or monument—packed paths of sand or gravel, a low cement curb, the dust-covered leaves of prickly hedges and swaying cypresses, even the particular maroon paint with which to mark a garden feature—these were all identical now to the days when Irini's nanny, a stalwart woman from Epirus in the north with blonde hair and pale eyes, had straightened her pinafore whenever she ran back from skipping rope.

She knew exactly where to go, what route to take through the garden's winding paths in order to avoid the dead end of the Prime Ministerial palace and circle back to the same boulevard as before, now at the entrance to the city's central square. Here,

there was change. The concert hall was now a Public selling lap-
tops and books and smartphones, and the building beside it, once
equally grand, was gone entirely, replaced by an atrocity in glass
and metal. The square itself was equipped with benches she knew
to be designed for crowd control, bolted into the marble paving so
as not to be used as weapons in the frequent demonstrations that
occurred there. The cafés that once ringed the square and set up
tables in the center were now prohibited from doing so lest their
furniture become projectile. The regulations had not prevented
the protesters—from the left or the right, it didn't matter—from
prying up marble tiles from the square and its stairways. So, as she
descended into the square now from the boulevard, she saw patches
of bare cement and grout where marble had once been.

There were refugees camped in the square, and the scope of them
was new to Athens in the last few years. There had, of course, always
been some refugees in the city. Islanders from Naxos and Anafi who
had claimed entire neighborhoods as their own, Greeks who had
fled Asia Minor in 1922, Albanians who had poured across the
border as soon as it opened to let them out of their prison country,
and now the tens of thousands who came from Afghanistan and
Syria and Pakistan and Iraq and Somalia, and immigrants like
Oumer and Tamrat. Performing that error of well-meaning people
everywhere, Irini scanned the square for the two Ethiopians,
assuming that, as foreigners, they would be wherever there were
any people like them. Oumer and Tamrat were not there but in an
internet café a few streets to the west where Oumer was building
a website for his planned Ethiopian-style coffee shop and Tamrat
was checking his email for confirmation of a wire he had sent home
to Addis Ababa.

Irini returned to Plaka by the pedestrian streets that had been
created in a panic of shame at the city's poor score in a test of

hospitability to its inhabitants. It was the time of sales in all the shops, August being at once one of the holiest times in the religious calendar, the most popular vacation period, and the best time for the clearing out of merchandise. A low price on a skirt or blouse could be someone's reward for enduring the city's greatest heat. Irini dawdled before a few windows but the shops catered mostly to the young and to styles that she would never even want to wear, and the shops that did appeal to her were too expensive. She determined to wait until later in the month when the prices would drop further and when she would likely have been able to set aside more funds. She did her shopping at the little markets in the Plaka, gathering eggs and fruit and cheese and yogurt and a small collection of vegetables in her string bag. As always, she was praised and admired by the shopkeepers, and as always, she tipped her head in her gesture of mock royalty and offered some small compliment in return.

But she was back in the little square too soon and she had hardly done anything to break up the routine of her day except to visit the park she had known since childhood. The day was still far too young. The cafés still held their first wave of customers, the old men who gathered daily to discuss the newspaper. She had joined a group of them once, but from up close she had seen how old they really were, these widowers with no one home to correct them on their shaving or their laundry, and one of them had farted unapologetically while joking about the austerity measures and Irini had never returned again. She skirted the men's café now and made for the other corner of the square to check the schedule for the rooftop cinema. Because it was August, the husband and wife who owned the cinema and had remained married despite the wife's affair with Father Emmanouil's predecessor indulged their son in his desire to screen European films to nearly empty seats. Attendance would be low in summer anyway, the young man reasoned, with natives mostly gone and tourists mistakenly preferring clubs and seaside bouzouki bars. So, the son chose to edify the few customers who persisted. This week and next he was screening a series of Truffaut films. *Jules et Jim* this evening. Irini had seen the film with her husband when it had first premiered. It had been just the two of them then, no child yet and no third person in the marriage. Irini had been twenty-seven and her husband twenty-nine and they had been married barely two years then—a little late in life for that, because the war had stretched the time for everything. They had not yet been past the high passions of their own romance, though Irini thought that neither Jules nor Jim nor this Catherine they were both besotted with need behave with such histrionics. She kept looking over at her husband in the dark—it was a winter screening and they were indoors in velvet seats—and delighting in his handsomeness in his turtleneck sweater and his sideburns. By any objective measure he had been a handsome man and Irini herself was a handsome woman. They had made a glamorous pair in those days, lounging over patisseries at Zonars or sharing drinks in the lobby of the Grande Bretagne.

Irini made a quick and unsettling calculation that she could forego something later in the week—she did not identify what, in the same failure to pin down the economics that had contributed to her husband's mismanagement of their budget—and to that part of herself that knew better she insisted on the importance of the cinema to her cultural life and to the cultural life of Plaka. She could not imagine Plaka without the cinema, and she could not imagine the little square without its offered glimpses from below at night of the glow from the projection on the large blank wall of the adjacent building. She purchased one ticket for the early show at nine o'clock that evening. The son of the owners knew to assume that

she had seen the film before and knew to express astonishment
that she had already been married in 1963 when it had first screened
in Greece. She could not possibly have even been born then, he
exclaimed, and she gave that tip of the head and praised him for
his good taste as a cineaste among the philistines of his generation.

It was barely lunchtime now—it was barely past morning—and
she did not know how she would fill this day that suddenly seemed
so stifling. No, that is not quite right. Irini knew exactly what
would break her out of the pattern of her life. She turned her mind
to frivolous options, to creature comforts that would delight and
amuse. She could go to the new cultural center and stroll the olive
grove that had been installed on a vast sloping plane rising to the
arts complex itself. She could browse the books in the national
library there and watch the sun set over Salamis from the rooftop
pavilion. At sunset it was easy to see where the Athenian fleet had
hidden behind the land mass of the island, lying in wait for the
Persian ships lured into the strait. This was one of Irini's favorite
of Greek victories, the sneak attack, the deception that won out.
However, like a true Greek, she admired the tragic losses almost
as much, and Ephialtes' betrayal at Thermopylae ranked with her
among the finest tragedies of ancient times, with its cunning and
improvisation, characteristics she saw around her in the city every
day. She had made the trip to the cultural center soon after it had
opened, along with seemingly everyone else in Athens, lining up
in the city's main square for one of the shuttle buses and riding in
cramped delight down the boulevard to the coast. She had felt like
a figure on an opera stage descending the long flight of stairs outside the giant building after ascending in an elevator made almost
entirely of glass. The place had sung with a liveliness she had not
seen in years. Children had ridden bicycles around the reflecting
pool where sailboats—full sailboats!—zigged and zagged at the

direction of the inexperienced, and couples had kissed by the olives, and entire families had leaned over the rail of the broad rooftop pavilion to gawk at the sea, the city, the Acropolis, the olive grove and the yoga classes and soccer matches and picnics below. If she could have gone there every day, she liked to think she would have. Or Irini could go to Hydra on the fast boat and reach its harbor town in time for lunch at the same taverna she and her husband had frequented in those summers when the Canadian was there writing his songs. He had been quite famous then and had become even more famous since, once his songs kept being redone in modern variations Irini found insipid.

Of course, she could do this—she could even fly to Paris or Milan, if she had the time and money. But she had lived too much time and possessed not enough money and not even the sharpness of her desire could balance the equation. And on top of all this, it was hot. She took her groceries up to the apartment and sat with her Proust and her French-Greek dictionary—though she hardly ever needed to consult it—and tried to concentrate on everywhere Marcel was going—which was difficult because he himself never went anywhere except in describing others—and not on everywhere that she was not.

⁂

If Irini had widened her walk that morning by even just a few more blocks, she would have seen Anna sitting at the counter of the café near Monastiraki where Oumer worked as a barista. Anna liked to stop there on her way to the gallery in Psirri and to chat with Oumer outside the confines of the church, and by now he knew her order and began preparing it as she arrived. A French coffee, which was what Greeks called the kind of simple coffee one had in America. She had been up late the night before sketching out a new project on a wall Oumer himself had told her about. In his parkour travels, he often spotted likely spaces for Anna's graffiti writing, and she, in turn, was learning to recognize good routes for free-running in the staggered levels of the city's buildings and park walls. Anna's daily stops for coffee had become exchanges of information: routes for Oumer and concrete canvases for Anna.

Earlier that week he had told her about a good wall on the side of an empty lot in Metaxourgeio that was used during the day for parking. The wall had texture to it—the lower half being of amalgam and the upper covered in plaster.

"Did you check it?" Oumer said. She would have to act quickly, given the rarity of an unpainted surface in that neighborhood where some of the world's best graffiti artists did their work.

"Yeah. Here."

She tugged her sketchbook from her bag and opened it to the page where she had done a marker drawing of her idea. In fuchsia, blue, and yellow she had drawn a design that worked with the wall's existing lines. Anna's style—if she could be said to have one—was neither the angular energy of wildstyle nor the tongue-in-cheek lightness of bubble writing. Nor did she paint images that were beautiful in themselves and simply took the urban hardscape as their canvas. She worked, so far, with the lines of the wall or building as she found it. This was not a particularly inventive approach. In fact, it could be said that such obedience to the contours of the building was a sign of creative weakness. In Anna's case, such an assertion would be correct. For, as avid as she was in her commitment to her art, Anna was only a middling artist and had, in fact, arrived in Athens not as a street artist but a collagist. Her creative output in college and the years after had consisted of cutting up images created by others and arranging them to her liking. Her liking tended toward the obvious: a stiletto overlapping a gun, a beach scene intercut with snow.

In Athens, she had made the friends who had in turn made her into a graffiti artist, plying her moderate ability and her willingness to venture to the empty lots and broken-down buildings of the city into murals they enjoyed. The walls of Athens were covered with art—or defiled, depending on one's politics and taste. Along with the rampant emblems of a particular seating section of a particular soccer club, or the slogans of the far left or the far right, murals and tags covered nearly every available wall of the city. Visitors to Athens who marveled at the whiteness of the Parthenon's marbles needed to look no further than the city's graffitied walls to see what the ancient temple must have looked like in its time, painted in bright reds and golds and greens. Anna's friends, who saw that her work was hardly better than what they themselves could make, nonetheless encouraged her. A few had become regular escorts for her painting sessions, holding the flashlight or scouting for police or property owners while Anna worked, and in this way they sometimes hid suggestions for improvement within their praise of her colors or her attitude.

Oumer swiveled the sketchbook on the counter for the right orientation.

"Cool," he said. "I like the pink."

Oumer was not a particularly keen judge of art, but this suited Anna better than a sharper critic who might have crushed her spirit. Anna was not a bad artist, but she was only average, and like many who do not rise above the middle of their craft, she could not see how far below the peak she stood. Which was, for Anna, just as well, for she rode the wave of her own enthusiasm into cheerful action and creation, instead of idling in the resignation that she would never measure up.

"Thanks, Oum," Anna said. "I stayed up way too late to do it."

She called Oumer by this nickname, though the abbreviation made as much linguistic sense as her shortening of the priest's name to his first syllable. Oumer did not have the heart to correct her, though Tamrat raised his eyebrows at Anna—who did not notice—each time he heard the sound.

She asked Oumer for a refill and he obliged, pouring the second French coffee into a paper cup with a plastic lid so that she could take it with her to the gallery. This practice was hardly common except among foreigners and tourists, for most in the city knew that there was always a coffee shop nearby and it was still possible to summon a waiter from across the street to bring coffees to one's office on a nickel-plated tray he swung from his hand like a giant censer.

Anna took her coffee from Monastiraki to the gallery in Psirri where no one came to look at the art, not a single person. She busied herself leafing through the art magazines the gallery owner used as decoration in the waiting area. There had been times when the gallery had been full enough for visitors to sit in the three beautiful but uncomfortable leather chairs and wait for space to clear in front of an intriguing work of art. In January, soon after she had arrived in Athens, they had had a show that had been quite successful, even garnering a review in the culture section of the center-left newspaper, and the gallery owner had been pleased enough to give Anna a tip simply for taking coats and handing out drinks and programs. But today she was the one who sat in one of the beautiful chairs and tried and failed to make herself comfortable.

In her bag from which she had pulled her sketchbook to show Oumer she had one of Father Emmanouil's silvery photocopies and an English-language Bible. She wanted to make headway on the readings. This would be her first Assumption in Greece, not counting the summer she had been fourteen. But that year her relatives had simply taken her with them on the beach holiday where she had fallen from the Vespa and scarred her knee. Those cousins now were long gone from Anna's and her family's life, the younger generation having emigrated and the older having either died or returned to villages from which they ceased to keep in touch. Anna would be on her own for the Assumption, and she wanted to make the most of it, delving as deeply into the holiness of the time as she had delved into its secular version years ago. But she resisted her urge to pull the paper and the book out lest a customer arrive and find the gallery assistant engrossed in a religious text. She sensed it would not do to be revealed as a believer. She thought back to the lunch Father Emmanouil had hosted after church five days ago. She was no fool. She knew what had run beneath the conversation, sensed Nefeli's worry about her, her defense of her, sensed the inexplicable—to Anna—disdain the older woman suddenly seemed to feel for her after having spent so many hours happily in her presence. Anna had told her friends how much she had liked this unusual old woman and now she wondered if their lack of interest in the old woman meant Irini was not unusual at all but a type, and her quick but fleeting embrace of their young friend was to be expected.

But still, Anna believed she had understood something correctly about the woman. Anna believed in many things. She believed in God, she believed in herself, and she believed today that she could befriend this old woman just as Nefeli and Father Emmanouil had intended her to do. And she believed that the old woman needed Anna's friendship. The woman had no one—there was obviously a daughter but, save the photos of her and her son, there had been no sign of her, no note on the refrigerator, no jacket on the hook forgotten from another visit, no figs the daughter herself might have brought. Anna resolved to try again soon, and, because she had been thinking of Irini and because she was too tired from her late night to attend the party she was supposed to attend, and because in her fatigue she suddenly missed the consolations of a television and its ersatz peopling of one's quiet space, on her way home at the end of the day, she stopped at the cinema in the little square and bought a ticket to the early show.

Neither woman saw the other at the cinema at first. This had to do in part with the dusk and in part with their different arrival times—Irini coming early so as to claim a favored seat among the folding deck chairs arranged in rows across the sloping roof, and Anna arriving late after a phone call with the friend whose party would occur later that evening and to which Anna had declared she was too tired to go. Irini stopped at the concession window at the high, rear end of the roof and purchased a small bag of passatempo, melon seeds roasted and salted so they could be cracked between the teeth. This had been her custom at the cinema for decades, as it was the custom of all Greeks, and she refused to adopt the American import of popped and buttered corn kernels. Anna bought a large bag of exactly this, surprised and delighted to encounter this reminder of home even in this place within sight of the Parthenon. For indeed the temple was on full view from the rooftop cinema. Irini had often registered her boredom with a film by simply turning to watch the lights play on the ancient stones instead.

Tonight, though, Irini was not bored. She slid down ever so slightly in the canvas sling of the deck chair and tilted her head back as if to be kissed. And as she watched the film's opening scenes and saw again after a passage of five decades the ease of these young people in their talk of love and sex, she felt an almost amorous closeness to the woman she had been during that first viewing and to her husband as he had been then. In the film, the woman had two men—obviously the Jules and the Jim of the title—a situation that was just as complicated and dangerous in real life, Irini knew, as in the film. To Anna, the film was an artifact not unlike the psalms and icons of the church. This was life from before, a life her great-grandparents could have known, could have replicated in their own Greek way. Her great-grandparents had been far too conservative to have lived at all like this. But Anna pretended otherwise as she watched and let herself be carried back to a previous time as if it could be her own history.

To Anna's surprise, there was an intermission, complete with a short, animated advertisement of dancing popcorn bags and cola bottles. When she turned to walk back up to the concession window for a Coca Light to slake her thirst after the popcorn, she saw Irini sitting in a chair on the aisle halfway up.

"Good evening," Anna said, opting for this rather formal greeting. "I see we both had the same idea."

"I never miss a chance to see Truffaut," Irini said.

"I'm getting a Coke," Anna said. "Can I get you something?" Anna chose her question carefully, selecting the Greek word that meant to offer rather than simply to bring, as she wished to make up for what she felt was the fiasco of their lunch together as the priest's guests.

"No, but thank you."

Irini reconsidered her reply, thinking that perhaps it would be a small kindness to allow the girl to treat her, and thinking, too, that she did not usually buy a beverage to go along with her melon seeds and so this treat would make a savings for her in the end. She began to speak just as Anna, of her own accord, turned back to Irini's row.

"In fact," Irini said, "they have a beer here that I like."

"Beer!" Anna said. "That's what I'll get. One for you as well?"

"Thank you. That would be lovely. I prefer the Mythos."

Earlier that day, in her restlessness, Irini had not gone to the new cultural center or to Hydra on the fast boat or to Paris or Milan, for these options were all equally fantastical given the state of her life and her finances. Instead, she had sat for hours reading the Proust and bits of the priest's selections from the Bible. The bottle of Mythos beer would be her sole indulgence, besides the cinema, the sole thing that would serve as an exception to the pattern of her days. She determined not to allow the sadness of that fact to diminish her enjoyment. There was, however, one problem with the fact that she had accepted—invited, really—the girl's offer of the beer: now the girl would have to linger and chat and it would be unspeakably rude of Irini not to make a more explicit invitation to the girl to join her. Her savings would not be without cost.

The cinema was practically empty. There was one middle-aged man sitting at the very front and four teenagers, two boys and two girls, who whispered and giggled at the back and paid no attention to the film. They had already completed the time-honored tradition of all teenagers in a Greek rooftop cinema, which was to roll their empty glass bottles of Fanta—guzzled just before the intermission—down the slope of the cinema roof so that the bottles trundled slowly and noisily but inexorably toward the edge of the raised platform at the front. Irini wondered why the owners of the cinema continued to order glass-bottled Fanta at all, considering that every night they had to sweep up the bottles and the occasional bits of glass if the Fanta rolled fast enough to break. The son of the owners had tried many times to discontinue the Fanta but his parents insisted, as they understood that the rolling of the bottles, more than the films themselves, was what compelled the teenagers to purchase tickets.

It was, then, in a virtually empty cinema that Anna returned with the beers, each one opened and topped with an inverted plastic cup, and made a little shuffle step to indicate she did not mind returning to her own seat. When Irini said, "Please. Join me, won't you?" and waved a hand at the deck chair beside hers, the girl fought to conceal the extent of her delight. As Irini was on the aisle, Anna performed the dance of theaters everywhere, shimmying past and desperately hoping not to touch. She took her seat, and both women filled their cups from their respective bottles—Mythos for Irini and Amstel for Anna—and toasted each other with a muted clink of the edges of their plastic cups.

In the film's second half, the situation of the lovers became dire, as each pull toward the one meant a rift with the other, and the connection between the two men remained a thing unspoken in 1962 when the film was made but palpable enough now to give the story a new meaning. There was a moment when the pain of it all for Jules and Jim and Catherine became so great that Anna and Irini both sighed and then turned to each other to agree that Jeanne Moreau was *so good*, and then they laughed at their identical reactions. Not much later, during a tender scene, one of the teenaged boys let out a belch—the product of the Fanta—and the middle-aged man in the front row jumped up—his silhouette entirely blocking the film that he was there to see and now defend— and shouted that he had had enough of their behavior and that they should go home and watch *The Lion King*. It was impossible not to find this funny and impossible not to support the teenagers as they ordered the man to sit down and stop blocking the *program*. During the next quiet moment in the film, one of the boys, the friend of the one who had belched, began to sing one of *The Lion King* songs in falsetto.

"That's it, I've had it with you," the middle-aged man said, and strode loudly up the aisle past Irini and Anna and continued straight out of the cinema altogether.

Not even Truffaut's classic could compete that night for drama with what had occurred on the rooftop, so as the film wound to a close, Irini leaned toward Anna and whispered "Look." They shifted in their deck chairs equally and evenly so that they spent the final moments of the screening watching not the conclusion of the doomed love triangle but the slow and stately rising of the August moon.

*

When the film was finished, Anna remained seated so that Irini could rise first, unhurried. The girl took her time descending the three flights of stairs to the lobby and from there out into the square, allowing the older woman's pace—which was not slow but not especially speedy—to dictate their progress. Once in the square, the two women faced each other directly for the first time since the Sunday lunch, and in both women there was a new surprise at the recognition of something shared. The film had been new to Anna, though she had at least heard of Truffaut and had purchased her ticket in a belief in educating herself about the culture of her elders. Irini explained the story to her and explained, too, the film's importance to the New Wave—for which she was obliged to provide a definition—and to Truffaut's *oeuvre*. She pronounced the French word with an accent Anna could only assume was quite correct, and in this she was right, for this was the same accent that led French tourists to respond to Irini with such respect. Because Anna did not speak French, she had been forced to read the subtitles, and her ability to read the Greek, especially when the letters blended into the background image, was not adept enough for her to keep up with the story. She had misunderstood certain crucial moments, it became apparent, and now Irini offered her some clarification. As she explained the meaning of one particular dialogue, the women drifted away from the cinema and found seats almost without realizing—Irini never patronized any establishment without realizing or without reasoning out every order and expense—at the café at the far end of the square. Irini was not as well known to the waiters in this café, as it was diagonally across from her apartment and from the taverna the priest took them to, and, in the cartography of small neighborhoods, might as well have been a continent away. The waiter, an old man whose muscled forearms suggested a lifetime of bearing piled plates, barely glanced at Irini or at Anna as he took their orders—a lemonade for Irini and a coffee for Anna who was rethinking her plan to skip the party with her friends and thought the coffee would serve as useful prelude. Irini continued her explanation of the dialogue that Anna had misconstrued and this required some elaboration on the nature of the love triangle among the principals. It all hinged, she told Anna, on one word and how one understood it.

"Your French is so good," Anna said, without having in fact any way to know whether Irini's translation was correct. "Did you live there?"

"Sadly no. It was a hope of mine once. We were taught French in school, and sometimes I spoke it with my parents at home. Of course, my husband and I visited Paris in our youth. But then—" She shrugged.

"Was it the war?" the girl asked somewhat breathlessly. Anna had found that most disappointments in a Greek person's life seemed to have something to do with the war, which one named as if there had been only one war, *the* war, so as to preserve a certain degree of political civility.

"Goodness, no," Irini said. "The war was why we stopped speaking *German*."

Anna waited for Irini to say more, but the older woman reached for the lemonade that the waiter had deposited along with Anna's coffee and a small glass in which the bill lay curled. Irini took a sip and sputtered at the taste. She had expected something home-made, with sugar added to the pulpy liquid and still granular at the bottom of the glass. She had forgotten, confused by the historical period of the Truffaut film and by the era when it was filmed, that she was in Plaka in 2018 and not in Siros during her childhood or in the same part of Athens more than fifty years before.

"This is dreadful," she said. "I can't drink this." She addressed this last to the waiter whose legs had not carried him away with the vigor that his arms possessed.

"Do I care?" he said. "Old fool."

Irini knew she was supposed to have no answer to the man's insulting question that should have put her in her place. But she refused to be chastened—if she had a philosophy it was precisely this: a refusal to be chastened—and so she replied.

"I'm sorry," she said. "I didn't hear you. Can you please say it again?"

"What?"

"I didn't quite catch what you said. Something about a fool. Did I hear that correctly?"

The man frowned at her with a disdain that was losing ground to confusion.

"Which one of us is the fool?" Anna said, leaning forward in her chair and hoping Irini noticed the emulation. "Was it me? I'm so sorry."

The waiter shook his head.

"Feminists," he muttered illogically, and turned for the kitchen.

It took little more than this gambit of mock sincerity and the look on the waiter's face to make the two women burst into laughter. Something had happened at the rooftop cinema—their paired bemusement at the middle-aged man who had stood in a silhouette that blocked the screen, the solitude of the two of them in the rows of seats filled only by that man, until he stormed away, and the four teenagers, and most of all their shared attention to the transit of the moon across its ancient backdrop. All of this had brought Anna and Irini together and led Anna yet one more

time to change her plans about the party. Fueled by caffeine she
would not need now for the party, she sat instead with Irini in
the square until the lemonade was gone—Irini knew never to
waste food or drink, and this might have been another pillar of her
philosophy—and until the restaurants at the other end began to
turn their chairs upside down onto their oilcloth-covered tables.

What did they talk about all this time? What was worth more to
Anna than taking her motorbike to Gazi to dance in the strobing
string lights of a friend's loft? Irini told Anna about the French
New Wave and Jean Seberg and Belmondo, and Anna described
the art collections at the gallery where she worked. They dis-
agreed briefly over what Anna called her murals and Irini called
vandalism. Irini warned Anna that though the city had very little
crime she must still watch herself during her vandal's outings at
night alone. They spoke of Father Emmanouil and agreed that
his homilies had lately lost their energy. They wondered about the
burdens upon him of this holy time of year and whether his sons,
who, as Irini pointed out, were beginning to display certain signs of
loutishness, were weighing on his mind. Anna had made less progress in the Assumption readings than Irini. They promised each
other they would do their best with the dolphin-gray photocopied
list so as not to hurt Father Emmanouil's feelings, though Anna did
not add that it was for her own spiritual benefit and not Father E.'s
that she would complete the assignment. It was after one when the
grumbling waiter, making no pretense to simply jog their memory
of the bill with a distant presence, came to stand quite frankly
by their table and glare at the bill curled in the little glass. They
placed their coins on the table—four euros from Anna's wallet for
the two of them—and rose. Before they parted for the night, they
made a plan to see the rest of the Truffaut series together, with the
next film to screen the very next night.

PART TWO

I f someone were to ask Irini how she could so suddenly become friendly with a young woman whose enthusiasm she had just days ago disdained, she would have said that expediency tipped the scale. She had lived long enough to know that strict adherence to a point of view was never guarantee of its survival. Sometimes that which was most rigid in a person's mind became precisely the notion that was easiest to upend. So it was with Irini's resistance to the girl. On the day that Anna had brought the figs, Irini had not realized the girl would take an afternoon's conversation as invitation to invade. But Anna had invaded—though the girl would never put it that way—and now that she had cracked the door open a second time, she was well inside Irini's little world. Irini had allowed her in, discovering that it was more pleasant to sit in the cinema as the guest of a young person you could educate than it was to sit alone.

Father Emmanouil asked the same question of Irini after the service the following Sunday, the day after the screening of the second film in the series, *The 400 Blows*. The son of the cinema owners had made an error in his chronology and was screening his Truffaut films out of order. When the middle-aged man had alerted him to this, during a daytime visit to the cinema's office, the son had refused to change the schedule, not quite believing that the middle-aged man was right and refusing to consult the internet for confirmation. The son was a cineaste but not a very good one. So, the second film in the series had been made before the first, and Anna and Irini had gone to see it and then had sat together at church the following day. Irini had joked that they should have passatempo and popcorn for the service. Anna had laughed but felt the joke a bit sacrilegious.

Father Emmanouil took Irini aside and left Anna to chat with Tamrat who was without Oumer that day.

"I thought you didn't want to spend time with the girl," he said.

"Me?" Irini said. "Nonsense."

"You said precisely that you didn't like her." The priest made little effort to conceal his smile.

"I said no such thing." Irini was right; she had not. "I said I didn't have time to babysit her."

"So why are you fast friends now?"

"Don't gloat, Father. It's unbecoming to a man of the cloth."

"You're not answering my question."

Irini shrugged, though she was in fact annoyed to have been found out as so easily converted.

"She's a good girl," she said, "and she needs someone to teach her about French culture."

Irini turned away then with a coy smile, leaving the priest to call after her.

"*Greek* culture."

Irini joined Anna and Tamrat, skirting the two widows who were now moving toward the priest.

"Where is Oumer?" she asked.

Before Tamrat could reply, Anna spoke up.

"Tamrat says he's hurt."

"He was training with the team," Tamrat said. He spoke with a slight accent but his Greek was nearly fluent. "Had a bad fall, I guess."

"Is he all right?" Anna said. "What happened?"

"He's fine. He just twisted his ankle."

"We need to tell Father E."

"No. Please don't," Tamrat said. "He'll be fine. He has a friend who was a doctor in Addis and he took care of it."

"Where is he now?" Irini said.

"I set him up in Tsaldari Street."

Irini frowned at the thought of Oumer sitting on the sidewalk with a crutch beside him. Tamrat could see the mix of hesitation and embarrassment on the old woman's face.

"On the computer," he said, not without some irritation. "We go to a place at Tsaldari Street for the internet."

"Oh," Irini said.

"He's researching tournaments," Tamrat said. Oumer had his own tablet he brought everywhere and used whenever business at the café was slow, which it was often as customers had the habit of making one inexpensive coffee last for hours. But the café Wi-Fi was not always strong enough to load the graphics of the best parkour videos, and so he had resorted to an internet café in Omonia. Neither he nor Tamrat liked spending time there, for the once-dynamic quarter of Omonia with its large park inside a roundabout had become the city's place for those most on the fringe. Refugees spent their first days there, until they found their footing, and junkies spent their last days there until they overdosed. Neither Tamrat nor Oumer considered themselves refugees—they had each left Ethiopia too calmly and with too much money to be called refugees and they resented the persistent label. But at least in Omonia no one would kick them out and fabricate a reason for the workstation to be unavailable or suddenly double-booked.

"Can we do anything to help?" Anna said. "Bring some food so he can rest?"

Tamrat laughed. He had bright hazel eyes and a thin mustache that gave his expression the look of an etching.

"He is fine and he has friends who are helping him. He will not starve, I assure you."

"Anna." This was Irini, who exchanged a look with Tamrat who, in turn, considered Anna with a tolerance bordering on dislike. Tamrat had met Anna early in her time in Athens when she had first come to the church, and he had seen her innocence then, her display of a certain type of kindness that, because it went along with self-assurance, often became unpleasant. He had expected that innocence to fade, but it had not, and he did not consider this a positive situation. Anna would have been mortified had she understood the effect she had on Oumer and Tamrat, whom she considered her friends.

"Anna," Irini said again, for Tamrat kept his opinions to himself. "I'm sure if there is something Oumer needs, you can give it to Tamrat to give to him." And as a formality, she asked Tamrat, "Is there anything? Aspirin? Does he need crutches?"

"He's fine."

The old woman knew not to encourage Anna to go in person to bring something to Oumer. Tamrat was certain Irini did not know exactly where Oumer lived, but he sensed she knew enough to keep the girl from visiting. If Anna were to see the crowded building where Oumer lived in an apartment with three other men, she would pity him and her pity would charge her to some sort of action that would only assert onto their relationship a false dynamic of authority. Even if Oumer had lived in a penthouse, Tamrat was certain the girl's visit would have been an intrusion. In this, he was wrong, for Oumer had come to like Anna as much for her combination of confidence and naïveté as for her tips on where to run. But Tamrat could not shake an annoyance at Anna he had formed early on. And now, again, he saw how the simple act of leaving your home country could erase your class and education and experience. It was like being a piece on a game board with your value set to zero because you had begun a journey.

❧

Between that day without Oumer and the following Sunday when he returned, Irini and Anna were to go to the third and fourth screenings of the Truffaut series. They attended the third film together, *Fahrenheit 451*, but as they were saying goodnight after yet another visit to the café—with Irini this time also ordering a coffee—Irini remembered her book club. It was because of the Proust that she had drunk the coffee to stay awake and read.

"I can't come with you on Wednesday," she said. "I have plans, I'm afraid."

"Oh." Anna was visibly crestfallen, and this gave Irini some pleasure and even pride that her absence would be so great a loss.

"More French, I'm afraid. It's my book group and we are reading Proust." She had already told the girl about her club but had forgotten. "If I don't attend, they will be angry with me."

"No, of course, you have to go."

"Invite one of your friends," Irini said. "Didn't you say they are all art students? One of them will want to go."

Anna agreed that this was a good idea but she had no intention of following through. She liked the rooftop cinema and the Truffaut as something she did with Irini, and the idea of bringing someone else even in Irini's absence seemed like a betrayal—of Irini and somehow of herself as well.

On the Wednesday, as dusk fell on the city and the cinema would soon be opening for the evening, she gathered her bag with the intent to see the film alone, but then she set it down again and opened her laptop to check email. She told herself she still had time to reach the cinema before the title credits, but she knew not only that she had actually run out of time but also that she did not wish to go alone. Yes, she had gone alone the very first time when she had stumbled on the French film and on Irini. But that night had been different. Now she had established herself in her own mind as part of a pair and she could not find the solitary pleasure in what she had once thought she would enjoy. So, she took her phone out of her bag and checked her texts, answering a few, and put a frozen curry in the microwave and sat with the container on her couch. She wasted time with her phone and then her laptop, looking at a shopping website and at her Instagram feed of artists and galleries and friends with cats, and then she looked up the plot of the film she would have just finished seeing and read a few reviews from the year it had first come out. It was the story of an affair, she learned, and ended with the betrayed wife shooting her husband to death. Anna expected Irini would ask her what she thought of the film's final scene, and so she began to look for clips online. But she stopped short of clicking any of the links. Instead, she imagined Irini and her husband sitting in the very same cinema she and Irini went to now, watching a film about the destruction of a marriage. She pictured Irini's husband sending puffs of cigarette smoke up into the night air, his face—she remembered his image from the photographs in Irini's apartment—glowing in sudden flares over the matches struck to light the next one and the next. Irini did not smoke, but she had said her husband had been a smoker. Anna did not know how or when he had died, but she assumed it had been cancer.

It would be safe to say that Anna missed Irini, even though she had seen her just one day ago and would see her again in two more for the next film. Irini did not, however, miss Anna that evening. For there was the discussion of the Proust—they were on the third volume now—and Irini was intent on upholding her reputation as the most difficult to please. She read every page while keeping a strict schedule of time's passage. It was all very well for Proust to be searching for the time he'd lost but she was more than searching: she was accounting. She read the books as if with a balance sheet, weighing her time spent reading against the beauty she had purchased with that time. There were days when she felt it was the Proust and not the Bible that could stretch her life to fit everything she needed to put into it, and there were other days she nearly panicked at the thought of all she could have done in her life if she had not been reading. She said as much now, after taking up a bite-sized piece of spanakopita.

"He's wasting my time here with his Odette and his lack of money." She did not like to think about how much Marcel's concerns with funds mirrored her own. "I could have been doing something else instead."

"What would you have done, Irini?"

This was said by a woman named, rather incongruously, Pamela, a name her parents had not been permitted to use within the regulations of the church, which governed such things in Greece no matter one's religion. Irini always wondered what her name really was, and when and why she had adopted this one.

"I'd travel."

"Where would you go?" Pamela said, and Irini did not like the hint of a sneer in her expression.

"I wouldn't tell you, Pamela, in case you wanted to follow me."

The others laughed at this, for they found Pamela—whose given name was the old-fashioned Pelagia—pretentious. But Pamela persisted.

"Well, anyway, I do some of my best reading when I'm traveling. Last month in Crete, I just sat by the pool and read and read."

"Let's not ask why you sat by the pool when you had the Aegean at your feet," Irini said.

"There can be problems on the beaches," Pamela said. "You know the north coast of Crete catches all the garbage."

"And life jackets now," the hostess said.

Irini looked across at her to see if she expressed this with fear or disgust and saw instead sadness and concern. Irini took another one of the little spanakopitas. The hostess had made them herself rather than buying them frozen from the supermarket, and they were very good. Irini would not need to make herself a bowl of yogurt when she got home to her apartment.

"It's awful," the hostess continued, and for a moment they all spoke about the problem of the refugees crossing the Aegean by the thousands and of the tragedies that had sent so many people on a perilous journey to a place so ill-equipped to take them in.

"Can we talk about the book?" Pamela said. And for a time longer, they did. When Irini corrected the translation—she had her French copy with her—the hostess asked about the Truffaut for she knew of Irini's new habit.

"Yes. I've gone to all of them so far. I would be there now if it weren't for this."

"I saw you going in the other day," the hostess said. "With your daughter. That must be nice."

"That's not my daughter," Irini said before she had a chance to think.

"Oh. I thought you were there with that young woman."

"I was. She's a friend. From church."

"How is your daughter?" the hostess said. "You never talk about her."

"She's fine. She's on holiday."

"Where?" Pamela said, hoping Irini would name a resort she had been to so that she could tell everyone she had been there.

"Siros." Irini took another spanakopita and busied herself with chewing.

"Lovely," the hostess said. But the conversation on that topic ended there as neither she nor Pamela had ever been there and it was also not one of the fashionable islands, nor was it one of the islands newly fashionable for never having been in fashion.

"So, you see the man has done it again," Irini said. "Wasted more of our time by leading us into this distraction." She brandished her French copy of the book. "Shall we?" In deference to the hostess, she looked in her direction as she asked, but everyone knew that not only because Irini spoke French and was reading the book in French but also because she walked all over Plaka with greater ease than any of them, and now also because she had a young friend who was not even related to her—for all these reasons, Irini was the unofficial leader of the group.

"Yes, of course. Back at it, ladies," the hostess said.

❦

When Irini entered the little square on her way home from the book group evening, she glanced up at the rooftop cinema, though from this angle she could not see the projection on the blank wall of the adjacent building. She wondered at what point the film was and wondered what Anna thought of the film's star, the older sister of Deneuve. She would tell Anna when she saw her next how the woman had been the brighter of the two film stars and how no one had even realized it was Deneuve who was the greater beauty until after the sister's tragic death. Briefly Irini considered persuading the son of the cinema owner to let her in and not charge her a ticket since it was already past ten. But she decided it would be good for the girl to claim the Truffaut, at least for tonight, on her own, to reckon with this culture from an older generation on her own, without Irini. And she herself was tired. These conversations with so many people in one room left her drained. She thought she might like from time to time to go to bed early, like Marcel, and let the world come to her in portions she controlled, rather than have to go out into it to find it. This, she supposed, was yet another reason that she enjoyed the church. The place was thick with saints and martyrs and the ghosts of all the faithful, but she always had her conversations with one soul at a time. Lately she was doing all the talking. There was some blessing in that. If your God ignored you, at least you didn't have to listen to him blather, and you didn't have to guard against what he might say to condemn you.

She leaned into the heavy door to the lobby of her building and hit the light switch with her elbow as she pushed the door shut—forcing it faster than its automatic closure—behind her. Anna would not like to hear her say that God was blathering.

Anna was, of course, not at the rooftop cinema, though she planned to pretend to Irini that she had gone. She had sat with her laptop and the scent of the curry wafting from its empty container and then she had grown restless after all. She texted a friend to check if anyone was at the bar with the birdcage above the espresso machine and, the answer being yes, she unlocked her motorbike and rode it slowly—she felt a sort of lethargy even in the bike—across to Metaxourgeio. Two of her friends were there, just two as the rest had left the city ahead of the planned camping trip to the Ionian coast. They, too, were in a mood of lethargy, sitting so low in their café chairs that they almost looked asleep, their cigarettes leaving long worms of ash on a plate. The place was nearly empty, though Anna reminded herself that it was a Thursday and it was August and this bar was not frequented by tourists. Still, though she understood this, she remained surprised that even young people like her parea, who had little money to spend beyond what their parents indulged them, could somehow afford to go away. It was true that their trips were not lavish. The camping trip would turn out to be an affair of sardine tins and loaves of bread and so many peaches and tomatoes purchased at the lowest price that they were all sick for days with only the toilet of a nearby bar for solace. But they were trips. Everyone acted on the presumption that, no matter their financial status, they must go away. So, there were only two friends at the bar that night—Sophia and Mel, whose full name was Melpomene but who preferred not to evoke the Muse of tragedy each time she was introduced.

"What's up, stranger?" Mel said when Anna arrived. She reared herself up for the obligatory kiss on both cheeks, and Sophia did the same. It was clear to Anna that, for all their lassitude, they had been in some serious conversation before she had arrived. Now they told her they had missed her the other night—the previous Saturday—at the party and they relayed an anecdote or two about new hookups and old jokes. She told them she had thought of coming over after her thing—by which she meant the second Truffaut—and they told her it was a good thing she had not because by then they had all decided the music at the party was too boring and they had gone to a club instead.

"Oh." The information struck Anna as if she had actually showed up at the party and found the apartment dark and quiet and had stood on the sidewalk texting to ask where everyone had gone—texts that, had she sent them, would have buzzed unheeded in the pounding loudness of the club. She had to remind herself that that night she had been having a good time at the cinema with Irini and then talking at the café with the angry waiter.

"What?" Sophia said.

"Nothing. Where'd you go? Was it good?"

"Gazi," Sophia said. Her conversation was running to only one word at a time and she had left to Mel the more elaborate answers and explanations.

"It was OK," Mel said. "The DJ's kind of an asshole but who cares."

Anna ordered a beer and drank it while her friends recounted bits of further gossip. Mel sat up and reached for her cigarettes to light another and Anna accepted the offer of one from the pack. Before arriving in Athens, Anna had been only an indifferent smoker, but now she partook with her parea and her clothes held the odor longer than she was aware. This was what accounted for the fug Irini had perceived on that first day when Anna had arrived with the figs in the basket.

Mel blew a smoke ring—she was quite good at this—and Anna followed its jellyfish-like movement in the still air toward the birdcage that hung beside the espresso machine. The cage was draped with cloth for the night. It occurred to Anna that it had been weeks since she had actually seen the bird, a parakeet like the kind she had once had as a pet. Her parents had chosen it for her and she had wished instead for a kitten or a dog or even a mouse or hamster like everyone else's pets. Her parents had bought her a parakeet because they were Greek, she knew now, and their language of pets had been made up of different words. They had had in mind, when they had brought the bird home from the pet store, not this particular bar, of course—it had not existed in her parents' days—but similar establishments in Chalandri where they had grown up, places where old men played backgammon to the tuneful chirping of a resident songbird. Anna's bird in the Astoria of her childhood had chirped no more than listlessly, as if it had known its keepers had found it disappointing. This bird, the bar bird, could have died weeks ago for all Anna knew, and the bar owner might have continued to drape a sheet over the cage to preserve the fiction of the bird and the unofficial branding of the bar. How would they know, without whipping the cloth from the cage, whether the bird was dead or alive or even there at all?

Anna's thoughts ran to these questions as she stared out at the birdcage and at the sweat on her beer glass and at the ash curling in its plate, but they ran, too, to the sunny kitchen window in Astoria and the old issues of the *Hellenic Voice* with which her father helped her paper her pet's cage.

"So, where've you been these days?" Mel said.

"Busy."

"In August?"

"Family stuff," Anna said, and she was in fact not lying. She liked that she had said this to cover not just the homesickness she felt now, but everything else. Her time with Irini had already begun to feel like time with a family member, and her time at church offered the solace that was particular to families—of being seen while not always approved of.

"You're being weird," Mel said, for she had noticed a tension in Anna's pressed-together lips.

"Just family stuff," Anna said. She chose her fabrication well, for these two young women were no different from any Greek of any generation and they understood the total authority of the family over any of its individual members. In practical terms, family was the most powerful entity in a Greek person's life, more powerful even than the State or than God for those who believed in that concept. Everyone was part of a family, the reasoning went, and in Greece that meant that everyone was bound as tight as a piece of cargo strapped into the hold by cross-hatched and ratcheted ropes. So, when Anna told her friends that she had family stuff, they understood that, in this fundamental way like all of them, she had no agency and no recourse.

Anna's most recent Skype conversation with her parents had not gone well. She had been brimming with excitement about her outings with Irini and had been proud to show, in her experience of classic French film, her newfound cultural maturity. She had spoken of the Truffaut films, two of them seen by that Sunday conversation and two more on the way, expecting her parents to understand the references and to be impressed. Who, now? her mother had asked, in English, using the expression Anna thought made her sound as though she was trying too hard to sound young, and when Anna's attempt to clarify had consisted of simply repeating the proper nouns at greater volume—Truffaut; *The 400 Blows*; *Jules and Jim*—her mother had pulled back from the screen of the household laptop and waved a hand in irritation. I can't understand you, she had said, lying in one way but not in another. Who's this friend? her father had asked. Anna had described her again in even greater enthusiasm than at the beginning of the call. But Anna's parents stuck on the facts. She's how old? You met her at church? Anna assured them she had other friends her age that she knew from those random meetings that were the province of the young, and she told them, to their relief, about the planned camping trip to the Ionian coast with her parea. But she could not keep from returning to Irini, to some remark the woman had made or some line she had uttered to put a waiter in his place. And who pays for her tickets and her drinks? her father said. You said she lives in the church apartment for free, so who pays when she goes out with you? She pays her way, Anna had assured them. But this was not true. Anna kept a loose accounting of the ticket stubs and the receipts curled into the little glasses at the café and knew that she had already picked up Irini's share on almost every occasion. She told herself she would have been spending that money anyway on herself if she had spent more time at the bar with the birdcage or bought more cans and markers for more murals. She told her parents Irini always paid.

The conversation had concluded on the topic her parents were most focused on: when was Anna coming home. Her citizenship meant she had no visa to overstay, and this worried her parents. They feared their journey to America and all that it had gained for them would be unwound, set back to zero, if their daughter made the journey in reverse and stayed in Greece. So, they asked again when she was coming home and what could she possibly be finding to support herself in a country where fully one quarter of her generation had no employment during an economic crisis of historic dimensions. Anna gave the gallery and the low cost of living as proof of financial solvency and when she insisted she was, economic crisis or not, making enough money to pay for her life, they reluctantly let the issue go until the next call when their deep love for their daughter would mix so strongly with their fear for their idea of themselves that they would bring it up again.

Now Anna looked across at Mel and gave her a wry smile.

"Yeah," she said. "My parents."

"Are they OK?"

"They're insisting I come home."

"Fuck that," Sophia said, expressing far greater filial independence than she showed in her real life, which involved a regular schedule of obedience to her mother, including coloring her hair for her now that she could not afford to visit a salon.

Mel reached for her beer. They all drank beer instead of cocktails or even wine as it was the cheapest option besides soda, and none of them deigned to drink a soda after six in the afternoon. Mel took a long gulp and, while she was drinking, Sophia gave Anna a stern look and said, "So?"

"What?" Anna said. She considered her outfit and her hair in case they were the subject of Sophia's attention. Mel answered her.

"So, when are you going to paint again?"

"To paint?"

"Yes. Hello? To paint again. When's the next one?"

Anna had been neglecting her graffiti writing the last two weeks, since she had met Irini, and had made no plans for further work on the wall in the empty parking lot whose sketch she had shown Oumer. She had not gone to the hardware store to stock up on cans, not drawn more designs into the sketchbook she now always carried with her. Irini had charged that what she did was vandalism and not art, this spray-painting onto public and private surfaces of images that often had to be removed through the efforts of the mayor's new anti-defacement task force—though this last was true only in the more moneyed regions of the city, while areas like Exarcheia and Metaxourgeio were left alone. An embarrassment had crept into Anna's thinking, a hesitation, and she had almost told Irini of the collages she had done before. She had defended her new art, but what, she wondered, if Irini was right? Now Anna knew an Athenian property owner—it did not matter that the property in question was damaged and uninhabited. For the first time in her new career as a graffiti artist, she considered the effect of her nocturnal artwork on those who owned the surfaces she took as her canvas.

"Yeah," she said. "I've been taking a break."

"Why? That's no fun."

Anna shrugged and took a long drink from her beer even though the bottle was mostly empty. She set it down and signaled for another.

"No fun," Sophia said.

"I'm thinking maybe I should knock it off."

"Why would you do that?" Mel said.

"We like watching you paint," Sophia said. "Besides, aren't you supposed to be making your mark on the city? No better way than to do it literally." She sat up and made a flourish with her arm to accompany this surprisingly long stream of words.

"I'm not *supposed* to be doing anything."

"Ah," Mel said. "You need another project. Come on." She stood and fished in the pocket of her jeans for coins she laid on the table. "Pavlos," she called to the barman, "this is for me. Come on," she said again. Sophia pulled a five-euro note from a wallet stamped with the fake logo of a French designer. Mel took Anna by the arm and hauled her upright.

"What are you doing?" Anna said.

"We're leaving," Mel said. "You're paying."

Anna dropped more coins onto the table than were necessary to cover her beer—Pavlos had never brought the second one—and snatched her helmet from the ground before Mel swept her away from the table.

"My bike," she said.

"Bring the bike."

Mel and Sophia watched Anna unlock the motorbike and Sophia threw the padded chain across her shoulder like a bandolier. First one and then the other young woman dropped onto the bike, Mel in front of Anna and Sophia behind, and they did not stop shouting and exhorting until Anna throttled up and rolled the bike slowly down from the sidewalk into the street. There was a distinct possibility that Sophia—who held onto Anna's waist with only one arm, the other catching her hair into a ponytail against the wind—would fall off the back of the bike before they arrived at their destination. Yet they had no destination until Mel called out that Anna must stop.

"Here?"

They were at the base of Lycabettos Hill, but on the back side, far from the expensive neighborhood of expats and shipping heiresses. As on the front side, the streets here were stepped, with long platforms between each new level, and the cement was pricked like a pie crust as if by the tines of a fork, in a fey attempt to provide traction for the locals. In the winter, heavy rains rushed down these streets and swept them clear of a year's worth of cigarette butts, and people simply stayed inside until it was all over. Unlike on the front side, several of the streetlights were dark and the garbage and recycling bins had been allowed to overflow.

"Go left."

Mel directed them down an alley even narrower than the terraced street and then commanded Anna once again to stop the bike.

"There." She waved an expansive hand but Anna had to lean around her to fully see what lay ahead.

"Where are we?" Anna said.

Mel wrenched her phone from her pocket and tapped the flashlight on.

"I used to date a guy whose family lives here. It's perfect for you."

In the beam of the phone light, Anna could make out a retaining wall some eight feet high and, just over the rim of the small parklet it held together, the Parthenon, its lights dimmed now in the wee hours but the shape of it marked out like a stencil against the bright city that spread to the coast. The retaining wall was covered with slogans and shapes. An anarchist A, the green clover logo of the local soccer team, the acronym of the radical left party, the initials of the communist party, and a skilled shadow-line rendering of a hammer and sickle.

"So?" Sophia said, as if determined to regain the consistency of her monosyllabic conversation.

"I don't know," Anna said. "It's someone's house."

"No! It's not. It's totally not."

Mel knew that her ex-boyfriend's family were regularly infuriated by each new mark on this wall that faced the front windows of their home and, because he had cheated on Mel and refused to apologize, Mel ignored that fact. She did not know—nor did her ex-boyfriend's mother—that the ex-boyfriend's younger brother was responsible for the anarchist As.

"I don't know," Anna said again. She was not sure whether she hesitated because of Irini, or because of the beauty of the view and a thought that her painting might mar it, or a doubt in her own ability to come up with something good. Mel and Sophia knew that they would have to help Anna with more than simply looking out for passersby or property owners and handing her the cans. They would have to nudge her in the right direction for a good design. They could have simply done the piece themselves, but they were the kind of people whose best expression came in the guidance of others.

As for Anna, the truth was that she had been long enough away from the painting and the cans—two weeks might as well have been a year in Anna's life—long enough immersed in these French films from sixty years ago and in the Bible reading for the feast of the Assumption, that it seemed not a bad thing at all to Anna to simply allow that side of her life to fall away. She had come so lately into the street art that her commitment to it was hardly as deep as she even thought, spurred as it was by a partly borrowed enthusiasm. There would be no loss if she simply went to church, saw Irini, went to work, and spent time with her friends. She would no longer have tips for Oumer on where his team could do their parkour training. But that would be all right. Why did she have to make a mark upon the city?

Mel hopped off the bike and darted to the wall to stand before it as if she were about to be executed. Sophia tapped her phone light on and shone it at her friend.

"If you don't use this wall," Mel said, "I will."

"So, do it," Anna said. Mel crumpled.

"Come *on*." She groaned. "You're better at it than me," she lied, "and I'm bored and it's August and we're still here."

Through the darkened columns of the Parthenon, Anna could see the glow of spotlights from the new cultural center by the coast. When the complex had been built, just over a year before Anna's arrival, it had been positioned as a deferential gesture toward the ancient building. But now, with its lights on after a performance of the National Opera and the Parthenon darkened already—because it was a Thursday night and it was August and the tourists went to bed early—the new building rose up against the old like an upstart cousin. There was no ignoring the beauty of the scene. For all its alleys and its traffic and its cramped balconies that had to hold so much of its residents' lives, Athens had a gift for expanse. It was a city of high views, from the tops of Hymmetos and Parnitha, from Lycabettos, and tonight from this retaining wall for a little patch of pine-needled ground on the wrong side of Kolonaki. Anna reached a hand into the flashlight beam and watched her fingers send bars of shadow across Mel's figure on the wall.

"OK," she said. "I'll do something."

"Hooray," Sophia said.

"Before the camping trip," Mel said. They were to join the others in five days.

"We'll see."

Sophia snapped a photo of Mel who stood, arms wide, in the sudden double flash. She texted it to Anna then and there, and the three young women briefly paused to contemplate on Anna's screen the image they had just witnessed and that Sophia had seen on her own screen. Two beats of a camera flash—the warning and the real thing—and then two quick revivals of the image in the dark on one phone then another. A miniature resurrection of the modern age. They pocketed their phones and took their places on the motorbike and Anna set the bike rolling. She kept the engine off at first, so as not to disturb the neighborhood, but really out of a sort of advance stealth, as if the painting was already done and she must sneak away. But the weight of the three of them and the slope of the hill gave them surprising speed and for an instant they were racing down the hill in the dark on the back side of Lycabettos, and it was fun to feel the wind on their faces and the hush of the deserted streets. For an instant Anna had a feeling of suspension in both time and place as if she had been hanging there above the city forever and could go on hanging there into eternity. And then she switched the engine on. She took charge of the bike once again and she was once again Anna in the city with an internship and with a passport and an apartment and a Sunday Skype call to her parents in Astoria after church.

They came down the hill and met the boulevard whose width made it one of the preferred locations for protests and demonstrations, then turned left past embassies and homes that had once been palaces and now were museums so that everyone could come and see what the wealthy families still owned. Now Sophia held on to Anna's waist with both arms and rested her cheek on Anna's shoulder, letting her hair sweep across her eyes. Anna dropped her off at the Metro station by the war museum where spotlights illuminated two fighter planes on the front lawn. Sophia waved from the station entrance and took the stairs down to the platform where she would wait seven minutes, as the sign said, for the train to her parents' suburb. She opened the picture she had taken of Mel at the wall and zoomed in on Mel's expression of mock alarm and added the photo to her favorites. Across the tracks from her, an employee of the Metro reached beneath the seats to clean the underside of the molded plastic. The woman was glad to have the job, though she could not afford to keep her own home as spotless as the station she was assigned to—a station that, she was certain, was only cleaned to this degree because the tourists rode this line to and from the airport. In fact, all the Metro stations were this clean, and all of them had a cleaner who felt her own station was the exception.

Anna switched Mel to the back of the bike and rode with a little more speed now to Mel's street in Exarcheia, almost back to where they'd been. From there to Anafiotika, Anna rode the backstreets, avoiding the poorly timed lights of the boulevards. She remembered the photo of Mel in Sophia's flash, Mel standing with arms and legs spread like a star or like a cross, depending on one's point of view, and she had an idea for what to paint on the retaining wall: the silhouette in blacks and whites, all grayscale, of a figure as if in a strobe light. She lacked the skill to achieve the effect she was aiming for, which would have been in the style of Duchamp's cubist nude, but she did not know that, and she had instead a willingness to try that might outweigh that shortcoming.

*

When Anna had first embarked on her street art, she sought answers from the internet so as not to reveal her ignorance to her friends. She learned that it was possible to begin by using something called wheat paste, a paint designed to appease everyone by building into a painting its own impermanence, as a few heavy rains or a month's worth of scouring wind and rubbing shoulders would soon wear the art away. But Anna didn't like the idea that her work would be something transitional, a way station between her ideas and the photographs she would be required to take in order simply to preserve her creations for her records. She needn't have worried, as long as she planned to paint in the days between May and September, for rain was so rare as to factor not at all in the permanence or impermanence of art. But she didn't know this yet, so as she considered leaving collage behind for this new medium, she assumed she would be good at it, and she assumed her work should be designed to last. She would have had more success as a graffiti artist from the start had she accepted the temporary nature of the genre. Anna would have been better temperamentally suited to sculpture, though a trip to the new museum near the rooftop cinema and the little square, or to the Acropolis to see the broken faces of the caryatids, should have reminded her that stone, too, broke.

Why, then, had she turned her energies to this mode of art that she found so much fault with? An instructor had told her once that she had a poor command of line, and another had once called her timid, so she had turned to collage as a safeguard against such inadequacies. Her job at the gallery had led her to the birdcage bar and that had led her to the art students who gathered there. One night soon after meeting them, she had followed the parea through a gap in a fence around a warehouse and had stood guard while one of them—a tall man with round, gold-rimmed glasses—painted a design. Over raki in a nightclub as the sun came up, they had draped arms over one another's shoulders for the photo taken by the waiter, and she had gone home to the little place in Anafiotika

with paint on her cheek. She had been getting into bed in the daylight when the text had come through from Mel and there was the
photo. Six of them crowded around a little table, the tall man, Mel,
Sophia, two other men, and Anna. In the photo it was impossible
to tell that she had not done the painting too.

So, with Mel and Sophia's nudging, she had turned to street
art of her own. On her first supply run, she had bought as many
cans as she could carry home, not knowing whether the law
would come to stop her. It did not, and so she was able to keep
buying her paint and storing it carefully in the coolest part of her
apartment—which had for a time been the balcony—so that the
cans would not explode.

At first, she had great hopes, if not expectations, seeing the city
as suitably lawless and defiant to allow for bolder work. But it was
her skill that stopped her, most of the time, and not the laws or
regulations, which were, indeed, lax and unenforced. It had been
clear to her from her very first ride in a taxi from the airport—she
had not known she could save money and take the Metro—that
spray paint must be readily available in Greece. The highway
from the airport to the center of the city was haunted by empty
billboards covered over—now that the crisis had made advertising
irrelevant since no one could afford to buy things—with mournful
and cryptic aphorisms in bold black paint. Her first walks through
Metaxourgeio and Exarcheia had shown her how high the standards were for graffiti art in Athens. She had sunk into the timidity
her college instructor had identified, and she had decided to
paint her work in humbler, less obtrusive places. It was in pursuit
of these that she found new parkour locations for Oumer, as she
roamed beyond the usual areas for art and innovation.

On Thursday, the day after the trip on the motorbike to the back side of Lycabettos, she went to the paint shop after work at the gallery and bought three cans each of black, white, and gray. She would work on the design until Saturday when she would have to do the painting all at once, with Mel and Sophia as her lookouts. That Thursday evening, in her apartment and with no plan to meet Irini—for the next and final Truffaut film would not screen until the following night—she sat on her balcony on the metal folding chair of a sort that one associated with France and not with Greece and that had been purchased by the Airbnb host at a Swedish store. She propped her feet up on the railing, feeling it give a little and briefly wondering if she would one day plummet from the balcony, riding the broken rail into the street. She lit a cigarette and though she had the intention to sketch and color a design, she took up her phone instead and found there the Bible readings Father Emmanouil had specified for the day. She would not tell the priest that she had tossed aside the photocopy whose slick paper had annoyed her and had instead marked the required passages on an internet Bible.

These assigned passages were very short—so short that Anna wondered what she was supposed to do with them. She began at the beginning of the week, reading again the passage set for the past Monday. Here was Matthew speaking of a high mountain and two friends and looking down from a great height and the figure of Jesus revealed to them in brilliant white and then the vow to keep the secret of his appearance. Anna knew she was still ill-educated in the ways of religious thinking. Or so she thought, feeling that the others around her during service had access to a part of their brains she did not have. They had a way to listen to the spirit that she did not even yet know how to hear. Even Irini who protested against the bad bargain she had made with her God, a bargain she was always on the point of getting out of—even Irini seemed to know where the spirit lay, while Anna was still looking for it. She knew she did not know these things, and yet at that moment on her balcony she dropped her feet from the rail and sat forward to read the Bible passage for the third time. Had she not been with two friends on a hillside just the night before? And had they not looked out over the city below—it was not terribly far below but in the calculus of visions it was far enough—and had not one of those friends flashed bright white in the beam of the phone's camera? And had they not, like Jesus—as Matthew told the tale—made a plan they must keep secret? Anna remembered the feeling of suspension just before she turned the motorbike engine on, just before the bike's ungoverned inertia sent them into freefall down the hill. She knew there was simply physics to it, but she could not help wondering now whether she was not intended to see in all this something more important. Had it not been precisely the kind of discovery, the kind of revelation, she had hoped for with her work all along? There had been that instant of belly-flipping that comes from an elevator's quick rise or fall and that had come last night in a second when she hesitated with her hand on the ignition. Anna wondered, as she sat on the balcony and looked across at the red-tiled roof of the neighbor's house, whether that instant had not brought her some connection to God's spirit.

It had not, of course. She would not find the spirit until later that summer, and its appearance would be fleeting. But for a short time that evening, Anna remained under the impression that she had been transfigured, in a way she did not yet understand, and that counted for something. She determined to speak to Father Emmanouil about it on Sunday, but to say nothing of it to Irini when she saw her at the cinema for the fifth and last Truffaut. Irini would have told Anna she had fallen into the habit of every fanatic—this would be the word she would use—everywhere of becoming a magnet to draw all the pieces of experience into a shape of one's own self. If Irini ever said this, she would be correct. Anna would have aligned her night's adventures with any reading Father Emmanouil had assigned for that date, and what mattered was not any divine symmetry in the priest's selections but Anna's own determination that she did not even know she had. A determination to find meaning and wholeness when there was only chaos and coincidence. This was what made Anna's art more pedestrian than insightful—though Irini did not know this yet.

Irini would have labeled Anna's reaction to the Bible passage and its similarity to her experience a display of enthusiasm. Irini possessed not only a French-Greek dictionary but also an etymological dictionary of the Greek language, and she would have intended this word *enthusiasm* in its full and, in her mind, proper meaning: a feeling of inspiration, or possession by a god. Enthusiasm, fanatics: Irini had long experience of them both, and she would soon fall victim to their manifestations in Anna's quicksilver soul.

Irini's husband had been a fanatic, though his religion and his God had been jazz. A trip to Berlin soon after the war had toppled him head over heels like a statue from a devotion to Mozart and the various bouzouki masters from the Pontic region of his family origins into an unwavering love of Miles Davis. Before the husband's trip, their home had rung with Mozart's symmetry only occasionally interrupted by skirls of Pontic mixolydian modes and halting time signatures. She allowed him the bouzouki music as a tie back to his homeland to the east, buying his Athenian allegiance with these reminders of the far-flung province. But after the excursion to Berlin where he had been taken by his German colleagues to the dirty, smoky bars to hear the cool jazz exports from America, he listened to nothing but Miles and Coltrane and DeJohnette. Irini did not mind the Miles who sounded more like Coltrane—she could not tell them apart—but when Miles traveled into rhythms and melodies that were, in her view, neither rhythmic nor melodic, she hated both the music and, it must be said, her husband. It seemed a blow he struck at her, a whip lashing at her with each flight of the trumpet up and down the notes, and she could not convince her husband to stop doing it. He filled the house with albums and bought more and more equipment on which to play them and through which to listen to them. The neighbors never complained of the noise, no matter how much Irini hoped they would, and their daughter had begun spending enough time out of the house that she was not bothered. Only Irini seemed to be an apostate to her husband's new faith—or, rather, a resistant convert. She went as often as she could to the Concert Hall for Mozart, to bask for a short while in the order of it. The world was full enough of chaos. Eventually, Irini won the victory of the headphones, but this was in fact no victory, for all it accomplished was a sealing off of her husband from her in silence. Once he stepped into that world, he became lost to her and she saw how much she preferred even the trying days when she stood on the sidewalk on Goura Street and heard the Miles trailing through the windows. The headphones sent her to the sidewalk again and from there she drifted further and further from their home.

Now, when Irini sat in her tiny apartment and read the passages Father Emmanouil had prescribed for the past few days, she laughed out loud at Matthew's tale of Jesus silencing his friends about what they could not yet understand and then making another one of those promises the devout loved so much—that good things were coming. And in the passage for the previous night, here was Saint Paul sounding like a bureaucrat at a public hearing, deciding who should speak and in what order and only one at a time and none of the women. She was certain Nefeli would have something to say about that, as she did every year, and she looked forward to this Sunday's lunch when she would enlist Nefeli in cornering the priest. And during the liturgy Irini would try again with that God of hers who had enough to answer for before one added secrets and false promises.

۶

Anna and Irini met in the little square on Friday just in time for the nine o'clock show. The son of the cinema owner had bungled the chronology of the Truffaut films so badly, with the third film first and the first film second, that now he would show in fourth place Truffaut's second film: *Shoot the Piano Player.* There was little time for more than pleasantries before the film began, and in the intermission—which the son of the cinema owner would never relinquish, thanks to the greater concession sales—the two women spoke mostly about the film itself, for Irini was captivated more than usual as she had never seen the film before. Delighting in the fact that they were meeting this cultural artifact on the same footing, Anna in turn expressed her reactions with more assurance and assertion.

"I get it," Anna said. "It's got to be such a huge deal to have to live with a decline like that." She spoke of the protagonist, a concert pianist fallen into a gritty life as a barroom entertainer. "How do you accept yourself," she said. "Or do you?" Anna was thinking of her own position and what it would be like to achieve the heights as an artist that she sometimes hoped to achieve, only to fall away from fame and ease and happiness. She wondered, did you lose all three, or could you give up one to pay for keeping the others?

"And Aznavour," Irini said, with a satisfied sigh, and for a moment Anna mistook the actor's last name for a Greek word she did not yet know.

"Aznavour is the perfect actor for this role," Irini said. Anna did not know why this could be so, and Irini explained the man's fame as a singer, his origins as a son of immigrants, and the noble work his family had done with the resistance during the war.

"He was just in Italy last fall," Irini said. "He should have come to sing here, too. His sister was born in Greece. So, you see, he has a connection."

"I'm sorry," Anna said, as if the man's failure to include Athens on his tour had been a personal affront to her friend, and it did seem so from the look of genuine hurt on Irini's face.

"He was a teenager when I was born. I can't remember a time without his music."

This was not correct, as Irini had been almost twenty by the time the man's first songs were played on radios in Athens. But his songs had been the music of her youth and of her courtship by her husband. The husband had sung them to her in a poor French accent but a lovely tenor voice as they rode in his car to Sounion for the sunset or to Faliro to stroll the corniche by the sea. He had sung them as they moved about the high-ceilinged rooms of their first apartment, and when they had taken up residence in Irini's family home, he had played the albums—heavy platters of thick vinyl—at their parties. Just a few months from this night when she and Anna watched the sad eyes of his young face at the rooftop cinema, Aznavour died at ninety-four, outstripping Irini then by twelve years.

Anna looked across at Irini who had gone silent, and she saw the woman's eyes rimmed with tears.

"Irini, I'm so sorry. Here." She pulled a napkin from the pile she had been given at the concession window. "Should we go? We can leave if it's too much."

"No, no. Please. Let's see how it all turns out."

It did not turn out well for the piano player and neither woman enjoyed the film's second half, Irini because she was immersed in longing—for her husband, for Aznavour, but most of all for the life she and her husband had had in those high-ceilinged rooms before the jazz and the silence and the drifting away—and Anna because she was worried for her friend and suddenly feared that having a friend of Irini's age meant she might die suddenly while they were together. Anna spent the film's final moments worrying that she did not know the Greek equivalent for 911. She couldn't ask Irini lest the question imply, correctly, Anna's concern for the older woman's health, but she determined to ask her friends or Father Emmanouil at the first opportunity.

They reached the cinema lobby and made their way through the small crowd into the square. The audience had swelled to almost twenty this night, most of them lured by the film's title and by what they assumed was its promise of action. Across at the café, most of the tables were occupied, it being Friday night. The women hesitated for a moment and Anna, whose thoughts were full of sudden descents from health or happiness, saw in her friend's face the lineaments of its youth. The long straight nose, the sharp brows, the oval shape of the jaw, and the slightly down-turned eyes made Irini a near likeness of the Greek actress with whom she shared a name—though Anna did not know that and only saw that she had been a woman of strong beauty.

"Irini," she said, the old thought coming upon her newly. "I meant what I said about seeing your family home. Are you sure you couldn't show me?"

"Why? We can't go inside."

"All your stories. And tonight. Telling me about the music and the parties. I'd love to see it."

"The house is empty. None of that is there now."

"I think you'd fill it for me with your stories."

Irini shook her head.

"It's not like that," she said. "Don't get ideas that you're going to see some dream of the past. I can't do that for you."

"I don't believe you."

Because Anna's words and tone surprised Irini, and because she knew the girl was right, and because she had in fact spent the last moments of the film seeing, as if on a brighter, bigger screen, the façade of her family home with her husband and her passing in front of one after another lighted window—because of all this, she took two breaths and said to Anna,

"Fine. I'll take you."

Anna jumped and began to thank her.

"If you do that," Irini said, "I'm going to change my mind."

Anna composed herself.

"You know you can go by yourself, don't you?" Irini said. "It's a public street."

"I know, but I want you to show me," Anna said. "I can come at lunch tomorrow."

"No. Not at lunch. It's too hot."

Anna said in that case she would close the gallery early—it didn't matter as there would surely be no customers—so she could meet Irini the next day at six o'clock.

❧

Anna could barely contain herself during the next day at the gallery. She checked the time on her phone and on her laptop at intervals that were far too frequent and only made her more aware of the slow passage of the time. She was to meet Irini at the door to her apartment building and they would walk together from there. Anna looked at Google maps of Plaka and dropped into various intersections the little orange man who could give her a view of the street, not knowing exactly which street the house was on. The alleys and passages of Plaka were the oldest in the city, some of them the very same that were trod by the ancients. This was a quarter of the city—there were, in fact, several such quarters—where any attempt to dig a new foundation or a Metro stop or to repair a water main could reveal an amphora or krater in fragments of red and black. Anna tipped the street image on her screen up and down, scanning in this virtual way the very buildings she would be walking past in a matter of hours and that she had been walking past for months. All this time, she had quite likely stood in front of Irini's family home and never known it and the thought gave her a shiver.

Anna knew her interest in Irini's house was a little strange. She understood that there was something excessive in her eagerness. But she could neither explain nor stop it, and she saw no compelling reason to alter her attitude as she was doing no one any harm. She was simply trying to connect to the very authenticity that she had gone aslant to with her choice of Anafiotika as her current home. She was in search of a past time she could attach to. She felt certain there could be little wrong with that. Anna did wonder about Irini's daughter who must surely have a claim and a connection to the house, which, after all, would have been her childhood home. Anna felt she should meet her, too, as if she too had granted access to the house.

Anna buzzed Irini's bell a few minutes before six. The buzzer clicked and she tugged on the door that she assumed had unlocked. But the door would not yield. Instead, Irini's voice came through the intercom.

"You're early."

"I know."

"I'm not ready yet."

The intercom switched off and Anna received no further explanation. Irini went back to the chair she had been sitting in with her Bible and the gray photocopied sheet, though she could read with no greater concentration than she had possessed all day. She knew that it was nearly time for the meeting she had allowed the girl to arrange and knew she would make no reading progress in the few moments remaining, but she could not simply let the girl in yet. She knelt on her sofa and peered out the window to the street and saw Anna standing with her back to the opposite building. She was not looking at her phone, and Irini understood this to indicate the girl's high level of expectation. She scolded herself for having given in to the girl and for being in a position now in which it would be churlish to cancel. She had by this point in her acquaintance come to feel protective of the girl not in spite of her enthusiasm but because of it. Anna's was an enthusiasm that sought to join and bind her to places and to people, and though Irini wished to maintain the girl's bonds to her—for a variety of reasons best left unexplained for now—she worried also about what the girl would do should her connections fray. And so, against her best desire and better judgment, Irini would keep the promise she had allowed the girl to convince her to make.

But there was more to this that even Irini was not yet ready to consider. There was good reason for Irini not to wish to show the house to Anna, and there was good reason—the same reason—she herself had not walked down Goura Street in many months. She made a habit to avoid the street and had no real need to walk down it as there were other, shorter ways to reach the garden of the Zappeio by the Parliamentary palace.

Later she would blame Aznavour and the spell he had cast on her with his sad eyes and small frame and the memories of his songs playing in the family home before everything had altered. She had in fact forgotten the facts of what she was about to see. She had slipped—and as she saw it Aznavour had been the one who tugged—into the lost time of her youth, the time of before the earthquake, of before the little apartment where she was the unpaying tenant of the church.

She gathered up her bag and swung it across her shoulder. She did not understand the other women her age in Plaka who insisted on holding their bags in one hand, off one shoulder, even as they expressed alarm at what they viewed as rampant purse-snatchings perpetrated by *migrants*. They usually said this as if the term signified bands of roving would-be criminals, as if they believed the purses of old women on fixed incomes to contain riches no migrant could resist. Irini's habit was to sling the strap of her bag across her shoulder and if a thief wished to try to take it, he would have to pull her down too.

"All right," she said, when she reached the street and exchanged cheek kisses with Anna. "But if you do anything annoying, we are turning around."

"I won't."

They walked for no more than five minutes, past an intersection that widened around a palm tree, and toward the ruined Temple of Zeus whose fifteen remaining columns rose into the pale August sky. Everyone in Athens knew someone who had heard the sixteenth column fall with a rumble that made people fear an earthquake or a bomb set off by one of the country's many radical organizations. This was not true, for the sixteenth column had been blown over in a gale more than a century ago. Facing the columns of Zeus' temple across the end of the street, Irini made a sharp right turn and then a left onto Goura Street. At the fourth building down the street, she stopped.

"Here?" Anna said. They stood before a postwar building painted in ochre and white. A brass plaque by the door announced a lawyers' office.

But Irini was facing the other way, and Anna looked across the street to a building she did not understand how she could have missed. Where their side of the street was bathed in late-afternoon sun that lit a row of newly painted buildings, the opposite side lay in a shadow that befit the darkened stone of its façades. Bracketed by buildings in a severe modern style was a three-story structure in the traditional mode of neoclassical Athens. A tall front door bore a large brass knocker and was framed by tall windows, two on each side, covered with louvered wooden shutters. The pattern was repeated on the two upper floors but with a balcony in place of the front door. The building was crested by an elaborate cornice that angled out over the sidewalk. But none of this was intact. On the top floor, the louvered shutters hung open and it was possible to see through the window openings to the sky where the roof had fallen in. On the middle floor, a large crack snaked diagonally from right to left and dry grasses jutted from it here and there. The façade itself was pockmarked as if it had suffered the gunshots of street fighting during the war. On the door were spray-painted initials and numbers, and along the base of the house on either side of the door were purple and yellow tags in the jagged and nearly indecipherable lettering of wildstyle.

Anna took this all in and tried not to let her reaction show. She had known to expect a damaged house. Both Irini herself and Father Emmanouil had made it clear there had been damage, and she knew that whatever damage had been done was sufficient to keep Irini or anyone else—even squatters—from occupying the place. She realized now she had had no notion of what that kind of damage would look like. Now she saw an edifice whose grandeur and whose disrepair were undeniable. She glanced at Irini for a sign of what to say and saw the old woman was looking at the house with a kind of ease, as if she had found again a necessary object temporarily misplaced.

"The only one of its kind left on Goura Street," Irini said, and Anna felt this was setting the bar for accomplishment quite low.

"Built in 1886," she went on, "and designed by a student of Ziller."

Athenians of the older generation spoke the name of the architect with a reverence that Anna did not understand. The man was responsible for a mansion here, an opera house there, a palace somewhere else, and he had perpetrated a kind of sanctioned colonization of aesthetics. He and those in his employ had taken the forms of the Greeks' very own architecture and sold them back in costly foreign translation. But there was no denying the balanced proportions of the house and a pleasing grace, even in the cramped confines of the old Athenian street.

"It's beautiful," Anna said finally, with another glance at Irini.

"It was, once," Irini said with a hard edge to her voice. "Now it's just *this*. Look what your fellow *artists* have done to it."

"I'm sorry," Anna said.

"Why? It has nothing to do with you." Irini glanced across at her and then back up at the house. "It's still here at any rate. Hasn't crumbled yet. Like me."

"I can see why you love it so much," Anna said, but she was lying and Irini knew this.

"Don't humor me, young lady," she said. "I'm not living in some altered reality."

"No, no, of course. But I can see how it used to be."

Irini stepped back and looked up at the façade, shielding her eyes against the sun.

"Well," she said. "You can't because you haven't seen anything like it before in your Astoria or even here."

Irini turned to walk away but Anna called her back.

"Please, tell me about it," she said. But the old woman continued walking, and it was clear to Anna that if she wished to hear anything about the house she would have to follow. When they reached the first intersection, she offered Irini coffee and a pastry.

"Please?" she said.

It was only a little past six and therefore the time of day when anyone who had rested in the afternoon—there was sadly no good translation for this practice except *siesta*, which Irini objected to. Why borrow from another language to translate into yet a third?— anyone who had taken a *siesta* might have a snack to begin the next part of the day.

"My treat," Anna said.

Irini sized the girl up, balancing Anna's enthusiasm against her own very real desire for a pastry and for an audience to listen to her stories of her grandest years.

"Fine."

She led Anna to the café where they had known Irini for decades, though she had little opportunity to visit, and she began to tell Anna some of the same stories she had told her on the day the girl had brought the figs and during the movies on the rooftop. She described the room in which her father wound the clock each day before the evening meal and described the room where her mother played the upright piano and the living room where they held soirees behind the two large windows on the right. She told Anna how people sat in rows of chairs pulled in from the dining room table and listened to her mother play. It was easier to tell these stories in the absence of the house in its current ruined state. She conjured the grand building for Anna like an image cast upon another wall.

"Mozart," Irini said, as if she could hear that music now.

"Did you play too?"

"Not at all. But after we were married, my husband and I were always playing music. Records. You could always tell my husband was home from the Mozart coming through the windows. And we had parties, of course, and we played music. Lots of swing bands. Benny Goodman. Duke Ellington."

"And Aznavour," Anna said, wondering if she had pronounced the name correctly.

"Yes, of course," Irini said. "Aznavour."

Aznavour's music was not of the dancing sort, but she did not say this to Anna, and she did not tell her about the jazz. Even before the jazz and then the headphones, there was a chair in the corner of the study where she sometimes sat when she was alone in the house and she would play the Aznavour records and sing along and cry.

Anna asked her what the house was like inside, and Irini took the rooms one by one and listed all the contents. A woman passing by caught Irini's lively voice and stopped for a long moment before moving on, listening to what could have been her own list of lost things.

"And at the very top floor were our servants. They were from Hydra," Irini said. "A brother and a sister from a family my husband's people knew."

"What happened to them?"

"I don't know."

Irini said this with no signs of sadness or embarrassment. Anna knew no one who had servants, though she gathered that Sophia's family had a housekeeper from Indonesia who lived with them. Sophia was adamant that Noor was not a servant in the old-fashioned sense and offered their friendship on Facebook as proof.

"Were they hurt in the earthquake?"

"They were gone before that."

The servant brother and sister had returned to Hydra a good decade before the earthquake and had opened a boutique hotel. The sister had married and the brother lived nearby with his partner and often babysat the sister's child. For nearly a decade after they had left, Irini and her husband and their daughter had fended for themselves in the house, eventually limiting their use to only two of the three floors, except when Irini sought higher ground away from the loud and anarchic music. She sat sometimes on the edge of the bed in the brother's room and tried to keep herself from listening to the trumpet from downstairs.

"And the piano?"

"What about it?"

"Is it still there?"

"Of course not. You don't leave a grand piano to rot in a place like that."

"Oh."

"We gave it to the Concert Hall. They sent men inside to get it. It took six of them to swing it down the stairs with a crane."

"Oh."

Irini expected a more emphatic reaction from the girl at having heard this tale that evoked one of the very first Irini had told her—about the day the statues were moved from the old Acropolis museum to the new and cranes had swung the bundled artifacts out over the rooftops.

"I've talked too much," she said, and when Anna made polite noises, she insisted they ask for the bill, which Anna alone would pay for.

"Thank you for showing it to me," Anna said.

"You wouldn't stop asking about it. You gave me no choice."

Upstairs in the little apartment, Irini sat on the couch with her back to the Acropolis and took in the contents of the place. There was barely room to move, between the dining set in the other room and the sideboard jammed into the hall and the bookcases in the bedroom. And this was all that she could fit, all that she could keep, from an entire three-story mansion's worth of furniture. Added to her few things were the items the church insisted must remain with the apartment. It was not customary for the recipient of the church's charity to have so much and such fine furniture as Irini, and so the kitchen came with a Formica table and the living room had been furnished with an armchair of hideous upholstery and ungainly shape. No, most of the recipients of the church's charity had had almost nothing. Irini was the first but she would not be the last resident of the little place to arrive with all the possessions of a comfortable life but without the life itself. Irini looked at these possessions—things she had barked her shins against until she had grown accustomed to the smaller space. They were not even her favorites of all the things she had once owned and she was stuck with them now. What she had loved most she had given up, though the sacrifice had done her little good so far.

Anna sat on her balcony once more with her bare feet pressed against the railing that was still warm from the day's sun. With no air conditioning and with a fan that only suggested politely to the air that it might move, the apartment had succumbed to the August heat. Anna's only respite was to open the door to the balcony and prop the transom window open into the air shaft at the center of the building to create a draft inside her space. The air shaft was a conduit for conversations held in many languages but mostly English and Greek and German. Tonight Anna watched the twilight sink over the rooftops while she listened to the doleful pleading of a young man that someone on the phone with him come back to yoga class tomorrow. She thought about Irini's house and of the stories she had peopled it with, window by window, as if to fill an Advent calendar. Anna was caught for an instant on the piano and found she could not picture it correctly. But she could picture the young Irini. Anna's training in figure drawing had taught her how to see the bones within a face, and she needed no photographs from Irini's youth to tell her she had been a beautiful young woman. It made her happy now to picture a beautiful Irini moving through the rooms of her grand home, and to imagine the handsome husband singing along to French songs or waving an imaginary baton in time with Mozart.

The house was, however, a disaster. In an American city, it would have been condemned, perhaps torn down by eminent domain. These words passed through Anna's head—condemned, eminent domain—as she heard the air shaft conversation shift now to a litany of affronts from which the young man was attempting to recover. Anna did not know it, but Irini's house was, indeed, officially condemned—that was the meaning of the numbers painted on the walls. A stay of execution was in place, allowing the owner to find a means to rescue the property.

One large crack snaked up the house, from the right of the door up to the base of the top-floor windows. In another building, it might have been a decorative feature of the sort Anna had seen in Manhattan when her parents took her in each year to see the Christmas decorations. Projections of holiday garlands draped across the front of Bloomingdale's or Bergdorf Goodman. Anna wondered if she could do something like that here, something to please the old woman by casting a familiar image from the past onto and over the losses of the present. A projection could mask the graffiti along the base and draw the eye to something more in keeping with the building's former beauty. There must be something Anna could do. She could make something beautiful for Irini to undo the very marks the old woman hated. One of the parea ran lights at a disco and another was a photographer who might know where to borrow a projector. Anna swore she could bring her parea together to do something more important than an August getaway to the coast. When they returned from their holiday, she would propose this idea to them—it was already taking shape—and this project would become the high point of their summer.

Before she could embark on the first phase of that project, Mel and Sophia texted her throughout the day on Saturday to be sure she would not back out of the plan to paint the retaining wall. Mel's urgency was driven by the discovery that the ex-boyfriend had hooked up with someone she didn't even know. Anna promised she would be there, and she met Mel and Sophia that night at the Chapel of St. George at the top of Lycabettos Hill, where they ordered drinks on the terrace that overlooked the city's southern spread. Anna considered telling her friends of her plan for the old lady's house but kept the idea to herself for now—in part because she feared that they would tell her the planned piece was nothing special, and if this was true, Anna did not want to know. They watched the zigzag-shaped cars of the funicular blunder up the track like oversized caterpillars—they had to pass the time until it was late enough to paint—and Anna thought of Jules in the

Truffaut and the giant hourglass he overturned for every occasion. When they were finished with their drinks—they had ordered cocktails—they left Anna's motorbike locked to the fence and went down to the alley they had visited before.

"You're sure your ex's family isn't going to come out and yell at us?" Anna said.

"I'm sure. And it's not *us*. It's you. You're the one who's going to have the can in her hand."

"Gee, thanks."

Anna wore a backpack she had filled with several cans of paint. She had tucked half of the cans into the knee socks she had brought with her in January when she first arrived in Greece expecting cold. The cans clinked dully against each other in her pack as she walked. The work of painting the mural—for it had achieved this status in her mind now—unfolded quickly. She and Mel and Sophia said virtually nothing to each other once they had established which of them was to hold the light for Anna when she needed and which was to stand guard. Anna sprayed with a staccato rhythm of short and long strokes, filling with long strokes and outlining with short jabs as she had learned to do from watching grainy videos online. She checked the design she had folded into her pocket and made sure the outlines took the proper shape. She painted three figures, each stepped before the other in a shifting grayscale from black-outlined white, through gray, to white-outlined black. The intention was for the three figures to be at once one and multiple, a group and an individual. Mel and Sophia offered tweaks to the image based on their sense of graphic design. But Anna held in her mind the words from the August 6 reading Father Emmanouil had given them and that had so aptly fit the events of the other night on this spot: three figures and a vision and a secret that must be kept.

What was the secret here? Anna did not know—and that was one of the weaknesses in her painting. She needed to understand the power of a secret kept and to understand precisely what she was withholding. That absence would have fueled the piece she was in the middle of creating now. But with Anna's graffiti work and with her personality itself, everything was always available—she prided herself on this, in fact, and this was why certain of her relationships were stronger while others were more strained. And while it is not necessary to be a liar to be a proper artist, it is necessary to fashion art from a curation of inaccuracies.

When she finished, she made a little alpha overlaid on the initial of her last name and this was her signature. She had struggled with this graphic as the alpha writ large resembled too closely the anarchists' symbol, and writ small evoked the fish image of devout Christians. She was, of course, devout, but this fish would have turned her murals into something completely different, and it was a symbol she associated more with van-driving parents in America than with graffiti artists in a large European city. So, she had settled on tagging her work with both initials, which seemed to her uninspired, and was. She rocked back onto the heels of her Converse and crouched down at the wall. She pulled her phone out and tapped the camera. Without seeing yet what she had done, she took a picture. In the double flash, she saw the mural's three grayscale figures framed by a kaleidoscope of shapes and shadows.

"One more," she said, and tapped the camera once again. "OK," she said, though the flash made it difficult for them to see in the darkness. "Now run!"

They ran on their rubber soles out of the alley and up to the start of the hill and around to the fence by the road where Anna had left the motorbike. They went on, laughing and out of breath, up the path to the church terrace. It was quiet here. The funicular hissed to a stop and let its tourists out into the cooling air. The stalks of giant mallows nodded below them on the hillside. The conversations from the terrace bar had a muffled quality. The night was humid and the damp lay on the hill like a blanket.

"Now what?" Anna said. She spoke with the anxiety of those who know they will be asked for even more.

"Now we go *out*," Mel said, and they ran down the path to board the motorbike again and Anna drove them into Gazi.

⚜

Anna's question—now what?—had not been about the next item in a sequence of small events. She had been asking that in part, yes. But her question had to do with things she could not even voice, even if Mel and Sophia had been inclined to listen, and even if she told them then about her plans for Irini's house. So, as they found their parea at the club and as they pushed their way into the crowd to dance, she wondered what she should do next with her art now that she had painted this image. What *could* she do now to match the idea and the execution—the first of which had been good and the second only solid—of the piece she had just finished. She was no genius. She knew this. But, as she joined Mel and Sophia beneath the flashing lights, she felt she had accomplished something on the retaining wall, and there was, she could not deny, that idea of the passage from Matthew that hovered over what she'd done. The blinding white of the flash preserved in her mind this notion of the figure who appears and then is gone, the one who is revealed but just as quickly lost—the implication being that the viewer has not deserved a clearer vision. She felt she should speak to Father Emmanouil about this, to ask if what she had experienced could be considered something of a divine revelation—even to articulate the thought made her blush with sheepish excitement. Still, would not her priest reassure her that, like any one of his congregants or even those who were not members of his church, she was thoroughly deserving of a vision?

Anna's completion of the painting on the retaining wall had set up an expectation in her. It had given her a sense of responsibility to a certain level of achievement, if not to a certain kind of project she should next undertake. She had been coasting, she realized now as the DJ shifted to a new track. She had been coasting, but without the kind of incline that could send her speeding down a hill. She had been gliding along, pushed forward every now and then by a nudge from the parea or a look or smile from the priest or even lately a comment from Irini. But she had no direction. She did not know what to do next. She did not fully understand whether her question was artistic or theological, but she knew now at least that she was looking.

❦

Irini could have told Anna what to do. The girl hadn't asked her, but that had not stopped Irini yet or ever from voicing her opinion, and she needed only the next opportunity at church to speak her mind. On Sunday, she took up a seat on her customary side of the aisle after a curt nod at the widows and greetings for Tamrat and for Oumer, who was back at church after his week of resting and recovery. Irini could not see whether he was still limping—the church was so small that it required only a handful of steps to enter and sit down. Anna joined her with a rush of heavy breathing and big smiles, and Irini's first question of the day was to ask her had she run there. Before the priest began the service, Irini leaned toward the girl.

"I need to tell you something," she said.

"Me too!"

"No. I need to say something to you and you will listen."

"OK." Anna twisted to look at her. "Are you all right?"

"Of course. I'm fine."

Irini kept her eyes on the priest who had begun to chant the first psalm of the liturgy, and she kept her head turned in rapt attention until she felt Anna settle back into her chair.

There was much Irini could have told Anna besides what she planned to say—about pressing her no further about her family home. We might agree that there was much she *should* have said. She should have explained the markings on the façade and the padlock and chain that looped through the handles of the double front doors. She should have explained the piano and the Mozart, and she should have explained the brother and the sister from Hydra who had lived twenty years with her family and then left Athens together in mid-winter when the crossing to the island was choppy and gray-skied. This was the conversation she was having with her God while Father Emmanouil went through the service and Anna seemed to hum with a strange energy beside her. She should tell the girl these things. But why? What was the point of certain stories taking their turn ahead of others? The priest had told them to read this passage from Saint Paul about, of all things, parliamentary procedure. Wasn't the man—or apostle, it didn't matter much in this case—saying someone decided which story was told and when? If they were all living in a lesser time—trivial moments that would be bundled into the significance of afterlife—what difference did it make what you told to people and when? It would all be *one* time, past, present, and future, once you died. And wasn't that the point of living, for someone who believed—which she was trying to see if she could do—to get to an afterlife where all the moments of your life were reunited at once in an eternal present?

Proust, Mozart, Truffaut, the priest. What were they telling her? Or maybe the better question was which of these would help her more—and it was true that she needed help. Did she really want to string every moment of her life like a bead on a necklace whose pattern moved in one direction only? Or did she want to snap the string and pour the beads into a basket and sift her fingers through them for the colors and the shapes that most delighted?

When the service ended, she took Anna by the elbow to pull her outside and away from Oumer, who the girl was beginning to go and greet. She led Anna to a corner of the tiny courtyard that lay a few steps below the level of the street.

"Now, listen," she said.

"Did I do something wrong?"

"I said listen and the first thing you do is ask a question." Irini waited to see if the girl would be so obstinate as to speak again. She was not.

"There is something I need to tell you."

"OK."

"You must not ask me about my house anymore."

"Why?"

"You must not ask me. I know I'm the one who agreed to show it to you but there won't be any more."

The girl appeared relieved.

"I get it. That's fine."

"What do you *get*?"

The girl appeared less relieved now that she was put on the spot.

"It must be hard to relive all those memories. I loved hearing the stories and if you had more, I'd definitely be into it. But I get it."

Irini released Anna's arm.

"Yes. That's exactly right. It's easier for me to keep my memories here." She placed a palm on her chest. "And let me tell you one more thing. Because I think I know you now a little bit. If you do decide to push me on the house, there will be no more cinema."

She said it with a smile. She knew this would be lure enough to keep the girl from balking.

"The Truffaut is over anyway," Anna said, smiling back.

"Your cinematic education is far from complete," Irini said. She had managed to use as collateral the very thing she herself wished not to lose. Her arrangement was, for now, complete: Anna would keep away from the family home and would continue to fund Irini's share of all their outings. "Now," Irini said, "let's go welcome Oumer back to the fold."

They were all happy to have Oumer among them again, and it turned out that he was indeed limping a little, injuries to the soft tissue being notoriously difficult to heal. But he was back at work at the café and had been keeping up with Father Emmanouil's assigned readings, and he had for now taken on the role of coach for the parkour team in its training for the coming competitions. The mood of reunion, except with the two widows who, as always, kept themselves apart, was strong enough that Father Emmanouil invited everyone for lunch at the taverna. The widows declined, morally opposed to such expansiveness on the part of the priest and also dubious as to his finances, but the rest of them made their way across to the taverna where Nefeli joined them with the priest's two sons. Nefeli greeted them all with pleasure, surprise, and questioning silent looks at her husband who she knew would have to forgo something—his weekly soccer match, perhaps, with the chipped-in tip for the referee—to make up for the expense.

Once they had ordered and once the boys had taken their ball out to the square, Father Emmanouil cleared his throat and pressed his palms onto the table.

"I have an idea," he said, "for an adventure."

"An adventure," Irini said. "Yet we're trusting you with the safety of our souls."

"An excursion, then," he said.

Father Emmanouil paused as the waiter and his mohawked assistant came with the basket full of bread and silverware rolled up in napkins.

"After this season of adoration of Mary Mother of God, I would like us to move to a contemplation of Last Things."

"Is someone dying?" Irini said. She looked around the table to catch the smiles of the little congregation.

"We are all dying, dear Irini," the priest said. She ignored the fact that they were all likely considering her as the one who would die soonest. "And that is precisely why I propose we take a trip, as a congregation, to the island of Patmos."

"Why Patmos?" Anna said. "I'm sorry if I should know this."

"You should," Irini said.

The priest set a hand on Anna's arm.

"Don't listen to her. There is a time for everyone to learn these things."

"Patmos," Oumer said, "is the island where Saint John wrote the Book of Revelation."

"Allegedly," Tamrat said.

"Yes," Irini said. "Allegedly. We don't know *who* wrote any of it."

"Irini," Father Emmanouil said with enough sharpness for Nefeli to speak up.

"We *believe*," Nefeli stressed the word, "in the writers of the Gospels and Epistles."

"Or perhaps we believe in the poetry of Seferis who gave us such a beautiful translation," Irini said.

"Seferis?" Anna said.

"One of our two Nobel Prize winners," Irini said, only slightly concealing her concern that this girl in possession of Greek citizenship was not also possessed of this proud knowledge.

"We *believe*," Father Emmanouil began again, "in the Gospel writers. And Saint John was among them," the priest said. He gulped a long drink of water. He knew it was his job and his calling to welcome all his congregants into the church but this was one of the many times he wished Irini would stay home, in the apartment he sometimes regretted securing for her. He resumed.

"Saint John was allegedly a refugee." He looked across at Oumer and Tamrat with an expression Tamrat found universally annoying. Having come to Greece two years ago, before the current crisis, and having arrived in Greece with a bit of money, he and Oumer should have stopped being thought of as refugees, and yet there it was, the well-meaning but incorrect assignment of a label. "But," the priest went on, "Saint John was definitely the writer of the Book of Revelation and he was definitely—"

"In your view," Irini muttered.

"In my view he was definitely the same John who asks Jesus who it is who shall betray him, and the author of one of the Gospels. Therefore, I propose a period of study of this difficult book of the Bible and then a trip to visit the very cave where John experienced and transcribed his visions."

"Were they visions, Father, or was he telling a story to make a point to Rome?" Irini said.

"Ah, I see you have been studying already." The priest pretended her question had not been yet another challenge. "There are some who see the imagery of Revelation as coded messages to and about Rome. But others believe them to be the report of John's visions."

"Which do you believe, Father E.?"

Anna had been silent all this time and had to clear her throat before she spoke.

"Should I tell you now? Or should we all discover this together?"

"A revelation of the Revelation," Irini said, taking up the silver-ware bundles and sharing them out around the table.

"Yes," the priest said. "I knew you'd come around, Irini."

"An apocalypse?" Anna said. In Greek the words for revelation and apocalypse were the same, and what Anna meant with her question was what was meant in English: destruction and devastation.

"An uncovering," the priest said, to explain the Greek word. He made a gesture as if opening a box. "Theologically, it's quite the same."

"But, Father," Irini said. "The apocalypse is always waiting for us. Why do you want us to confront it *now*?" And for want of a better explanation of the oddness of his proposition, she said, "It's summer."

"God takes no holidays, Irini, you know that."

She did not like that he felt so certain of this—not God's behavior, which she allowed him to be entitled to know something of, but the extent of her own knowledge.

"But *you* do. Why do you want to spend the last days of the summer pondering the end of the world?"

"What better time?" he said, though this idea had only just come to him. "What better time than the end of summer to consider the end of days?"

In fact, Father Emmanouil had arrived at his idea for the study of Revelation because he sensed in himself a growing distance from divinity, and this worried and alarmed him. He had always felt his congregants were better off with all that tethered them to this world than with flights up and away into the next. But he had of late begun to wonder whether he was not sliding down a path if not to excommunication—he was hardly as bold as that—then to a sort of apostasy from the very faith he loved. To study Revelation would be to force himself back to the contemplation of essential questions in a way that was almost punitive and would, he hoped, restore him to his God. And for the others? There were fewer Greek spots in all of Orthodoxy more powerful than the Cave of the Revelation where God had made Himself apparent to John—even to think these words made goosebumps rise on Father Emmanouil's arms. He would be a poor priest indeed if he did not determine to bring his congregation to this place of light and grace.

"I'm not sure I want to contemplate the end of days at all," Irini said. The end of her days often seemed far closer to her than she wished, though sometimes further away than she could afford—it took money to live, and she was running out of it. She did not know that she wanted to spend time contemplating what the apocalypse would mean for her, and she had accounts of a spiritual sort that she was not yet ready to settle.

"I'm not sure about this Patmos," Tamrat said.

Father Emmanouil did his best not to jump from the table in exasperation. He felt he could manage Irini's small rebellions, but if she had pulled Tamrat into her defiant current, he thought perhaps he should give up on the idea altogether.

"The church will fund the trip," Nefeli said, and reached a calming hand out to her husband. She did not have to look at him to know that he was becoming flustered. "Father has persuaded them to cover the boat fare and the hostel."

"I can pay for it," Tamrat said. "And so can Oumer."

Irini, who knew she could not pay for the trip, was glad to hear Nefeli's information without having had to ask.

Oumer was saving money for a different trip, hoping to go to Santorini for the parkour championships sponsored by a company whose beverages packed more caffeine than his strongest pulls of espresso. But if the church was going to fund the trip to Patmos, Oumer would go to Patmos happily, and he would scout the island for free-running spots while he was there.

"What's the objection, then?" Nefeli said.

"I'm just not sure we should be going," Tamrat said.

"I want to go," Oumer said. "Speak for yourself." Oumer understood that when Tamrat said *we* he meant *we Ethiopians, we Africans, we black men, paler than many Greeks but who are always black to them.*

"Oumer." Tamrat turned to him. "With everything that's happening, I don't really feel like going on a trip."

They all knew that what Tamrat meant by this generalization was the way economic anxieties boiled over into anger with those seen as new or strange.

"So, we're supposed to hide?" Oumer said.

"No."

"We live here," Oumer said. "This is our home."

Tamrat made a dismissive sound and then leaned into the table.

"Look," he said. "Maybe we'll join, Father. Maybe Oumer will come and I'll stay here. He has his own life. But Athens isn't my home. Addis Ababa is, and I'll go back to my work there some time soon." And seeing the concern on Nefeli's face, he unrolled his knife and fork from inside the napkin. "Besides," he said, to make her smile, "no offense to Oumer, but the coffee in Addis is much better."

"Father," Oumer said, "I think this is an excellent idea and I would very much like to study Revelation and then see the holy site of its creation."

"Thank you, Oumer, and bless you," the priest said.

"Me too," Anna said.

"Yes," Irini said, "I suppose I will come as well."

"Of course you will," Nefeli said and Irini heard in the words exactly what Nefeli intended her to hear. It was a warning, but of what exactly Irini could not be certain yet.

*

Before they could begin the study of Revelation, however, the congregation and their priest had to conclude their preparation for the Assumption of Mary, which was now only three days away. On the day of the Assumption itself, the little church's stubby nave would be packed wall to iconed wall with celebrants, for every Greek in Plaka and many Greeks in other neighborhoods whose churches were not as old or as pretty or located in so dramatic a setting would make Plaka the site of one of their two yearly visits to a church, the other being midnight mass at Easter. Tourists who happened by during the service would add themselves to the throng, and some, to the chagrin of most of the Greeks in attendance, would chime in with what they thought were the proper vowel sounds as the priest and the cantor—brought in special for the holy day—sang the mass. Irini was on guard for this behavior and was known to press a finger to her lips and let out a sharp hiss to shush a tourist.

There had been, of course, plenty of years when Irini had not attended church on the Assumption. She and her husband had often spent the holiday on Hydra, and they had preferred to align themselves with what felt new and outward-looking. This meant

leaving church celebrations to the old women of the island or to
the younger locals of a certain class. It had been a given then that
educated people could not be believers, or if they were believers,
they adopted a rather casual attitude toward the rituals of the
church itself. Irini had worn a cross around her neck even in those
days, but she did not make the sign of the cross upon embarking
on a journey or at the start of a meal and she viewed August 15
as a day to be away on holiday, nothing more. Even once she had
begun attending the church with the stubby nave after having
made her promise to the God she didn't trust, Irini made a point
of exercising her freedom on that day in the religious calendar.
If it was raining—which sometimes happened even in Athens
in August—she might stay home. Or she would walk the perim-
eter of the Acropolis, past the ancient theater, to the cave where
Socrates had drunk his poison, and past the Agora and back again.
As she walked, not minding the rain, she savored the dusty scent
of moistened earth that smelled in Athens like nowhere else she
had ever been—though she had not been to that many different
places. If she saw a crowd already spilling out of the church as she
arrived for the service, she would turn back home. She had made
her promise to her God, but she could only continue to keep it if
she exercised these capricious independences from time to time.

This year, she had a feeling as the 15th approached that she would
not attend. She had read enough, thanks to the priest's photocopy,
perhaps too much. As the photocopy was the same each year, and
thus the readings were the same, Irini's thoughts too remained
unchanged. If she was to learn something, she would find it else-
where. And Irini wanted to learn. She had a sense that she could tuck
bits of knowledge between the seconds in the clock, the days of the
calendar, and push further and further apart with those increments
so that her knowledge would expand her time itself.

Hence now, as before, the Proust. And hence the Proust in French, a language that she spoke much better than she understood. (She had in fact relied on the subtitles of the Truffaut much more than she had let on.) This week the book group was held at Pamela's home, and Irini was certain not to skip the session as she knew the food and drink would be both plentiful and good. There was the added benefit of the meeting coming so close to the August holiday that talk of everyone's vacations would offer ample opportunity for Irini's amusement. Neither Pamela nor her food were a disappointment, with the coffee table spread with cheeses and dried fruits that, though a rather wintry spread, were quite filling. Pamela announced she would be going to Paros, a bland enough destination that no one had much to say about. The woman who had hosted the previous week's meeting offered the mountains as her vacation spot, and Irini knew immediately that this was why she had always found the woman so appealing. From the looks on the others' faces, one would have thought the former hostess—whose name was Lydia—had announced her plan to go to North Korea for her holiday and not a village in the Zagori region where the air would be cool and the walking would be lovely.

"That's my kind of holiday," Irini said, though until this moment it had never occurred to her to vacation in the mountains instead of on Siros or Hydra, and it was only her sudden spark of allegiance to Lydia that had made her speak up. Now she thought that she might like a place like that where she could walk and smell the dust and the pine needles when it rained.

"Where are you going?" Pamela asked. "Are you going to be able to get away?"

"Of course," Irini said, because she always liked to meet Pamela's inquiries with the opposite of Pamela's expectations.

"Where are you headed?" Lydia asked, with an enthusiastic curiosity that pleased Irini.

"Patmos."

The word dropped like a spill of champagne.

"Really?" Pamela asked.

"Yes, really."

Irini helped herself to another bit of cheese and, knowing the rest were waiting for more details, took her time arranging the slice on a cracker.

"What?" she said. "It's an island. Perhaps you've heard of it."

"We know where Patmos is, Irini."

"Good."

"But it's so—"

Irini suspected—correctly—that Pamela was going to comment on the island's exclusivity, and thus to imply surprise that Irini would be admitted there.

"So far away," Irini said instead. And to appease them all by appearing to them as the person they knew her to be, she went on to say of course she couldn't afford to take a helicopter there, like the uber-rich who had of late made Patmos their playground, but would take the ship overnight from Piraeus. "Saves the cost of one night's lodging, too."

"And will your daughter be joining you there?" one woman said. "With her son?"

"Yes, as a matter of fact," Irini said. "She will."

This satisfied most of the women—filial ties asserted and extended—and irritated only Pamela who did not feel she should be upstaged in her own home, not least by Irini, and especially because she already knew she had put out an array of food that did not go well with the season, nuts and dried fruits being reserved for the coldest time of year. The group was able to return to their discussion, only diverting from Swann's house once to discuss the pilgrims who would be traveling to Tinos on the same boat that would be taking a woman named Demetra to Mykonos for the holiday—no one dared express astonishment that this rather matronly member of the group would be spending her August holiday on an island full of Instagram influencers. Instead, they all commented briefly on the way the most ardent in their devotion to Mary would disembark from the boat in Tinos harbor and fall onto their knees right on the dock and would crawl the seven hundred meters to the church on padded kneelers. None of the women could fathom such extreme devotion, not even Irini who had shared a boat with them for all the years she had traveled to Siros. Siros, Tinos, Mykonos had been the itinerary of the sturdy boats that worked the Aegean route all those years. Anyone continuing to Mykonos like Demetra two days from now and anyone sharing the route to Siros would see the pilgrims either in the height of their anticipation or the depths of their deliberate and sacrificial suffering. Patmos was a route of its own and a story of its own, and none of them around the coffee table had any experience of the place except from the society pages and from a long-ago lesson in school about Saint John the Revelator. With Patmos, Irini was on her own, as she knew she would be, and she had won back a little something from them in their talk of hotels and rented villas and family visits.

All of them knew which one was Irini's family home. All of them had been there for parties, and one or two had been inside even before Irini had married. They were old Plaka ladies like Irini, and they had known her mother and her family and had seen their parents coming home from card games with Irini's parents at Irini's parents' house. Through the terrible ill fortune of a fault line and the poor work of a mason in the nineteenth century, and a period after the war when the blasting for a new foundation across the street had weakened something in Irini's family home but not in theirs—through all of this, their homes had been untouched and had remained assets to be shared or handed down to children and grandchildren. So, all of them knew that, without the tricks of circumstance, they were no different from Irini. In fact, she was better than most of them—if by better one meant better educated, better informed, healthier, more agile, more attractive. They knew all this and, in some way, they did her the kindness to resent her for it still. Though she had almost nothing, they never let their guard down in her presence, for she was, unarmed, a stronger adversary than they were with all their weapons of security and wealth.

Obviously, Irini had not told the truth about her holiday. Or, we could say, she had stretched it, shifting the location of a journey into a different moment in time from which it took on a different meaning. And populating her future experience with different people so that she herself took on the identity the book group ladies wished to see. The book group did not like to think of her as a student of religion, as a pilgrim to Patmos, this spot of strangeness in the Christian faith. They preferred to think of her as a mother and a grandmother. She had given them what they wanted. Was it wrong of her to make these substitutions? The question is not rhetorical, much as Irini herself might have wished for it to be. Was her tale of a Patmos holiday a problem for anyone? We will find out soon enough.

That evening, she took up the Bible and flipped to the Book of Revelation, but she felt there was not much that she could learn from her reading of these images of sealed books and doors and beasts. She had perused the thing before and seen the brief text mostly as a work of fantasy—which from time to time she felt to be the state of the entire Bible. Now she tried to concentrate on the images for what meaning she could glean. There was to be an apocalypse and the end of days. This was clear. But Irini felt she could not muster much alarm about this fact, being confident—though not pleased—she would be long gone by its arrival. The images and symbols seemed to her like something out of Bergman, whose films she had watched with curiosity the summer before last when the cinema owner's son had chosen the Swede for his film series. There was fire, and plenty of it, and Christ with gold trimmings and brass feet, and there were tribulations and warnings and plagues. The verses were so dense—and she had had enough of that with Proust—that she could not read them in their proper order and instead let her eye catch only what was familiar to her from her life outside the church: the Alpha and Omega, the seals, the death.

And yet. And yet Irini felt a personal scolding coming from the Book, a chastisement that seemed aimed directly toward her, even as John pretended not to care whether she paid attention to his words or not. She did not want to mind the condemnation, and yet she did mind. This John who had written all these symbols and terrors was pretending he didn't even care if she took heed of him or not. She would be doomed no matter what. What then, she wondered, was the point of committing to believe him?

But the more she read, the more her resistance dwindled. Here were horses and strange riders and flames and doors, and she began to shuffle and shift the images in her imagination. The earth shook and the world cracked open and something—but she had no idea what—was revealed to her, the covers thrown from a large lustful bed or from an ancient statue shown to the light, or as with a document exposed to air that shriveled to dust just as its meaning became clear.

She jolted from the dreams that had overtaken her and flung the book onto the couch beneath the window, jumping up to set the book down once again with the care befitting a holy text. The lights were still shining on the Acropolis and she looked to the golden-colored lines and triangles of Kallicrates' stones as the home of reason. She rubbed her hands over her eyes and went to the bathroom to splash her face with water, for it occurred to her that the apartment was quite hot. It would be good for her to get away from Athens. Had she not just recently been wishing for the means to take a trip? She could sit on the deck of the boat to Patmos and let the breeze hold these frightful images and dreams at bay, at least for a while. She could take the sea journey as a time out of time, the boat dipping over and over into the same water and never coming to a final shore. She could smell the salt of the Aegean as they crossed, and in the morning when they neared the island she could watch the sun rise over Turkey. She might suggest to Father Emmanouil that the church make next year's trip to Constantinople, and because she would call it that and not Istanbul, he might give in and the church might pay for that vacation too.

❦

The next day was a Tuesday and Irini had to walk. She had to put between herself and the Book of Revelation as much distance as she could. She left the thing where she had tossed it on the couch and from which she could still hear its whispers about the end of days, its accusations about all that she had done and left undone. And so, she fled. Why had she agreed to this entire enterprise? Why had she courted this look into the apocalypse? Was it truly worth it to endure these flights of terror for the sake of an island holiday on someone else's euro? These questions were not rhetorical, and she planned to come to the end of at least *this* day with some answers. The priest's urgency had spread to her, and now she felt all her days leading up to this one like a wave about to break upon her head.

She walked around Plaka with her string bag to gather groceries, for this was an act of practicality that could anchor her to the present. The fruit seller gave her chunks of watermelon on toothpicks while he rang up her grapes and peaches. The produce man threw in a bag of onions with Irini's eggplant and tomatoes. She felt confident enough to stop at the grocer for cheese and olives, selecting the saltiest feta and the briniest olives she could find. With the shops set to close for the August 15 holiday, the vendors could afford to be charitable in giving away things that would spoil if kept. Irini dropped her collection off at home and went out again. Only now the day was nearly violently hot and she realized she had forgotten to drink a glass of water at her sink. There was a blessing in this, for she would not need to use a bathroom and she had been able to leave the apartment again and the malevolent presence of the Book without delay. Because it was August 14, she ventured to the pedestrian street that was lined with shops—where, on her previous visit, she had found nothing she was interested in buying. The prices were much lower now and the merchandise deemed less appealing—but to Irini closer to classic—was now on the racks, brought out from the storerooms. Irini considered a pair of slip-on sneakers that masqueraded as ballet flats. These she felt would give her some traction for the rains of fall and winter and would replace an older pair that had worn thin. It took so much time for her to catch the salesgirl's eye that, when she finally ventured over, Irini put on the air of someone famous that the girl should know. She could see the girl puzzling over Irini's clothes that, though stylish, were neither fine nor fashionable, and Irini dropped a line about the stage—which was enough to convince the girl that she was serving an actress from the heyday of the Athenian theater.

Around the corner from the shop, Irini sat on a bench and switched the old shoes for the new, as she had no desire to carry a shopping bag with her. For she intended to walk all day. She intended to keep moving, pursued by reminders that her time—everyone's time—was running out, hounded by the beasts that had already appeared ahead of an even darker revelation. She walked through Plaka and through Monastiraki and into the Thisseio by the ancient Agora. She sought the shade whenever she could and she dipped a hand into a fountain and tapped her moistened fingers to her neck. In the square of the Agora near the ancient Roman library, the café in the middle ran a set of misters to spray the boxwood hedges by the tables and to keep the diners cool, and as she passed she dipped her head into the mist. It did not matter. The heat had dried it by the time she reached the next corner.

What was she doing as she walked? She was taking an inventory of the present moment. Here was Athens, here was the world on this day, on this eve of a holiday, with the city's people on the move or preparing to depart, and with its vacancies and closures and abandonments failing to outnumber all that was still there. Shoes discounted by 65 percent since it was August. A man selling paintings on panes of glass arrayed on a blanket by the sidewalk. A man and a woman in their forties arguing and then pulling in toward each other and the woman buttoning the top button of the man's collar. A child walking beside her mother, turning the grids of a many-colored cube. Women with bulging calves carrying yoga mats under their arms. And everybody everywhere talking or tapping on a phone. This was the city. This was the world. It was alive and it was on the move and it was lines of conversation tying each person to many others. Could she not find in this—she must find in this—some solace?

There were names to where Irini walked—Monastiraki, Ana-fiotika, Kerameikos, Gazi, Metaxourgeio—names that foiled the tourists and confused the locals who remembered the names when they meant places where you shouldn't go and remembered the places even before they had any names at all. Irini had known the area around the gas plant when it was a rough neighborhood of brothels, and she had known Metaxourgeio when silk was still made and worked there. Now she found herself mid-afternoon in this quarter of the city newly given over to collaborative art exhibitions and cafés and secondhand book shops and record shops—record shops!—that sold albums in vinyl, and she was starving and her feet were sore from the new shoes, but she had finally escaped the hounds and beasts of Saint John's visions. Across from where she stood, there was what looked like a bar where a birdcage hung above the elaborate system of valves and tubes the young people used to make their coffee. She didn't like the look of it—to have a bird leaving its waste in such proximity to a food source seemed unwise—and went instead to the café beside it where two men roughly her age sat playing backgammon. She peered at them as if at mannequins in a museum, and they were indeed real—can we help you, they said—though Irini was convinced the café owner paid them to give the place an air of old-time authenticity. These two men were among the not insig-nificant number of older people who still lived in Metaxourgeio, stepping from tidy two-story houses where the appliances still ran on old, two-prong wires and out onto streets fully painted over with murals and tags and posters. They had been coming to this café for decades and would continue to play backgammon there until they died.

Irini sat at a small table and ordered a Greek coffee with medium sugar and gulped down the glass of water that came with it—restrooms be damned—and danced the empty glass in the air for a refill, which the waiter brought in a copper pitcher. One of the men looked across the backgammon board and she could see that he found her attractive. She did not attempt the ruse of the old theater star here. The man knew how to read the signs of her clothing and her hair. But she wanted none of that, in any case. She wanted only to drink her coffee and rest her feet before the long journey home. She refused to equip herself with a mobile and so she had no way to ascertain the best way home except to ask—and she had scant enthusiasm for appearing ignorant or lost. Especially not in a city she knew like the back of her hand, and especially not in front of these old men. The men were both younger than her by six and seven years, and the one who had looked at her had a smartphone he would have been happy to use in her assistance. But she did not ask, and when she felt herself beginning to succumb to sleepiness, she dug a two-euro coin from the pouch in which she kept her change and set it on the table. She nodded and smiled a salutation at the men and twisted her way through the tables.

"Ma'am," the waiter called after her, and she patted her sides to see what she had left behind. "It's three." He saw her puzzled expression and, because his grandmother lived with him and his partner and he saw what had occurred, he wound through the tables to Irini and placed himself between her and the two old men. "It's three euros for the coffee, ma'am," he said softly, "not two."

"Oh," she said.

"Sorry. Trendy-place prices. I have to cover my tab, or else—"

"Here you go, young man," she said, and parted with another coin, wondering how the old men could afford their daily sojourns. The waiter fished in his apron for change and she told him to keep it. This was an act of utter folly on her part, to pay twice what she had expected. But it had been a day of giving free rein to the fool and not the judge, so let her spend by accident rather than skimp on purpose.

She did not know the way to the Metro, but she knew that even if she found the nearby stop it would take her first away from home before she could change trains and go back toward it. So, she walked. She became lost enough to ask once for directions, and she became afraid more than once when she turned down a poorly lit alley and when a man approached to ask if she needed help. In the shadows below broken streetlights, she sensed again the beasts and fires of Revelation and felt again the rising wave she had worked so hard all day to outrun. It took all her force of character not to hail a taxi or not to ask someone to let her place a phone call. And finally, she arrived in the little square and had never been happier to see the ticket window of the rooftop cinema, even if the place was closed for the holiday tomorrow.

Irini slept all night and until the heat of midday had fully invaded the apartment. She sat up and felt her throat crack with hoarseness. Some kind of folly had compelled her yesterday, even as her purpose in going out had been to confirm the foundations of logic and materiality that made up her world. Materiality had beaten her up, bruising her feet and wearing down muscles that had been pushed beyond endurance. She wanted nothing more than to sleep. She had to sleep. She pulled the sheet over her face to block the beam of insistent sun and lay on top of the summer blanket—which was simply a heavy sheet because no one needed a true blanket in August in Athens—and let sleep come back to her.

She missed the service for the Assumption of Mary Mother of God. Father Emmanouil's performance of the liturgy was notably poor and the widows would never forget this, and by summer's end would switch to a church in the center of Monastiraki, attending services in the company of the lost and the stoned who were still awake from Saturday night in the bars of that touristy quarter and needed someplace cool to sit. Father Emmanouil scanned the crowd for Irini, telling himself there were so many people in his church that she was simply hidden from his view. But he could not ignore the puzzled look on Anna's face as she caught his eye. He shook his head at her, and this caused the cantor to introduce a hitch into his singing, and because so few in the church that day knew the liturgy well from regular attendance, no one actually noticed the disruption except the two widows who were already disgruntled, and the cantor himself who had convinced his wife and daughter to come hear him today and who knew they would now think he was not very good at his new post. Anna twisted in her seat to look for Irini, but she could not see over the heads of the congregation. And Irini, for all her upright posture, was not tall, though most would have told you that she was, in that way that we remember true details far less well than what we wish. Anna snuck her phone from her pocket and glanced at the screen, but there was no point to this instinct as she knew Irini had no mobile. This had been the topic of one conversation that became oddly heated as Anna asked her how anyone could check on her and how her daughter could be expected to feel confident about her mother's health and safety. Irini had grown angry. Not angry in the way of the curmudgeon that she often was, who performs a greater anger than she feels, but truly angry with a downward set of the mouth and a rise of color to her cheeks. Then she had announced to Anna the news that her daughter and grandson had lived in Australia for many years. Anna had expressed surprise, but Irini had repeated that she was fine without a mobile phone and put an end to the conversation. Now Anna saw she had a text that her own mother had sent before going to bed in America and the preview on the screen showed a row of heart emojis and a puppy face with bows—Anna's parents did not have a dog—but of course there was nothing from Irini or about Irini and nothing from anybody in her parea because they were all asleep.

As soon as the liturgy was finished, Anna turned her back on Father Emmanouil, who she knew would understand, and pushed her way out into the sun. In two minutes, she was at the door to Irini's apartment building and she was sweating. The bedroom window was closed but the shutters were open, and this combination suddenly alarmed her. It was backward. It was something one would do in winter to capture heat, but no one would do it this way in the summer except by accident. Anna pressed Irini's bell repeatedly and got no answer. She pressed all the other buttons for the building until someone, without asking who she was, buzzed her in. She ran up the stairs past a man standing with his wallet ready at an open door and called back sorry, for she was not his breakfast gyro, and at Irini's door she banged and called. There was a doorbell here too and she leaned on the button.

There was a bang from the other side and Anna stopped.

"Irini?"

The door flew open and Irini stood there in a bathrobe with her face pale and eyes small without mascara.

"Good God, what the hell are you doing?"

"Are you OK? We were worried."

"I was sleeping. Do you mind?"

"You missed the service."

"I am aware of that." She began to close the door.

"Your window was shut. It must be baking in there."

Anna accompanied her words with a movement of her head toward the interior, and Irini swung the door almost completely closed.

"Stay there," she said. "Did I invite you in? I don't think so. Who asked you to come here?" She paused for an answer but went on. "I overslept. So what? I've missed the Assumption before and I'll miss it again. Mary is still up there," she waved a hand, "I'm guessing, whether I'm at church or not."

"But you were supposed to be there."

"Says who?"

"You wanted to be there. Are you sure you're feeling OK?"

Irini took a breath and forced it out through flaring nostrils. She stepped out onto the landing, never letting go of the door handle, and her mouth turned down and her face turned dark.

"You need to mind your own business, young lady. We keep company when I want to. And I do what I want. If I don't make it to some place you think I need to be at, that's my business. You have a mother of your own. Why don't you go bother her?"

And then she stepped back inside and shut the door and Anna heard the pure petulance of Irini looping the door chain into its track. She stared at the door for a moment, not knowing that Irini was staring at it from the other side and waiting for her heart to calm. Anna whispered in English as she turned to go.

"Fuck you."

She was trembling as she emerged into the little square, deeply ashamed and almost afraid that she had said this, and to a woman old enough to be her grandmother—though her grandmother had not lived past sixty-five. And to say it on a holy day was even worse, even if it had been in a different language. She could not return to apologize—Irini would not let her in, and might even call the police to make a point—but at least Irini had probably not heard her through the door, though if she had she would certainly have understood the words, her English knowledge being strong enough for that. But on this day of all days, Anna felt her actions did not go unseen. Should she not live as though she had to meet the standards of the God she prayed to? She determined to return to church, but first she stopped at the taverna where they had had lunch with the priest a week ago. She found the head waiter.

"Can you keep an eye out for Irini?" she said.

"Sure."

"If she goes out, can you just check on how she's doing?"

The man accepted this assignment, for his own mother was roughly Irini's age and was quite ill, and he took comfort in directing his attention here.

The waiter watched for Irini, and Anna's God was watching her, so she returned to the church, which was now empty of celebrants but remained illuminated inside by the many candles they had lit in memory or prayer or hope for members of their family. Anna dropped a coin into the box and took a long taper of honey-colored wax and touched its overlong wick to one of the candles planted in their tray of sand. She crossed herself and murmured an apology—though she could not be specific in her terms, for that would be to perpetrate a greater insult—and added a prayer before planting her taper in among the others.

She found Father Emmanouil outside the church in its sunken courtyard, looking up at the cloudless sky.

"She's all right," she said.

"Thank God." He crossed himself. Anna liked how, when the priest said this casual phrase, he meant it literally.

"She said she overslept."

"Hmm."

"Should we be worried?"

Father Emmanouil cocked his head at the girl. There was something so encouraging to him about her choice of pronoun. He was a man of faith, but he often thought the reason he had been drawn to his vocation was not the divinity itself but the idea of the *we* in the way believers anywhere became a group together and the way their superficial differences of humanity yielded to the common essence of their souls. In this thinking, the priest forcibly turned his mind away from the horrible things believers had done in the name of that common essence and its superiority to the common essences of all those who believed in other faiths.

"No," he said. "We should not be worried. We will be here to greet her when she returns, and we will in fact have never left her side."

"But what if something's wrong?"

"I'll check on her," he said. "And also, in a pinch, I have a key."

Father Emmanouil believed that the shared divinity of human beings was best supported by the conveniences and tools of the modern world.

"I'm sorry," Anna said, because she could think of nothing else and because her candlelit apology for cursing had not fully eased the guilt that still rested on her shoulders.

"We all do our best, Anna. Irini too, though it might not seem that way. Only her God knows what goes on in her soul, and she is the one who has to reckon with that." He saw a change in Anna's face and quickly went on to say he meant no criticism or condemnation.

"OK," Anna said. "What next?" And it occurred to her this was a question she had already asked once this week. She could not shake the feeling of being on the edge of something, these August days, in the near empty city.

"Settle your mind," the priest said. "And then turn to John and look for what he has to teach us of the mysteries of the end of days."

She smiled and said goodbye but had to admit that there was little comfort in this advice. The end of days. She was twenty-seven and had no plans for her life. It hardly seemed the time to contemplate its end.

Anna drifted south out of the little square with a glance up to Irini's window, now with the shutters loosely swung across it, and continued on to Goura Street to Irini's damaged family home. She stood across from it and let her eyes adjust enough so she could pick out the details in its shadowed façade. There was the knocker, the padlock and its loop of chain, the numbers and initials painted on the lower wall, the crack that marked the house like an errant ink line on a sketch, and the graffiti—not particularly artful—written all along the bottom. Irini had worried her and angered her and now worried her again, and Anna wished to do for her some act of kindness. In fact, Anna's impulse had as much to do with what she wanted to offer to herself, as she sought to atone for her own whispered outburst.

What if instead of projecting an image on the façade of Irini's house, she painted something added to the line formed by the crack? She could in this way turn the graffiti into something beautiful—to cover it entirely with her own work would be an act of disrespect to a fellow artist. What if she found a way to revive this house Irini loved so well? The damage to it did not have to be the end. Irini believed that the house stood at a dead end in its own history—that it could move neither forward repaired, nor backward razed to the ground to make way for something new. The cost of moving in either direction was too great, and so the house would remain like this forever. Of course, it would not, for little by little the mortar would crumble and bits of masonry would tumble into the street and weeds would expand the crack and the walls would lose their attachment to each other. Irini was not the only person concerned with the fate of the family home, but no matter who engaged in the debate, it was time itself that would win the argument.

But before any decay took place at all, Anna could do something to make the clock stand still for a bit and even appear to spin the other way. If she was good enough, she could. She was proud of her painting on the retaining wall and had ridden the motorbike home from the gallery out of her way more than once to pass by it. She was pleased at the memory of the moment of its creation, and her pleasure made her think the painting was far better than it really was. Anna embarked on a plan, and that meant sitting on the sidewalk on Goura Street with her back against the wall of the new building opposite and sketching Irini's family home in her notebook. She had a view between the bumpers of two cars, but it was enough for her to see what she needed.

Anna conceived of a trompe l'oeil design that would turn the right-hand side of the house, to the right of the crack, into an image of its former glory, using the existing graffiti as colorful leaves of a giant plant. She would paint the shutters to look like lighted windows. In the false window of one of them, the lid of a grand piano would be visible. In another, there would be figures in silhouette against the light, a man and a woman—her approximations of

Irini and her husband—and beside the figure of the woman, the outline of a little girl. Irini had said her daughter had emigrated to Melbourne, a city where there were almost as many Greeks as in the Greek city of Patras—so she hoped it would please her to see the daughter included in the design. The loop of chain for the padlock looked loose enough to allow a small person to climb inside the house, which meant that Anna could get inside if she needed to—perhaps to store her paints, ahead of time. But this also meant there was a possibility that others had gone in before her. From outside, there seemed no evidence of a squat—no cables tapping into power lines from inside a broken window, no sound of tarps flapping from inside where they would serve to create rooms from rubble—and this suggested to Anna that there was a strong enough police presence in the touristed neighborhood of Plaka to keep squatters away. In fact, it should have warned her that even squatters had deemed the place unsafe. But she was so enamored of her plan that she could not think the building itself might be dangerous.

She drew herself up from the sidewalk and crossed to the front door. She set a tentative foot onto the first step of the flight to the door and peered up at the padlock and chain. Through the opening, she could make out the cornice of a doorway and the base of what must have once been a grand staircase. She considered the possibility of doing some painting in the interior as well. If she could get inside through the gap between the doors, why not Irini too, and perhaps Anna could present her with something beautiful inside.

Her parea would be leaving tomorrow for the camping trip—to join the many who were already there and sending texts of sea waves and sunlit faces. She was supposed to meet Mel and Sophia and a boy named Andreas at Sophia's parents' house in Kifissia to get the VW Polo they were borrowing for the journey. She didn't want to go. Partly because she now had this project to do for her friend whom she had angered, and partly because she did not want to miss the trip to Patmos, and Father E. had not yet finalized the plans. She did not want to end up on the Ionian coast with no way back to Athens except a seat in the car of someone intent on staying put. She would tell Mel and Sophia at the birdcage bar that night.

In her Skype call with her parents that week, Anna told them about the service at the church and how they had all sung the Entrance hymn with its strange minor wanderings. It was one of the few times her story about something Greek made her parents happy, made them chime in with elaborations of their own drawn from happy memories. There was one time, her father said, this girl from my school's hair caught fire when someone leaned in with a candle. Only once? her mother said. Every year in my church someone ended up with a bob the day after Easter. Her father threw his hands up in surrender. I never win, he said, and they leaned into each other laughing and Anna missed them terribly and wished all of a sudden she was home. I miss you, Mom, she said, and then she wished she hadn't for she saw the tears in her mother's eyes and then she couldn't keep from crying. Oh, honey, her mother said, and while Anna reassured her she was fine and went to fetch a tissue and returned to blow her nose, her mother took their tablet in both hands and brought it close as if she were cupping Anna's cheeks in her hands. Come home, she said. Why don't you just come home? This caused Anna's crying to resume because she wanted in that moment to come home and also wanted to make a home in this place that was both new to her and familiar, and she wanted the church to feel again like the home it was before the strangeness of the Assumption. She shook her head. I can't, Mom. Not yet. But why? I don't know. I need to test myself. Her father spoke up. What test? It's Athens and you're Greek. You passed the test when you were born. Dad, I don't know. I want to do some things. Maybe in a few months. What things? Just things. I don't know, but in a few months, it will have been a year and maybe then I can come home.

In other versions of this conversation, this was the point when Anna would remind her parents that they had left their home at roughly the age that she was now and they had stayed away much longer between trips before they stopped returning almost completely. But this time she knew that they and she were afraid of exactly this and that rather than use her parents' exile as a benchmark, she should heed the warning that it sounded. I have to go, guys, she said, though she could not stand the thought of going to the birdcage bar on top of all this. Sweetie, her mother said, because she had heard the lump in her daughter's voice and would have been able to detect it even on the most muffled and staticky of phone calls. She felt the absence of her daughter, her only child, like a phantom limb—or, really, a phantom womb, as if Anna were still inside her and whatever the girl did, her mother felt it in her cells. So, when Anna said she had to go, her mother felt a pain that was not even quite a pain but a longing so deep it simply became her. She knew that if she did not allow Anna to sign off, Anna would begin to sob and she, Anna's mother, would have to watch and suffer. OK, she said. You do that. Go and meet your parea and have some fun. They told each other that they loved each other and blew kisses to their screens. Anna fell back against the couch and let the tears fall and the sobs come. She wanted to text Irini then, just to be sure the old woman was all right, but since she could not she texted Mel to say she couldn't come to the Ionian coast after all. She didn't receive a reply until an hour later. Bummer. We will miss you. And then emojis in a row: sad face, beach towel, heart, cocktail.

PART THREE

Anna looked for Irini at church that Sunday, but still the old woman was not there. By Wednesday, after two more days of checking her phone for the identifying numbers of an Athens landline and finding nothing but photos from her friends at their seaside campground, she decided to go ask Father Emmanouil what he knew. The priest had sent Nefeli to Irini with some apples that an aunt had brought back after visiting the family's village for the holiday, and Nefeli had found Irini fine. She had been reading among her many books and admitted she was looking forward to the Patmos trip. Anna was pleased to hear the news and was, of course, a little jealous too, as she could not help feel that Father E. had inadvertently replaced her with his wife, sending her to do the very thing he had sent Anna for a mere four weeks ago. She feared that in some way this meant she had failed a test—as if this was the very test she told her parents she wished to succeed at. And she had failed. Father Emmanouil had tried to match her with Irini, had sent her with the figs as the shibboleth of passage, and she, Anna, had not only been expelled herself but also caused a break in the pattern of the old woman's life. Now Anna expressed all this to Father Emmanouil and refused to let him reassure her. She was adamant it was her fault Irini had missed the mass for the Assumption and now this Sunday liturgy as well.

"No, no," he said. "It's true. She doesn't always come. Even on the holiday."

"But you were looking for her too that day."

"I know. I was. But that's simply what I do."

"It's all my fault," Anna said.

The priest crouched down so he could look up into her face, and whiffs of incense and sweat drifted from his cassock.

"If *you* don't show up for a holiday service, I promise I will be looking for you in the crowd. But," he said, "I'm going to have a hard time finding you because you're so short."

His words had the desired effect of making Anna smile.

"You have to let it go, Anna," he said, and then his expression became serious. "It's difficult to be a friend to an old person. They have lived so much that there's a lot of wear and tear and sometimes it just doesn't feel good for them and they won't say that's what it is. I wish our bodies didn't matter." He leaned in again. "That's kind of my job. But they do, and you have to remember Irini has a whole life behind her and yours is all ahead of you. It makes a difference."

Anna waited, but it seemed that he was finished. She wanted more absolution, more advice, though she resented, too, the implication—more than an implication, a statement outright—that she had not lived at all yet.

"Let's see if she comes this Sunday. We're going to have a planning meeting for the Patmos trip after the liturgy. What do you think? I bet she'll be there."

But Anna did not wait until the Sunday. She told herself she was not pestering Irini but would simply visit Goura Street again. She wished to measure her own enthusiasm for her project against the reality of the old house and its cracked façade. She waited until no one was passing down the street—an easy task with the city still empty for August and the day at its hottest—and stepped up to the loose loop of the padlock chain and, with one more look up and down the street, turned her shoulders sideways to see if she would fit. She did, and once her leading shoulder had passed into the house, she ducked her head in too. She took only a quick glance inside—fearing the police she wrongly assumed would be patrolling the decrepit building—but it was long enough to feel she was actually inside Irini's family home, and just barely long enough for her eyes to adjust so she could make out a chandelier and a set of bookcases or armoires that were built into the walls. She pulled her head out and dashed down the front steps as if just coming to the surface on a single breath. The street was as empty as before, but Anna had already had enough time to imagine it crowded with cars and taxis and, longer ago, horse-drawn carriages—she did not really know when people began driving cars in Athens—dropping off the many guests to the parties at the house. She realized she did not know Irini's maiden name, which would have been the name by which the house was known. She had been to the mansions of Athens' other wealthy families—she thought *other* out of a loyalty to Irini that equated her family with those far above her station—mansions that were now museums to house each family's collection of art. In the Benaki museum she had seen Cycladic heads thousands of years older than the Parthenon. It had all felt like a claim to continuity, as if with the collection the family was establishing a heritage to the ancients, from these mysterious heads of the Cyclades, to the ancestors who built the palaces, to the descendants who spent their summers in villas on the very same Cyclades where the heads had once been found. Anna had made the dutiful artist's tour of all these museum mansions when she had first arrived, spending winter afternoons over teapots in their high-ceilinged cafés. Now she pictured Irini's house on Goura Street with a collection of its own and with ticketed visitors arriving to see the canvases hung on its tall white walls. She was not stupid. She knew this was not possible. Irini had no money and her family was scattered or dead—the daughter had emigrated years ago to Australia, taking with her the grandson Anna had seen in the photograph that first day she had brought Irini the figs. Her collections had been in music, not in art, and Anna did not know where the husband's albums had disappeared to.

What, then, would Anna be doing with this project she had conceived for Irini's family home? She would not be restoring anything, would not be making anything with her art that Irini could use. Would the old woman consider it an act of vandalism or would she enjoy it? Anna told herself Irini would be grateful, and that the mural would bring to the old woman's eyes the tears she had shed during the screening of *Shoot the Piano Player*. In fact, the project was the kind of courtship gesture that meant more to the person making it than to its intended recipient. If Anna was being honest with herself, she would admit that the entire project was driven by her desire to have done something for Irini, without much consideration for whether Irini would approve. So, as she stood on the sidewalk in the scant shadow cast by the house in the high midday August sun, she gauged her enthusiasm for the project against the feasibility of its completion and decided to go ahead. This was no flash of delight, as with the mural on the retaining wall that had come from a moment of exhilaration—and, if she was honest, the art direction of a romantically vengeful Mel. This was the result of inspiration, yes, but planning and assessment, too. And Anna had found the spot herself. Yes, Irini had taken her to see the house, but she was the one who had seen the potential for the painting, not Irini—and not Mel or Oumer who had, after all, chosen many of her other walls for her.

From Goura Street, Anna could not resist the temptation to try her luck at Irini's door. She went to the little square determined to succeed in another visit—though she would say nothing about her plan for the façade of the house. She could make the mural a surprise with its own climactic moment of unveiling, and since she could not drape the house itself, she wondered if she might lead Irini blindfolded to Goura Street once the mural was complete. This time, when she pressed the button, Irini clicked on the intercom and asked who was there. Anna expected her to switch the intercom off after hearing her reply, but instead the mechanism of the door let out its long, insistent buzz and was still buzzing as Anna turned the first corner of the stairway.

"You seem to think that I was angry at you," Irini said, before Anna even reached the landing. Irini held the door open for her and stood crisp and smiling, her skirt in navy and her blouse a floral in russet and green. The truth was that Irini had, in fact, been angry with Anna. It was Nefeli who had changed the old woman's mood when she had come the day before with the apples. Admit it, she had said, all Anna did was wake you up by accident when she came to get you. With that in mind, and because she had felt the loss of the girl's hosting at the café and the cinema, Irini was now happy to see her. She could have called Anna from her landline, but she had not at all wished to reveal the dependence she had developed in these last four weeks and she knew, too, that a phone call placed to the mobile phone of a young person was both dire and rude. So, she had waited, once her anger had softened beneath Nefeli's indulgent smile, for the girl to come to her. And now that she had, Irini was determined to have the girl accompany her somewhere *out*. All week she had gone neither to the cinema nor to the café, mindful of the cost and of the inevitable added expenses of even a church-funded journey to an island where there would be the personal cost of souvlaki skewers during the boat ride, a ginger ale if she became seasick, a euro here, a euro there for every candle lit at every church—and they were sure to visit many. She had gone out for only short walks in the early morning, before the heat descended onto Plaka. In avoiding both heat and spending, she had seen few people and conversed with none.

"Sit and have some water and let me get my things," she said.

"Where are you going?"

"We are going out."

Anna was so relieved to learn her friend harbored no ill will toward her that she took twice as many steps as Irini as they crossed the little square, turning and facing the old woman and walking backward a step or two while she listened or while she told Irini about the two widows who had left the church on the Assumption never to return. Some who encountered the old woman and the young as they passed through the square would have been forgiven for imagining they were engaged in one of the traditional Greek dances with its halting rhythms and its backtracking and hesitation. When Anna and Irini reached the café that they had frequented during their brief season of Truffaut, Anna insisted they sit for a drink and that it would be her treat.

Anna's enthusiasm and Irini's satisfaction could not, however, change the fact that their conversation was conducted around double silences. They covered all their usual topics—the Church, the Truffaut films, Irini's reading, Anna's parea, the effects of the economic crisis on the youth and on the poor, with Anna not acknowledging that she fit the first category and Irini not acknowledging she fit the second. Anna kept from Irini the secret plan that fueled her happy mood, and Irini kept from Anna her worries about the economic cost of Patmos. Anna's deepest secret she kept even from herself: how relieved she was to have Irini back and how sad she was to be away from home.

"My friends are all away now," Anna said. "But you need to meet them sometime."

"They don't want to meet me." Irini was, however, flattered already by the compliments on her youthfulness she knew she would receive.

"I bet they do. You're cool." Anna remembered her friends' indifference to Irini when she had first described her to them that day she had brought the figs and then been tardy to the birdcage bar. But she was certain they would change their minds, especially once they learned about the mural on Irini's house, as if the coolness of the mural—assuming that it would indeed be cool—would drape over Irini too.

"*Cool.*" Irini said the word as if testing it. The word was used in Greece in its English form and Irini said it now with the tight sounds of her native tongue.

"See? That's what I mean," Anna said.

"Why are your friends away?" Irini said, by which she meant why was Anna not among them. She sipped her lemonade to hide a glance across at Anna, studying the girl's expression.

"I was supposed to go with them," she said. "But I changed my mind. You know. It was just going to be a lot of gossiping and drinking and lying on the beach."

"It sounds perfect. You should go."

"I can't." She said it quickly, too quickly, both women felt. "I don't have a good way to get there. And besides, it really is nice to see the city without so many people."

Irini cut a delicate bite of the pastry she had allowed Anna to encourage her to order. It was a chocolatina, layered with cake and cream and, while not as well-flavored as its appearance suggested, it was far more decadent than the pastry she bought for the priest's boys, and certainly more decadent than her Magnums from the kiosk.

"This cake reminds me of Zonars," she said.

"When you used to go there with your husband." Anna stated the words like a student reciting historical facts. Irini had told her about their visits to the grand café on Panepistimiou Street, but Anna still did not know the husband's name. Panepistimiou Street led to the main building of the university from which it took its name. Irini had stayed away from it since her husband's death, as, in her opinion, the closer to the massive entry gates one got, the scruffier the buildings, covered with what even Anna would have described as vandalism. In the neighborhood around the gates where protesters—some said seven, some said none and that the coffins had been stuffed with rocks—had been crushed to death in 1973, there seemed now to be only cafés and bars that made no attempts at style or atmosphere. They were places of utility where students and protesters went to stay awake or settle down.

"We should go there together," Anna said. She did not know that Zonars—which had been at the near end of Panepistimiou—had decamped along with the lifestyle that had produced most of its patrons.

Irini shook her head.

"It's gone."

"Oh no."

"Well, they moved."

"Let's go to the new place. I'll take you."

When Anna said this, she meant that she would make this outing, too, a treat for Irini. But Irini thought that she was offering to put her on the motorbike and drive her to the far side of the Acropolis. In any case, Anna did not understand that Zonars in a new location was not Zonars at all. It was the location that had made the place, and now that it had moved to a site adjacent to another restaurant famous for its entertainment of tourists, Zonars was floating free of history or reputation.

"It's not far enough for a motorbike. And I'm not so decrepit that I couldn't walk it." Irini said nothing of her daylong wandering around the city. Her calves were only now beginning to recover, and she recalled the day and its bewildering afternoon with shame and even a lingering fear.

"I should totally take you on the bike," Anna said, her one misunderstood offer now turning into two. Irini made sounds of protest and amusement—both of which she felt sincerely—but Anna insisted. She had stayed behind her parea in Athens, she had somehow led Irini to miss the holy day that they had all been waiting for, and she was planning a gift for Irini that she could not yet show her and that could possibly lead to her arrest. An excursion would solve all these problems. But none of them were actually problems that required solution. They were simply the facts of Anna's experiences. And wasn't this one of the things Anna needed to learn during her time in Athens—it was—to live with the facts of her life as she experienced them, not to keep looking backward or forward for significance? In the end, there was no trip to the new Zonars, or a trip anywhere with Irini on the back of Anna's bike. Anna did not propose the excursion again before other events intervened, and by then the journey became both unnecessary and impossible.

※

On the Sunday, Father Emmanouil rushed to the door of the church as soon as he was finished with the liturgy to intercept his congregants as they departed. He reminded them all to come back at six in the afternoon so that he could discuss with them the planning for Patmos. He had taken to calling the excursion simply this—the name of the island—now that their travel was assured. Because the trip was only partly paid for—by the lesser shipping magnate who had grown up in the neighborhood and felt he owed his success to godly interventions—and with insufficient church funds to cover all the group's expenses, Father Emmanouil preferred his congregation meet in the vestry after lunch so he could save the cost of feeding everyone an Athens midday meal on top of paying for their Patmos lodgings. Irini ate some cheese and cantaloupe at home and then closed her eyes against the white light from her living room window to nap a bit before the meeting. There were times when the August sun struck the Parthenon like a mirror and the heat reflected double into her small room, and she felt this was some act of the ancients to make her suffer for the advantage of the view.

She was the last to arrive in the vestry, finding Oumer engaged in small talk with Anna and the priest, and Tamrat scrolling through his phone. Nefeli sent the boys to greet her—which they did with the edge of boredom Irini had begun to see in their interactions with her—and then marshaled them off home. Nefeli was once again in the position of having to watch over her boys rather than leave them home alone, for they had grown enough to rejoin the tide of mischief they had left behind in younger childhood and find it stronger than before. In the space of just one summer, Irini had had to become guarded with these boys. The day before they had left for their grandparents' house, they had eyed each other with directed stares at Irini and at the bill, and the older boy (Irini could never remember which name went with which) had pushed his portion of pastry around the dish, his disinterest in it not one of taste like Irini's—though she masked her indifference as generosity—but one of moral objection. He had not wished to partake in Irini's gift that their father always paid for. So now when Nefeli sent the boys to greet Irini before taking them away, they

leaned in for the kisses on each cheek from a distance as if to touch
Irini would be to endorse whatever it was about her they objected
to. Nefeli rolled her eyes for everyone to see but did not compel the
boys to warmer salutations. "Come on, then, gentlemen," she said,
and in Irini's opinion the appellation was undeserved.

Father Emmanouil had placed on each seat in a circle of chairs
another set of photocopies from his ancient machine with the
slimy-looking paper. These were the itinerary and the details of
the hostel and the details of the ship journey. They were to travel
on a ship that took its name from its destination. Gone were the
smaller vessels that bore the names of saints and goddesses and
winds—the true holy trinity of Greece—and that took almost half
a day to make their journeys. Boats like the *Patmos* were faster,
steadier, more identical to each other so that the journey became
simply a journey—to be performed and completed identically no
matter someone's destination, and no longer given its own character
by virtue of the specific means taken to arrive. Irini listened to the
priest extol the advantages of their speedy itinerary—only seven
hours, and we will see sunset on the sea—and thought she much
preferred to have the trip be a destination of its own. Considering
the uncertainty of arrival—in this particular pessimism, Irini held
a kinship with many of her generation—it seemed wiser and more
pleasant that way. The priest seemed delighted in this daytime itinerary. His delight masked his concern that they would arrive near
midnight and have to find their hostel at that hour and that they
would make a somewhat motley crew of travelers. Irini did
not see the appeal of arriving so late at night. This was Patmos, not
Santorini. Everyone would either be asleep or settled at dinner
parties in their fancy villas. No one would be about to help them
find their way and Irini did not trust the priest's command of his
smartphone's mapping function.

"So, we must all bring flashlights and walking shoes," Irini said without looking up from the curling gray paper.

"Well, yes," the priest said.

"For the cave?" Anna said. That teenaged summer she had visited her cousins, they had taken her to see the caves in Perama in Epirus and she had been disappointed to see the caverns furnished with raised boardwalks and handrails. In college she had gone with friends once to a cave in the Catskills where the stone was rough and gloomy. She had realized only then it was the tinted lenses on the spotlights in the cave in Greece and not the stalagmites themselves that held the color.

"For the town," Irini said, "so we don't trip and break our necks."

"You're hardly going to break your necks, Irini."

"I don't see why we can't arrive in the morning, like civilized people." Irini knew, too, that the overall cost of the trip would decrease if they counted one night's lodging on the ship and not in the hostel.

"Those tickets are twice the price. They include a berth," the priest said. And with an uncharacteristic sternness she associated more with his new scolding of his sons, he added, "Or you could spend the night on the deck without one, but I don't think that would be very nice."

"We could certainly endure that, Father," Irini said, "if we wished to economize."

Anna glanced quickly at Oumer and Tamrat who she incorrectly thought of as having come to Greece on one of the thousands of dangerous vessels ferrying people across from Turkey or the north African coast, when in fact they had each flown coach on Turkish Air. They were unperturbed by this talk of decks and exposure to the dark. Tamrat was perturbed about having to spend so many days in the close company of the girl Anna, but

Oumer had reminded him that now that the priest had given her Irini—don't say it like that, Tamrat said—she would leave them alone. And Oumer reminded Tamrat, too, that he had formed a kind of friendship with the girl and had come to not mind her. He and Tamrat both believed that Father Emmanouil had brought Anna and Irini together as an act of kindness toward *them*, but the priest had not realized the men found Anna annoying and believed himself to be matching the women together for their own sakes.

Once he had settled the matter of the boat journey and of the tickets themselves—which were to be kept in Father Emmanouil's possession in a blue plastic folder printed with the logo of a travel agency, from the days when such agencies existed and when the church had budgeted more luxuriously than it could now afford—the priest moved to what he sensed could be the delicate topic of accommodations. The hostel had only double and quadruple rooms, and single rooms would not have been affordable, in any case. To put all four of his congregants in one room, as he had heard that certain church groups chose to do in order to preserve the atmosphere of the pilgrimage, would be unacceptable, and he suspected that the groups that booked the quadruple rooms had more pecuniary concerns in mind than they admitted. He could not take his need for savings to the extreme, so he had booked four rooms, one for him and Nefeli, one for their boys, and one each for the women and the men. Father Emmanouil had many worries on this topic, for he was not sure that Oumer and Tamrat were not gay and he had the incorrect notion that one of the reasons they had left Ethiopia was the danger of expressing a sexual identity the government deemed illegal. If they were gay, he was bound by his faith to find them sinners, though he did not agree with this doctrine. In this way he had drifted from the teachings of the church, and on this particular issue, he was not sure he wished to find his way back.

The priest explained the situation with the rooms and watched the faces of his congregation for signs of distress. Seeing none—each of them had small distresses they were able to conceal—he went on to the essential purpose of the journey.

"The Book of Revelation." He explained the schedule he had drawn up, composed of visits to the sites associated with Saint John as well as more than one visit to the cave itself, and new opportunities each day for contemplation. "Last things," he said, with a delight not usually associated with the end of days. "This is of great importance for us all, as Christians, as Orthodox believers, as human beings whose existences on earth are but finite precursors to eternal life."

"And when are we leaving, Father," Irini said, "so that I can be prepared?"

"I was getting to that. We are booked to depart on September 8. Will that work for everybody?"

The priest had put things backward. He couldn't announce the date of already-purchased tickets and then ask the travelers if they could depart on the departure date. His travelers were in no position to say no, since they all knew the priest's plans were all in place and this was not a schedule they could pick and choose. Oumer would have to arrange someone to cover his shifts, and Tamrat would need good internet so he could send in whatever opinion pieces he would file as an expat commentator. Anna could certainly close the gallery for a few days, especially in the very beginning of September when life was only just resuming after the summer's pause. But she made a sound of unease.

"That's two weeks from now," she said.

"Plenty of time to continue our contemplations," the priest said. "You can still come?" He cast a smile around the circle of chairs, certain his proposed religious pilgrimage was as irresistible to them as it should be to Anna.

"No, yes, I can come," she said, in that contemporary fashion that arrived at assent by negation.

"Good. Then that's all set and we depart on our adventure on the eighth."

Irini said little for the rest of Father Emmanouil's presentation and when it was time to go, she rolled the itinerary up into a tube—the paper's curl made this quite easy—and got crisply to her feet. She habitually blustered to the priest that she did not believe fully in his God, but things were more serious now, for she had ample reasons to wish for a secular absolution in her life. In the days since her long and exhausting walk, she had remained in the grip of the divine, difficult though she found her welcome there. She still could not shake the images from Revelation that came back to her whenever she set her Proust down for an instant. Had it not been that fallow time after the Assumption, she would have had distractions. She would have had another book group meeting to attend and she would have been at least able to chat with the grocer and the fruit seller or even the charmless man who sold her the Magnums at the kiosk. But the kiosk had closed for the holiday, as had the fruit seller, and the grocer, too, was away and had left a surly nephew to run the shop. So, she had been very much alone with the thoughts she could not do enough to shunt aside.

※

In the days after the priest's meeting, Irini took up the Proust but put it down. John's images of beasts and seals came flying at her, and she picked up the Book of Revelation as if to ascertain whether the images could retreat there within the words. She instantly put that book down as well. Now that the priest had stressed this idea of Last Things—which was, she had to admit, his job, but no less pleasant for her—she felt herself to be stalked by horrid creatures of her own imaginings and hopes. She took up the Bible and read again Saint John's strange narrative of seals opening to reveal yet more seals and new ones again. She did not even understand what he meant by this word *seal*. She pictured giant letters opening like doors, unfolding one after the other, and messages on them that she could not read but that spelled out all her crimes and misdirections. She wished she could find greater consolation in the Proust, in the specific comforts and ailments of Marcel's remembered days.

Anna needed Goura Street to be at its least busy so that she could work on her mural without interruption or arrest. It must be said that, in the face of all the graffiti throughout the city, Anna's concerns for the operations of law and order were rather quaint. It was not the police who would come catch her, but the neighbors who would fear the spraying of a profanity or a lewd image painted in their children's view. Once they saw what Anna had done, they would likely view the mural as an improvement to the house's cracked façade. But Anna did not know this, and so she felt that she must complete the painting before the end of August when everyone came flooding back into the city for the unofficial beginning of the end of the year. Greeks recognized only two seasons—winter and summer—and lived a little like Persephone in dread of darkness. It did not occur to Anna at all that the person most offended by her mural could be its intended recipient. So swept up was she in the generosity behind her plan that she was certain of Irini's gratitude. She was fashioning something the way a bird does who flashes gaudy plumage to attract a mate, while the mate rejects the courtship altogether. The matter would never come to this point, in fact, but if it had, Anna would have seen that she had trespassed on far more than someone else's property.

In the days after the meeting, Anna stole time from her job to work on the mural on Goura Street, and with the gallery owner gone no one noticed or minded her absence. During the days when she should be at work, she gathered her supplies and made the sketches she was going to use to match the building's actual façade to her invented overlay. Had it not been for the fact that Athenians would be returning from their August sojourns and that Father Emmanouil had booked their tickets for September 8, the first weekend of low-season discounts, Anna would have hesitated. She would have had time to become afraid. She did not like the thought of creeping around an empty house—not really—and she did not like working alone in the darkened city.

She had not taken up street art because of some innate passion for solitude and clandestine exploration, and this was yet another way in which she had chosen a medium that did not suit her. She had fallen into street art because of that photograph taken at the club over the raki, because of the people and the arms over the shoulders. She let herself be drawn into it because it was cool and she thought she should try to be cool even if it sometimes frightened her to try. Now, had she not felt the approach of the Athenians' return and of her own departure for Patmos, she would have stopped and changed her mind about the project. She would have taken Mel and Sophia with her to a different wall in a different, more secluded place—a place not so explicitly belonging to someone but also somehow safe, maybe another one of Mel's ex-boyfriends—and she would have painted something there with the vibrant colors she had intended for Irini's home. The façade on Goura Street was, after all, in a fairly busy spot. If she did her mural there, it wouldn't be just Irini who would see the thing at Anna's invitation. Tourists lost on their way to the Temple of Zeus would see it, and residents of Plaka taking a shortcut to the bus stops on the boulevard.

But because she felt the pressure of the deadline she herself had chosen, and because she felt she must do something that would earn the days she spent in Athens and would repay her debt to Irini, she went ahead with her plan. She had agreed to begin the new film series at the rooftop cinema with Irini. It was to be Rossellini, whom Anna knew as Ingrid Bergman's husband, and she assumed that Ingrid and the Ingmar Irini had talked about were related—they were not. She would meet Irini on Thursday for *Roma Città Aperta*, a suitable title for the two women at a time when Athens, too, seemed an open city, with its population gone. Before the film, she drove the motorbike around the back of Goura Street to drop off the supplies she had collected over the past days so that she would not be conspicuously loaded down on the day when she would do the painting. She parked the bike on the cross-street and walked in her quiet Converse to the house. She slipped through the loose loop of chain beneath the padlock, momentarily snagging her pack with the cans in it against the doorframe, and stood fully inside for the first time. The house was not as dark as she had expected. The glow of the city found its way in through enough cracks and openings in the roof and windows that she saw she would not need her phone's flashlight for which she had provided an extra charger. With her eyes adjusted, she walked over to the armoire she had seen before, an achievement of carpentry that rose to the full height of the ceiling. There must have been a ladder once, Anna concluded, to allow people to reach its highest shelves. She could not see from where she stood that the upper portion of the armoire was equipped with a set of false book fronts, papier-mâché and ormolu molded to resemble a fine library. There had never been a ladder for the armoire because there had never been real books for anyone to take from a shelf and read. Anna set her bag down and crept further into the house. Her work would happen on the outside wall but she could hardly be expected not to explore Irini's house now that she had her secret project as excuse. Again, Anna allowed her prideful generosity to carry her away into belief that her enthusiasm amounted to permission.

She had to see for herself what Irini had conjured for her with her stories. There was a carpet underfoot and it crackled with the years of dust and plaster that had fallen from the moldings. The furniture was gone and so the space seemed to Anna larger than it was. There was no piano, no divan; there were no armchairs. Anna wondered where these objects were, since Irini did not have them with her in the church's tiny apartment. She never spoke of these things being in a storage space or having been sold, or perhaps ensconced with a relative in another property, like the house on Siros that she only spoke of as a childhood place. Anna passed through an arched opening into what would have been the dining room, and she looked for these items from Irini's past, as if to move deeper into the house were to move further away from the present moment. As if today, an August night in Athens, took place in ordinary time along Goura Street while further in, toward the back wall that gave onto a tiny alley between the houses of Goura and Thalou took you back deeper and deeper into history. Anna had seen the ancient artifacts displayed in cases in the Metro stations where construction had unearthed them and then been halted until the completion of an archeological excavation. In Athens, to move deeper into the ground was to unwind time by hundreds and thousands of years.

The grand staircase was damaged. Anna had seen this when she entered and the space of its slow curve had loomed above her. But she came now upon a narrow stair that she assumed had been used by the servants. This was true. This staircase led up the back of the house, in tight angles, all the way to the rooms once occupied by the brother and sister from Hydra. She set one foot on the bottom step but heard a sound that could have come from the street or from the house itself—the brief two-tone peal of a car alarm silenced in haste and irritation. The sound called Anna back to the front of the house, to Goura Street, to the moment she found herself in, and she knew she could not be creeping up the back stairs of Irini's house when she was expected to meet her at the cinema. She glanced once more up the narrow staircase and turned back to the front of the house. She found a place to stash her cans so that if anyone were to venture in through the padlocked chain, they would find nothing.

When she arrived at the entrance to the rooftop cinema to see the first film in the Rossellini series, Anna was filled with the excitement of a surprise withheld. Irini approached along the cobbled street that ran along the side of the square and Anna watched her with a rising excitement. Irini had not seen her yet—or so it seemed—and walked with easy grace and her chin up, with no need to look down at the safe placement of her feet. She had a cardigan over her shoulders, and Anna realized upon seeing it that the air had begun ever so slightly to cool as August came to an end. She forced herself to keep quiet but almost blurted out that she would be painting a mural for her on the house. She would have liked to work with Irini as her audience. She could have been a conjurer for her, right before her eyes.

"What's up with you?" Irini said.

"Nothing. Just happy to see you."

They went through their routine with the cinema owner at the ticket window, where Anna once again paid for Irini's ticket, and at the concession window where Anna bought two beers—Mythos for both of them now as Anna had converted—and popcorn and passatempo. They took their usual seats in their usual row, and when the middle-aged man who had yelled at the teenagers passed them on his way to the front row, they wished each other good evening. On the nights when they had come for the Truffaut, the moon had given a slight haze to the picture, casting enough strong light of its own to dilute the projector beam, but tonight, the picture projected onto the blank wall of the apartment building was sharp and clear. Irini commented on this clarity and on how fitting it was for the neorealism of Rossellini rather than the romance of Truffaut. Anna did not quite understand how the stories about broken-down piano players and common thieves and beleaguered children could constitute romance—she allowed *Jules and Jim* into the category for the obvious reasons of its love affair—but she agreed with Irini, sensing it was too vast a question, too vast for whispered conversation while the movie played, to ask the difference between the romantic and the real. Anna believed that these could be one and the same. Though she had not yet had a grand romance—she was no prude and had had plenty of hookups—and had never had her heart broken, she was certain that the grand shape of her life, or anyone's life, followed the rise and fall and deepening of a love affair. Anna was too limited in her application of the term. She did not see yet that late-August night that she had fallen in love with the city and with one of its residents, and that the city and the resident were going to crack her heart in a way that would make her guard it overmuch for a long time after.

So, she ate her popcorn and she helped Irini slide her arm into her cardigan—there was a faint scent of a heady flower Anna did not recognize as the tuberose of Fracas but that she had come to associate with Irini—and she gripped Irini's arm when on the screen the Nazis fanned out into the broken-down neighborhood of the protagonists and shot the woman running after her arrested lover. Rome drifted up on the blank Athenian wall in front of the two women as a city stripped of everything that made it human. The city's people had been driven into hiding, strangers and exiles in their own streets and piazzas. Driven into shared apartments and basements, they filled those cramped spaces to bursting with grand passions that played out almost like a masque. There was the priest, the widow, the fighter, the lover. There was marriage, betrayal, heroism, death. Irini had seen Athens this way, though she remembered it mostly from photographs, not from her family but from commemorative spreads in the newspapers that featured wartime images taken from high floors and low corners out onto empty squares. She had a vague memory of being snatched up by the arm and hurried around a corner where, behind her and her mother—she thought it must have been her mother—came a scuffle and a shout. Irini had filled that memory with an image as of a camera turning to observe a boy writing a liberation slogan on a wall and a German soldier smashing his head with the butt of his rifle. She never knew if this was true and thought perhaps her mother had taken her back down the street and they had seen the soldier standing over the bleeding boy. Perhaps she had slipped from her mother's grasp and run back to see the blow as it occurred? In truth she had seen a photo of the slogan and the boy and she had filled in all the rest. But she had decided where the event had taken place, and when she did happen to pass that corner near Syntagma, her stride hitched a little, an instant of imagined past piercing through to snag her.

When the sign for intermission swam up onto the screen, the middle-aged man groaned his displeasure—the cinema owner's son was not especially adept at timing—but neither Anna nor Irini moved, and Anna could not fathom there was more to come. Irini was lost in contemplation of her other Athens, and Anna found herself overtaken by sadness and admiration. Here were people living in their small way like heroes, and they were just enough like people Anna knew—the priest, the fighter, the lover, the widow—that she had been drawn up into the empty Roman streets. When Rossellini brought the camera close, Anna placed herself just there, beside the actress who shared her name, and when he pulled it back, she was just around the corner, out of sight but living the same drama. She looked around her now and half expected to see the city in black and white and herself in grayscale clothing. Irini laughed.

"What?" Anna said.

"You fell asleep."

"No! I didn't." She wondered if she had dreamt herself among the characters. "It's just really good. I really like it."

Irini pulled her cardigan around her.

"I told you." She said this as if Anna had resisted attending the film when in fact it had been the other way around, Irini expressing reluctance and financial concern until Anna convinced her to accept the payment of her ticket.

Anna went to the concession window for the second bag of passatempo that had become Irini's custom.

"You see, though," Irini said when she returned, "how the priest is sometimes a meddler but a hero in the end. Father Emmanouil should see this."

"Don't tell me how it ends."

Irini made a face Anna did not know how to interpret, but with which she intended to signal a warning against hope. Anna did hope, though she was becoming hardened by these films where the lovers parted or the hero failed or a woman was killed, so often shot down as she ran. She would have liked to know all would be well for these resistance fighters and would-be husband and wife in a city open to what Anna could not see as anything but danger and loss. When she had been buying the tickets, she had seen the poster for the eleven o'clock show of a brand-new movie, a romantic comedy. The Rossellini poster was stark black with fiery orange and the rom-com sported fuchsia and pink and yellow and Anna pined for the sweet happiness it promised. But she was also proud to be a young person buying tickets for a classic. Still, she would have liked to have had a bit more happiness along with the importance.

She watched the film's second half with a growing despair not only for the resistance fighter and the priest but also for herself who was going to be—she would see—robbed once more of a happy ending. She turned once to Irini as if to ask her to alter the story, as if Irini herself was responsible for this tragedy before them. And when the film was done and all the people who had mattered were dead and the music swelled loud enough to strain the cinema's speakers, she turned again to Irini with her eyes round and full of tears.

"Oh, no," Irini said, softly. "Oh, sweetheart." And the sound of this endearment, stripped of the fastidious tone of nearly everything Irini said, shocked her so much that she stopped crying.

"You looked just like Anna Magnani," Irini said, "in that close-up." She handed Anna a tissue and peered up at her lowered face. "Here."

Anna knew the moment, when the widow told her lover the war was too much and she could not go on, and Rossellini brought the camera close enough to catch the tears glistening in Magnani's eyes. It was the moment that had made her begin to tear up herself. But now she dried old tears not new and scanned Irini's face, looking for the mood, the sentiment, that had let slip the nearly whispered *sweetheart*. She thanked Irini for the tissue and then asked the question she had been pondering nearly the entire time she had known the old woman—something prompted now by the tone in that one word.

"You must miss your daughter."

Granted, this was not a question, but the statement contained in it all of Anna's curiosity about this young woman who had emigrated to the community of Greeks most distant from her home, who had stayed away for years, not even sending her son back to visit with his relatives, this woman who managed to figure not at all in her mother's life, though Anna had seen those two photographs of her on that very first day when she had met Irini. Anna could not stand to think that she would do this to her own mother, and she could not stand to think of herself so stranded, so abandoned, as Irini had been by her offspring. So, she uttered the statement whose expected response was an implicit affirmation—yes, I do—and heard Irini say instead,

"We stay in touch."

"I Skype with my parents," Anna said. "It helps. You should Skype."

Irini shook her head.

"I don't have the gizmo for that. And I don't want to see the other person on a screen."

Anna waved a hand at the cinema's screen.

"You just did."

"I mean the tiny ones."

The cinema owner's son came to tell them he was clearing out for the rom-com and if they wanted to stay for that one too, they would need another ticket.

"Doesn't our ticket permit us to sit just a moment longer? Go away, Taki," Irini said. "We paid for the seats and we'll leave when we like." As on the previous nights, Irini had in fact not paid.

"Then how do you stay in touch?"

Anna was young enough to think only of all the digital ways a person could communicate with another. When Irini answered *letters* as if this were obvious—which it was—Anna felt both discovery and relief. Relief that Irini was not consigned to silence and discovery that her voice took the, to her, romantic form of letters written out by hand. Anna needed no rom-com on an August night, for Irini had just given her the romance of correspondence.

"I wish I wrote letters," she said, and now, released by this new word, she stood and led the way for Irini up the cinema's sloping roof and slowly down the stairs. When they reached the square, a dozen people clustered around the entrance to the cinema, waiting for admission to the rom-com, laughing and talking in the boisterous spirits that befitted the audience of a film with pink-and-yellow posters. For a split second, Anna felt the wrongness of her position. She should be with these people, ready to watch a movie in her native tongue that would make her laugh on purpose, not with an old woman, having just watched a film older than all of them and that had been full of tragedy and death. What would her parea say if they saw her now? Should she be proud or embarrassed? Irini stopped and looked at Anna.

"I don't understand this," she said. "You wish you wrote letters. So, write them. Save your wishes for something you can't control. And for the rest, *just do it*," she said in English. She was old and poor, but she picked up the old magazines at the salon where she sometimes did her hair, and she knew the advertisements. Now she began to cross toward their evening café.

It could be said that this was a fundamental difference between Irini and Anna, more essential than their relation to the country, or the church, more deterministic even than their different generations. Anna had wishes, but Irini had needs. Anna's soft desires did not compel her to action but cast a mist of hope over her existence. Irini either required something—and found a way to get it—or she didn't and had no thoughts for it at all. This was what made Anna such a better believer than Irini. Anna's wishes beckoned toward the idea of divinity and all the accessory hopes it carried. Irini seemed to move through her days like a passenger on the tram that went from Monastiraki to the coast. She was either on it or at one end or another, and she had only to ensure she reached the end with all her luggage.

And yet. Did Irini never wish for anything at all? When she stood before her family home and gazed up through the glassless windows, did she not breathe in a kind of hope about what had come before and might have been? Did she not worry, about her money and her time? And what is worry but a kind of hope? Of course, she worried and she wished. It was for Irini a matter of managing the wishes to offer up on the chance the world would grant them.

"So, what does she do there in Australia?"

"Who?"

"Your daughter."

"Raises her son, goes to work." Irini shrugged.

"Does she like it there? Does she miss Greece?"

"She has her life. She goes about her life."

"Oh."

Anna saw that this line of questions was getting nowhere so she turned to the reliable subject matter of the family home.

"She must have grown up on Goura Street, right?"

Irini flinched at Anna's words.

"It's odd," she said, "to hear you saying the street name as if you know it."

"But I do know it." Anna took a long sip of coffee. "It's a street in Plaka. And now I know it's where your house is."

"Now you do." Irini drank some lemonade and puckered her lips at the taste. She stirred the sugar up with the long spoon the surly waiter had brought at her insistence.

"My daughter used to slide down the banisters in that house. It's quite a long way," she said. "You can imagine."

"I never had a house with a stair like that." Anna had grown up in horizontal spaces, a brief sequence of larger and larger apartments in Astoria that culminated in the floor-through her parents still lived in now. The only staircases of any length she had had access to were the fire escapes of her college dorm.

"It was a good game," Irini said, mollified now by the sweetness she had stirred into her drink. "I used to do it when I was a child. But for my daughter, we put pillows around the bottom for her to land on. Just in case."

"Your parents didn't do that for you?" Anna laughed.

"I suppose they did. I don't remember. I just remember the excitement of it, sliding all the way down."

They sat in silence for a bit. Around them the square was livelier than in past days. Anna could feel the season changing with the return of Athenians from their Great Migration, their periodic internal diaspora unwinding itself. It was a time of cardigans at night, of the disappearance of lizards from the basking stones of the Acropolis, of the scent of mothballs wafting from winter clothes prematurely worn during these false winter days before being hung up again until the true cold.

"Was Athens ever like that?" Anna asked. "The way Rome was in the movie?"

"Like what? Athens was not an open city if that's what you're asking."

Anna was not sure what it meant to be an open city, but she was asking about the way the buildings had been deserted, hollowed out.

"With people hiding other people and all crammed into tiny spaces."

Irini could have scolded the girl for her ignorance. She could have given up that instant on the project that she had agreed to—she was now clear that the priest had sent the girl to her for a solid education in what it was to be a Greek. But the changed air of the little square made her react with a tolerance she guarded closely. So, she told Anna about the resistance and she told Anna how certain families were known to be hiding resistance fighters and how certain other families—those who collaborated with the Germans—might turn the others in. She told Anna of the great famine that befell Athens in 1941 when she had been five years old and how her family was more fortunate than others and how none of them had starved to death.

"You would walk down the street for an errand and a man in front of you would suddenly fall down dead. My mother used to tell me they were sleeping. There were a lot of sleeping Athenians then. It was like something out of a fairy tale if you believed my mother."

"Did you?"

Irini looked over at her sharply.

"I saw the flies. I knew what that meant."

"You said no one in your house died. Who was there besides you and your parents?"

"I know what you're asking, and I'm not going to tell you," Irini said. "If we had harbored resistance fighters, I wouldn't give up their secret even now. I will take that information to my grave."

She took another sip of the lemonade.

"Your house would have been perfect for hiding places," Anna said.

Irini cocked her head at this remark so suggestive of possession and intimacy.

"I had good ones there, yes."

"Come on! Just *good ones?*"

"I'll tell you that I searched the whole place—except the servants' quarters because I was taught to respect their privacy—and I never found a hidden passage or a secret chamber."

"No Narnia," Anna said.

Irini waved a dismissive hand.

"I'm afraid I don't know that one."

Anna knew enough about the author of those books to jump at the opportunity to tell Irini about his Christian allegory and the lion who was clearly intended to be God.

"You should read them. They're great. And there's the whole theology thing on top."

Irini took another lemonade sip that was mostly pulp oversweetened by the sugar that had settled at the bottom. She was a woman who read Proust for her entertainment. She had no intention of reading books with a talking animal and meant for children. But she was being kind now, so she simply made a sound of assent and smiled at Anna.

"Didn't your daughter read them? I bet they're in Greek translation. They're kind of huge." Anna had the egocentrism of the

enthusiast who cannot accept that what inspires passion in her is
not universally beloved by others.

"If she did, I would remember."

"I bet your grandson read them. In Australia. For sure. He must
be bilingual, right? Duh. Of course, he is. He's like me. Parents
emigrated but speaks Greek at home."

Anna's words sailed out from her without foundation like a great
cantilevered breath of sympathy. She had found a kindred spirit in
the boy as she imagined him—she had created her own kindred
spirit, as enthusiasts so often do—and her passion for the imagined
details of his life swept her up from the conversation she was having
with Irini to the disembodied room of a Skype call where she and
her parents came together. Later she would come to think of these
Skype calls as seances for the living where she could engage with
spirits that consoled her. Now all she knew was a kinship with this
boy and a certainty that he, like her, had gone looking around his
familiar home for a passage to the extraordinary world that lay just
the other side of it.

Because she was so caught up in her excitement, Anna did not
notice the change in Irini. The old woman had set her lemonade
glass down and pulled away from the table and tugged her cardigan
tighter around her shoulders. Irini did not want to hear the girl's
excitement. She did not want to hear about the books she may
or may not have seen her daughter reading and that her grandson
may or may not have read in English or in Greek. Her thoughts
had drifted back to the confines of the family home and all the
spaces in it she had occupied as daughter, wife, and mother, and she
thought of the way the place had cracked from side to side and
imagined the house splitting along the line of a secret opening
that she had never found. She had gone looking for hidden doors
and chambers as a child. And then as a woman, she had begun to

close the spaces off inside the house, her husband in one and she in another. Even then, even in the days of the jazz and the melodies that assailed her sense of melody, she had been looking for a secret passage out, a secret path to order. She had found one way out, but it had proved only to create greater disaster. Not for the first time Irini felt as though her every wish had passed through the Goura Street house like a hot knife, filleting the masonry with gaps and weak spots. All it had taken was an earthquake plenty of other houses had survived for the building to reveal its frailty. Or, rather, to reveal what she had wrought upon it with her longing.

Irini brought an end to the evening with the reasonable excuse of her great age. She tipped her head in that way she used with more distant acquaintances—something Anna noticed and which caused her a hint of confusion now—and pushed her chair back from the café table.

"At the cinema or church," she said. "Whichever comes first."

Anna began to tell her the schedule for the Rossellini but Irini leaned forward and kissed her on each cheek and said goodnight.

Anna watched Irini cross the square and saw in the trim figure and its upright posture a certain small heroism. She was eighty-two, widowed for an unknown number of years, poor, and thousands of miles from her nearest family. And yet she tended to her mind and her physical and spiritual vigor every day and she was—wasn't she?—open and accepting of the new and the different. Anna remembered with a certain pride the way Irini had put the waiter in his place when they had first gone to the surly café. This was her Irini, her old Athenian, and look how cool she could be. She wanted to do something for this old woman. She wanted to offer what she could—more than a movie ticket or a lemonade.

She had intended to take another day to finalize the design for her trompe l'oeil on the house on Goura Street. She had been set in her mind to do the painting Saturday night so that she could arrive in church on Sunday and, when the liturgy was over, take Irini by the arm and show her the earthly transfiguration that she herself would have freshly wrought. But she thought back to the instructor who had called her timid, and to the friends who had painted the side of the warehouse that day with the raki on a whim, and she thought of Sophia's question the night they had gone to the retaining wall: what are you supposed to be doing? She wasn't supposed to be doing anything, but now she had made a plan and according to that plan, she was not supposed to begin until the day after tomorrow. She checked her phone and saw that it was almost midnight. And then she told herself it did not matter what the time was. She would do it now. She had everything she needed. She would do the painting for Irini and for herself—this thought came to her like a jolt—*now*.

She nearly ran through the little square and out the other side, past Irini's apartment building and down into Goura Street. The columns of Zeus' temple glowed in the traffic lights at the end of the street, but at Irini's family home, the street was quiet and only one streetlight was working, the other having been caught up in the damage to Irini's home those years ago and its connection to the city's grid still and forever cut. Anna had ample darkness when she needed it and she had her phone to tap to brightness so that she could see just enough to step over the fallen masonry at the base of the front door. With a twist of her narrow shoulders and a duck below the loop of padlocked chain, she was in, once again, standing in the high-ceilinged entrance room. She cast a glance up at the staircase with its wooden banister and wooden finial post at the end and tried to picture Irini and her daughter, each as children, gliding down. She thought of all the places Irini would have explored in her childhood for a secret passage out, or in, and she promised herself that this would be her reward once her painting was complete: to explore the house as if she were the child allotted this potential treasure. It did not occur to Anna that the painting itself should have been reward enough, and that was indication of precisely the timidity her instructor had seen in her. A bolder artist—a bolder person—would have sensed her creation to be a gift not just for those it was intended for. A bolder person would believe her art to be more than a transaction, an assignment—even if an assignment she gave to herself. Her art should expand and exceed.

If she had been reading Father Emmanouil's text from Revelation carefully, her mind would have been teeming with images that grew and extended and grew again—those seven seals always incomplete for the addition of another seven—and she would have known her own art to have that possibility. If she had not been timid. But in her way, she fetched her spray cans from the space beneath the stairs where she had stashed them and she twisted back out beneath the padlocked chain to stand before the house. Her eyes had adjusted to the deeper darkness of the interior and now she could see the elements of the façade that she would need to cover up: the crack that snaked from lower right, up past a window, toward the edge of the door and across the lintel before angling upward again to the left and farther out of Anna's reach. Without a ladder, she had conceived of a design that would cover that right-hand corner of the house, turning the crack into a vine, including silhouettes of a small family in one window and adding another where the angled top of a grand piano could be seen. She began.

She had collected cans of green and black and brown and red and she used these for the larger foundational colors in the crack, laying down the blacks and browns and greens to make the vine and working with the wildstyle angles already painted on the wall. She had, for this occasion, purchased brushes she would use to blend the colors where she wanted flowers to appear. She could not always see as clearly as she liked. She should have brought a headlamp, and she should have had at least one lookout, and she should have waited until deeper into the night when there would be no chance of revelers taking a shortcut through the street. She was fortunate that the changes in the neighborhoods of Athens had made this edge of Plaka neither touristed nor entirely residential. If Irini's house had been undamaged, it would have been sold like so many others on the street to a law firm or a consulting office where modern pendant lights of minimalist design would have hung from the plaster medallions. Only once while Anna painted did someone walk down Goura Street and she did not even notice, as the hiss of the spray can covered the sound of the man's steps. He took the sound for the hissing of a cat and did not even turn to look where Anna reached overhead to paint the edge of the window frame.

Toward three in the morning, Anna realized that a project of such scope perhaps exceeded not only her abilities but also her allotted time. She was tiring, and she was beginning to see that she would have to compromise her design in order to complete it. But she could not simply stop halfway and finish the next night. With a site as public as this one, she had to finish all at once and then hope for the inertia of beauty that would keep the authorities from erasing what they would admire—and she dared assume they would admire it. And she needed time to fetch Irini—before Irini could happen upon the painting by herself. In this, too, Anna was fortunate—that Irini seemed to make a point of avoiding Goura Street and had only come to the house with Anna after considerable persuasion. She took a chance and turned her flashlight on and scanned the house.

The painting had been so clear in her mind, so beautiful and subtle. Here instead was a work executed in shapes that were too stark, colors that were too harsh. The vine failed to conceal the crack but only looked as though someone had tried to mark it out for engineers, and the breaks in the masonry of the window moldings were still visible despite the new outlines she had tried to make. The windows, however, were all right. She had not taxed her skills with the silhouettes of mother, father, only daughter, and she had captured with elegance the sweep of a piano's curving lid. She tapped her flashlight off and steeled herself for more work. She had five hours, possibly, until daylight, and on a Friday, there would be lawyers and consultants arriving early for work.

She sprayed the red and white paints heavily on the take-out containers she had saved for the occasion and dipped into the colors with her brushes, and she went to work on the vine, adding a flower here and there, adding some of the brown as well to shade the thing with nuance. The vine got better, slightly more beautiful, or rather something closer to beautiful, though she knew the wildstyle lettering she worked around showed greater artistry and skill. When Irini finally saw the façade of the house three weeks later, Anna's colors had already begun to peel and fade, but she could see even then that the girl Anna had made something if not beautiful then lovely and she wished that she could tell her this.

There was no denying that Anna was still tethered to the earthly matters of time and calendar. Her awareness that it was nearing six and that a faint gray had risen over the city with the coming sun affected her assessment of her work. She deemed it finished when another person or she herself in different circumstances would have admitted there was more to do. Had she continued to work on the mural, she might have actually crossed the line over into the kind of beauty she imagined. She stepped back into the street and could see, without need of her phone's flashlight, the effect of her work on the façade of the house. The mural, if nothing else, gestured at the kind of nearly successful deception of a trompe l'oeil. It would fool no one into thinking the house was whole again and grand, but it signaled that such imaginings were possible, and that in itself was something. That was the gift she could offer to Irini.

Anna snapped a photo. She would need to do another shot in daylight. But this was her proof, her sign that when the paint had not yet dried on either the walls or her hands, she had been there, present, as one said, at the creation. She approached the house once more and in the lowest corner of the wall, wrote her initials with a marker. Even these letters would not last to the next summer, but for the few weeks before things changed, they marked the work in a way that no one knew but Anna, as hers.

Now it was time for the reward Anna had promised herself and she slipped once more inside the house and tucked all her cans and brushes and take-out containers in a plastic bag she stuffed into her backpack. She crept through the downstairs rooms—a parlor, a dining room, and the room that must have housed the piano—and she wondered again where all the furniture had gone. What had happened to the piano and the audio equipment and the carpets and settees? From an imagination shaped by old movies as much as by the mansion museums she had visited across the city, she filled the empty house with these things. But the actual contents of the house had been systematically removed after the earthquake, not simply left behind the way one saw with houses after bombings or explosions. Here there was only plaster dust and chunks of masonry and even in some places dirt, where enough sun and rain had found their way in to summon vegetation. There were droppings of course, too, and in one corner there was a pungent smell of cat urine, and she dashed from the room with the shame she thought Irini would feel if she were to learn about this desecration. At this point in her story, Anna had not yet understood that her very presence inside the house was a greater desecration than the wandering of any cat.

She returned to the grand staircase with its big newel post and remembered the movie she had taught her parents was the one Americans watched at Christmas, and she reached for the post to see if, as in the movie, she could lift it up. She thought she might tell Irini about this detail and for once she would be the one to explain to her a classic film in black and white. She would have gone up these stairs and would have tried to slide down the banister as Irini and her daughter had both done, but she could not see how to do it with the post at the end. But she remembered the back stair she had seen on her first visit and thought of the rooms at the top of that stair where the brother and sister from Hydra had both lived. It was in these places—that housed people who were at once strangers and deeply intimate—that a house might hold its secrets. In this world of dumbwaiters and back stairs and basements and sculleries—Anna had watched with her parents the British show about the rich people and their servants—this was where a house might yield up a secret passage if one knew where to look or, not knowing, was bold enough to try. So much of Anna's life in the city was taken up with questions about this world and the next—she had chosen this preoccupation for herself and could have lived instead an Athenian life concerned only with the present—but now she searched for two worlds that could both be now, both be here. Could the eternity she was looking for, the connection to the great current of time that sailed onward from her and that she had ridden from the past into today—could that eternity be simply another layer added to the life she led? Could she touch it by stepping through a door or behind a cascade of water as she had done once on spring break in Jamaica, or by looking into the strobing flash of light cast on a wall that she herself had painted?

She found the back stair again and now it was quite easy to see. She could even hear sounds of garbage trucks and street cleaners—Plaka was kept clean for the tourists—and knew that Goura Street would soon be waking to the sight of her mural and if she did not wish to risk arrest, she should be leaving soon. She started up the stairs. And because of the noise around her, she did not hear another noise that came this time: the small crack that signaled the larger one. Her leading foot, once all her weight was on it, broke through the eighth stair tread that was rotten and she fell through the hole that opened as the staircase snapped in two, banging both arms and shoulders and the right side of her head on the broken wood. She fell ten feet, which may not sound like very much, but when one has fallen in the midst of a stride up a staircase, the landing is both painful and uneven. Anna cried out as her legs splayed beneath her, bent at an awkward angle, and it is true that she saw stars from the impact to her head. When she could breathe in again, she tried to sit up but found that there were too many parts of her that hurt. She lay back down to take stock of the pain and she began to cry, briefly and shyly, as if she should not even then disturb the silence of the house. She was bleeding from her right temple and this discovery caused her to panic, though it would turn out that this was among the least of her injuries. She scrambled up as if to run from the blood, metallic in her mouth, and, ignoring the stabs of pain in her ribs and shoulders and the thicker, juicier pain of her right arm, she made her way to the front door. The twisting movement she made as she approached the padlock chain took her breath away, but she did not want to cry for help from behind the lock—though that was indeed how the man who rescued her came to tell the story. The girl was trapped inside

the house, he would tell people later, and I saw her bloodied face
at the chain. God knows how long she'd been locked up in there
and I hope they find whoever did it. Never mind the fact that it
was clear even then that anyone of slim build could have passed
into or out of the house, and never mind that only its clear reputation as a death trap kept the squatters from attempting it. The
story that followed Anna's fall was a tale befitting tabloids or fairy
tales—which are often quite the same. In fact, Anna forced herself
through the chain, muffling her own cry, and sat against the front
steps of the house until she was spotted by a man who cleaned one
of the lawyers' offices on Friday mornings before work. He, being
a native of the city, from Ilioupoli, knew the number to dial for an
ambulance. And so, Anna—who was dizzy and in enough pain
not to think of her mural or the house or Irini—was taken to the
hospital near the war museum where she had last said goodbye to
Sophia on the night of the retaining wall. She was asked if there
was anyone who could come attend her and she shook her head
with so much vigor that the nurse told her to stop for the sake of
her brain. Her parea was all gone now and her relatives were far
away and strange to her and she felt ashamed to ask for help from
Father Emmanouil or Nefeli or Irini or Oumer or Tamrat and she
realized she knew hardly anyone in the entire city.

❧

Anna was well looked after in a ward that was as well staffed as
it was ill-equipped with modern comforts. By virtue of her Greek
passport and her parents' forethought, she did not have to rush
out to an ATM for cash to pay the fees for her health care, as it
was covered by the State. By Friday afternoon, when she had had
her tests and her treatments, she was released. Her diagnosis? A

broken arm, a lightly sprained ankle, two cracked ribs, and a head wound that had required seven stitches. There had been talk of a possible concussion, but there had been nothing the doctors could do about that except tell her to rest, and she was in no condition to do anything else. She was lucky that the ankle had miraculously not been more damaged, but the arm would take some time to heal and she would certainly not be painting or riding her motorbike for several days, if not weeks. She waited in the lobby for a taxi she had called—a nurse had loaned her a charger for her phone and she had used her app—and arrived, finally, home. Then she cried, but only as shallowly as her cracked ribs would allow her, and she knew she should not call her mother in this state but she was overcome with loneliness and with pain and that turned even the smallest wish into deep longing. She tapped out an actual phone number so as not to show her mother her stitched and bandaged face on Skype. On the phone, she could tell a story that would console both of them.

A phone call coming from her daughter at this irregular time on this irregular day, however, charged Anna's mother with alarm, and Anna fought back tears as she reassured her everything was fine. I just wanted to hear your voice. To keep from crying—in understandable self-pity and in relief at her mother's concern—Anna sent her voice into its highest register. She slid into the mistake of most liars and offered too much detail for why she had called instead of Skyping, why on Friday instead of Sunday. She was on the Ionian coast with her parea, having decided after all to join them in a rental car that was, she promised, larger than a compact, and the Wi-Fi at the campground was not strong enough for Skype, and besides, a group of Australian backpackers there was using all the bandwidth to check in with their families about the wildfires. So, she didn't mind running up a few euros on her phone plan just to say a quick hello. Her mother said to wait so she could run outside and get Anna's father who was on the patio with his tomato plants. No, Mom, Anna said—a touch too quickly. This time I only want to talk to you. Everything OK? her mother asked. Completely. Her only complaint was that she might have gotten a bit sunburned on her back. But why had she called? Anna's mother wanted to know. Anna slid into another tale about an excursion they would all be going on tomorrow until the Sunday that would make it hard for her to even call on the regular day. One of her friends knew someone who had a boat. Friends with a boat, her mother said. Her mother had not grown up with any friends who had a boat and she exclaimed upon this now with happiness for her daughter's social life. I know, right, Anna said, and she could not help but look around the room in her Airbnb in Anafiotika at the metal coffee table and the bookshelf with the chipped veneer and the balcony so small that it was more like a glorified ledge. She could not help give in to self-pity not only for the injuries and the pain but also for the lie as well. She wanted her mother to believe her and she wanted her mother to doubt and to worry.

Her mother doubted, and when they hung up the phone, with Anna claiming one of her friends had come to fetch her for a swim, her mother walked with care out to the patio of blue- and lavender-colored stones that had been fashionable fifty years ago and stood watching her bald and wiry husband pluck dead leaves from the tomato plants. Without stopping his ministrations, which he did on the evenings when he returned from the fabric company in the Garment District where he worked, he asked her whether she was going to say something—they spoke to each other in Greek—and she told him something was up with Anna. He stopped then and straightened and waited for more, but Anna's mother simply shook her head and told him something was not right and just wait and he would see. Her tone implied that something about the situation was his fault, but they had both been happy for Anna to spend some time in Athens and both were now convinced that the time for her to return home had come. All they had wanted was to go along with Anna's desire to see their homeland and, as an inoculation against further immersion, to let her take this three-month stay. Anna's parents liked America. Their lives were more comfortable there than in Chalandri. They did not want their daughter to be sucked back to Greece and thus uncoil the spring of opportunity that they had loaded for her with their own departure.

Anna held the phone in her good hand and sobbed like a child. Her neighbors heard her through the wall and briefly considered knocking on her door, and Anna sensed this—or, rather, suspected this would be the case—and brought herself to calm. She had a few hours to kill before night and sleep would put an end to this day that had begun in the midst of such hope on her part and ended with pain and sadness and—not to be overlooked—an endless half-second of intense fear. She had fallen through the floor. It was simpler to say it this way and this is what she had told the doctors. She had been in an old house and fallen through the floor. Though they had asked her about her partner and how safe she was at home—and Anna had been too dazed even to realize what they were asking—they had quickly enough come to accept an accident that, to them, seemed inherently Greek, given how many ruined houses there were in the countryside, and given how many young people had been driven back to their ancestral villages by the deprivations of the economic crisis. Anna had not told the doctors where the house was with the broken floor, and they assumed she had been brought to Athens from somewhere in the empty spaces spreading on the backside of Hymmetos. So, she had fallen ten feet through a floor. She had landed, more importantly, on a floor from ten feet up. Nothing like that had ever happened to her or to anyone she knew, and even as she leaned against the bathroom sink trying not to vomit as she forced down another painkiller, she lived again the half-second of her fall and sensed again the fear that had landed on top of her a second later.

The medication helped her sleep but she woke once with the shudder of a dream of falling and her breath came rapid for a long time after, and the primate spasm of snatching had sent a stab of pain through her ribs. Later, her dreams took on the figures from Saint John and she was vaguely aware that she was, in her dream, walking among beasts who burned with flames and that her escape from their flaming horns somehow depended on the opening of envelopes whose flaps her broken arms—both of them in the dream—could not undo. It was an awful night.

☙

On Saturday, while Anna spent the day in a waking dream of pain and medication, Irini went out into the neighborhood to do her errands. The heat was no longer as oppressive as it had been, even a week before, and she borrowed a sense of freedom from the coming weekend and the embarkation to Patmos. The trip was only one week away and she purchased her groceries with that in mind. Exactly the number of eggs she would require—seven—and exactly the weight of grapes she could consume—one kilo, for she found grapes refreshing—and exactly the weight of feta and the number of chicken thighs she could cook in red sauce in her tiny kitchen—300 grams and three, respectively. She would leave behind nothing that would spoil while she was gone. She purchased her week's supplies with the attention of someone measuring out the last of things—her last money, her last days—which, in a way, she was. All the reading of Revelation had cast a pall over her every action and she realized now, as she counted the eggs to put in her shopping basket, that she had confronted Anna on the night of the film with the anger of someone about to die. Again there was the truism of the thing and she could hear the priest's voice repeating, we are all dying, Irini. And what was she to do about it? She managed her purchases and her time so that she could have enough funds—including those she got from others—to live enough days. She had no financial debts, but she was compelled to move in lockstep with the money that, like breaths and beats of the heart, fueled her existence. If only she could command the end according to her wishes—her Orthodoxy was tailor-made to render suicide out of the question—and finish her entire life as she would finish out this week before Patmos, with nothing left and nothing spoiled.

Before her basket became too heavy—when she had bought only the grapes and cheese but not yet the eggs and chicken—she crossed one of the large boulevards and entered the garden founded by one of the old families of the city, a family Irini's grandparents had known socially, though they had been at the lowest edge of the super-rich of that era. She found a bench in the shade of a Seville orange tree and wished for an anachronism of the seasons that would scent this August day with the sweet fragrance of its blossoms. She had briefly worn a neroli perfume before settling on the darker aroma of Fracas. Her husband had had a good nose—she wondered what he would have tasted in Marcel's madeleine—and had preferred the orange to the tuberose, both of which he could discern. Her daughter had been born after Irini's switch and had only known her in the darker fragrance.

The idea of her daughter billowed up around her now like a dark fragrance of its own. Here was the exception that passed the bounds of Irini's tidy system. Here was debt. With her daughter, Irini could never muster that perfect accounting of resources and experience she achieved or planned for in the rest of her life. In the case of her daughter, there was much to account for, and with every day that brought Irini closer to Patmos, closer to Saint John and his beasts, the debt grew against the resources that could repay it. What would happen—this was not a rhetorical question—if Irini died without having settled this account? If there was indeed an afterlife, was there a separate room for the debtors of the kind Irini would then be? A debtor's prison from which one would be freed by a family member making sacrifices to collect the needed funds? Or would she be consigned to spend eternity in the kind of place like those sixth seals of Saint John, the ones that never seemed to lead to a seventh and final prize but always opened up to yet more stages in the process?

The whole thing, this apocalypse she often felt she was eagerly awaiting, took forever. As she had this thought—she was having a conversation with her God in just these words—she laughed out loud. Pigeons scattered and resettled in their grimy preens of fastidiousness. Was that not the point? To go on forever? Irini was not sure that this was what she wanted, after all. Wouldn't a better reward for true believers be one giant embrace of all one's loved ones like the final grand chord in Mozart, and then death, silence, and the end? It was a good thing she was able to go on this trip to Patmos, for this would be, it seemed to her, her chance to find the answers. She would light her candle—she had been able to save euros for them since Anna had been treating her at all their outings—and she would stand in the same cave where Saint John had seen his visions and written them down and she would ask her questions of her God. There was a chance that this time he would listen.

By early afternoon, Irini had returned to her apartment with her purchases complete, and Anna had begun to feel the pain in her arm as something she could provoke or silence. The cast did its work and, as long as she moved slowly and did not breathe too deeply, or laugh, or cry—her sobbing earlier had turned the pain of her cracked ribs into a strangely specific burning—she could exist in a state of calm. Except the spirit in her—for there it was—was restless with guilt and yearning, new guilt for what she must have done to fail so miserably as to fall, and yearning for that place or space beyond that she had been searching for before she plummeted. She had been reading from the Bible perhaps for too long, for she saw her life now as an allegory. And how could she not? She had broken into someone's home with the intention of a gift and she had fallen before she could complete her search for something deeper. Anna did not realize yet that neither the workings of the spirit nor its accounting followed such obvious patterns. It was the very nature of the spirit to be subtle. Anna would learn that soon enough, but that day as her pain receded and she thought the swelling at her temple had begun to disappear, she saw herself as a figure in a morality play whose outcome was still within her power, and she knew that one way or another she had to get herself to church and to Father Emmanouil tomorrow. She took the last of her painkillers—the doctors had been ruthless in their mission to avoid addiction—and curled beneath her summer blanket with great care and slept. She was still wearing the T-shirt from the night of the painting as she could not bring herself to raise her arms overhead and she lacked the strength in her one good arm to rend the T-shirt to remove it.

On Sunday as she made her way from Anafiotika to Plaka, her soiled and slept-in shirt as well as the cast on her arm and the bandage over her right temple—there was now a deep green bruise descending toward her cheek—elicited stares from people on the street. At least one woman dressed in black and on her way to a church in Monastiraki made a disapproving noise and crossed herself as Anna passed to ward off any trouble this beat-up young woman had endured or caused. As she neared Plaka, Anna was taken for, in order, an Albanian criminal, a junkie, and a refugee. At the corner of one street where the taxi rank at a hotel caused a small knot of cars, an older man asked from a considerate distance if she would like his help to cross, and when she smiled wanly, offered an elbow for her to take. He held an arm out to prevent the taxis from jostling into their path and the drivers heeded him because they were certain the old man was assisting his granddaughter.

Anna arrived at the church with the stubby nave with the relief of a pilgrim, and indeed her travel across this little part of Athens that morning was a far greater pilgrimage than what she was expected to undergo in just one week, in Patmos. Here was safety. Here was community. Here was the priest who had shepherded her into this whole new life in which she had undertaken a mission both spiritual and creative at Irini's family home. He would know what to do. The liturgy had already begun and so she slipped through the half-open door and let herself down gently into a pew at the back. Father Emmanouil looked out across the nearly empty seats and, seeing Anna with the cast and the bandage and her hair loose and unkempt, stopped completely in his psalm and then, because the divine demands of the liturgy compelled him to continue, he coughed as if his throat was dry, made an apologetic face to his congregants, and went on. Anna closed her eyes and listened, nearly falling asleep from the exhaustion of her injuries and her trek to church. She had seen Irini and Oumer and Tamrat in their usual seats, Irini's white bob and Oumer's close-cropped curls and Tamrat's locs, and she tried not to think of what they would say when they saw the state of her. She concentrated on the story she would have to tell—of her gift, her temptation, and her fall. If she could show them all the gift that she had made for Irini, they would understand.

As soon as Father Emmanouil finished the liturgy, he swept down the nave to Anna, arousing in his wake the other congregants who turned to see the girl in her bandage and her cast, her eyes slowly opening at the priest's exclamations.

"What happened to you, my girl?" he said, and began to lift her into his arms.

"Don't," she cried out. "My ribs."

"What happened?" he said. "Someone get a little water for her," he added, in the belief held by every resident of a country capable of tremendous heat that a little water could cure everything. There was a momentary confusion about where the water could come from and who would get it, but finally Oumer rushed to the vestry to fill a glass.

"Did you crash the bike?" Irini said.

Anna shook her head.

"Did someone do this to you?" the priest said, his tone lowered for the magnitude of the situation.

Oumer limped back with the water and held Anna's hand around the cup to help her drink.

"Don't tell me you tried parkour," he said, and she tried not to smile.

"I'm OK," Anna said. "I mean," she began to laugh but winced in pain, "obviously, I'm not, but it's OK." She drank the water. This was easy to do, and she had been drinking copiously with every dose of painkillers, as if what ailed her was a hangover from the birdcage bar and not a beaten body from a fall. "I'm better now. I'm just tired."

"But you haven't said what happened," Irini said.

"It's kind of a long story."

Because they were still in the church where it was their custom to listen to stories, they settled into the pews around her. Father Emmanouil took her good hand in both of his and he saw now for the first time the dabs of paint that stained her knuckles and, he noticed now, her shirt. He noticed too that she smelled of underarm sweat and metal and the plastic scent of acrylic paints—though he did not know that this was what it was. Anna began at the beginning, though her audience wanted only to know what had happened at the end and assumed the injuries had occurred at the tale's conclusion.

"You know your house," she said, stupidly, to Irini. "You know the big crack that goes kind of across the front."

"From the earthquake," Irini said.

"And you know I do street art." Anna made an apologetic face, still not certain how such activities were received by the general public. "So I thought I could do something nice for Irini since the house was so great and she loves it so much. Maybe I could even show people how it could be used as a gallery or something." She became excited at her own telling now and did not notice Father Emmanouil's frown or the stillness to Irini's look of attention. "So I painted a mural. I wanted to surprise you." She began to cry and fought to stop herself. "I can take you all to see it."

"But what happened?" Tamrat said, with a slight irritation at the girl's drama that was now threatening to eat into his plans to meet a friend for chess later that day.

"When I was done, I went back in to do some exploring. I know, Irini, it's your house and I shouldn't have without your permission but you told me all those stories—"

"You went in?" Irini said.

"I know. I'm sorry. I just wanted to see inside."

Irini jumped up from the pew.

"Irini, stay here," Father Emmanouil said.

"You heard the girl. She went inside."

"You know it's condemned, right?" Oumer said.

"What?"

Irini made an angry noise and pushed past Oumer out into the nave.

"It's condemned," he went on. "That's what the marks mean."

"You never said." Anna stared at Irini.

"Why should I have to? Did you not see the lock?"

"It's loose. I just walked in."

Irini was at the church door and then gone. Anna got up to follow her.

"Where are you going?" The priest made to grab her. "You can't go anywhere."

"I need to talk to her," Anna said. "I need to explain."

Anna was up and moving down the nave with as much speed as she could tolerate. Behind her she heard Tamrat say, "Just let her go if she wants to go."

Though her progress was limited by the need to keep her breaths shallow and the need to keep her casted arm from swinging, Anna saw Irini at the far end of the square and slowly gained on the woman as they passed through Plaka and headed toward the pedestrian boulevard by the new museum. Anna called after her to stop, but Irini would not even turn and Anna knew now that passersby were staring at her. Because Irini's name was the word for peace, they wondered at this battered young woman who seemed to be declaring or demanding peace from the battle she had clearly lost. No one thought the

white-haired woman striding purposefully several yards ahead
was in any way connected to the woman with the cast on one
arm. Anna kept Irini in her sight even as they crossed into a
neighborhood she did not know, though it was mere blocks
from the little square with the rooftop cinema. They were
behind the museum now, in a tight grid of streets that sloped
steeply away from the city's ancient hill. Anna was growing
lightheaded from the effort of the walk and only hoped the old
woman would soon run out of steam, for it seemed she was not
going *to* someplace but fleeing *from* the church and from Anna's
telling of her sorry tale.

And then just as suddenly as this pursuit had begun, it ended.
Anna followed Irini around a corner and saw her at the top step
of a low two-story house bracketed on each side by taller buildings of postwar concrete slab. Anna was closing the gap as the
house door opened but Irini made no move to go inside. The house's
stucco was blackened from decades of exhaust, but flowerpots on
either side of the door held bright red geraniums. Anna called to
her once more, and Irini turned toward her. So did a woman who
leaned out of the door and then said something to Irini in a tone
that was clearly angry. The woman appeared to be roughly the age
of Anna's mother and she dyed her hair in the deep auburn that
was a Greek woman's announcement that she had begun to gray
and was not going to accept it.

All the while, Anna had continued closer and she had reached
the point where she would normally have been included in the
conversation. Or, rather, the argument, for as she neared, she heard
Irini say loudly and with some agitation, "Haven't I respected your
wishes all this time? All these years?" Anna had never heard Irini
raise her voice like that. "You have to go there and do something
about it, Marianna. Please."

"Don't you ever tell me what to do. You gave up that right a long time ago."

Anna's mission changed from wanting to ask Irini's forgiveness to wanting to save her from this woman's ire.

"Are you OK?" she asked.

"This doesn't concern you," the auburn-haired woman said.

"You're kind of yelling at my friend."

"Your friend?" She turned to Irini. "Who's this one now?"

"I told you, Marianna. She got into the house. I'm only here to tell you you can't leave the lock like that. Someone is going to get hurt. Like Anna."

"Oh," Marianna said. "We wouldn't want any strangers to get hurt. God forbid we should hurt the strangers." She stepped back into the house and began to swing the door shut.

"You're the one with the key," Irini said. "Do you think I want to be here?"

The woman reappeared.

"You know what? That's right. I have the key because you fucked it up, didn't you? You fucked it all up."

"Hey," Anna cried. "Don't talk to her like that."

"Who're you?" The woman came toward her and Anna could not help but step back into the street. "Why don't you mind your own business."

"Marianna—" Irini said.

"She's my friend and she's old."

"Let me guess. Have you been taking your friend out for dinners and coffees? Have you been giving your friend museum tickets and books?" Marianna had seen the look that Anna could hide no better than the wincing from the aching arm. "Yeah," she went on. "I thought as much. Good job, Mamá."

"Marianna."

"Mamá?" Anna said.

"I'm her daughter." Marianna did not wait for this to sink in. "Where was I this time?" she went on. "Where was I, Mamá? Last time it was Germany, wasn't it? My husband and I were guest workers." She laughed, because she and her husband had been divorced since their son was eight and he was now in high school.

"This is your daughter?" Anna said.

The look that fell over Anna's face was one of such pure bereavement that it held Marianna and Irini and Anna too in a bubble, as though they had all three together suffered a great loss. Which in fact they had, though Marianna's loss had occurred on the day of the earthquake and Irini's had occurred in the days following and every day since. Anna's loss was new and stung with the sharpness of new wounds that carry pain and shock and even a degree of fascination.

When Irini broke the silence, she did so with a voice that barely rose above a whisper.

"Yes."

"And she doesn't live in Australia?"

"No."

"Did she ever live in Australia?"

"I wish, kid," Marianna said, her pity for the girl washed away by the returning wave of her undying resentment. "Maybe if everything had turned out differently, I'd be going on surfing holidays to Bondi Beach. But no, that's not how it works, is it, Irini?"

"I came here to tell you what you need to do. I'm leaving you alone now," Irini said.

"Oh no, you're not. Stay here and listen or I'll never lock that chain tight and if someone does die it'll be on you." This was an empty threat, however, for even if Marianna had not minded about the dire possibilities of litigation, she had no desire to endanger anyone as she herself had once been in harm's way. But Irini stayed, and Anna marveled at the daughter's power to command such obedience in the woman Anna knew—or thought she had known—to be so self-assured and independent.

The tale that Marianna told still sang with bitterness and hurt from the events of almost two decades ago. On the day of the earthquake, once the walls in her apartment had stopped trembling and the books had stopped spilling from the bookcases, she had seen on her phone that there had been unusual effects in Plaka, where at least one neoclassical mansion had suffered significant damage. She did not bother to look up the news reports that speculated on how this selective structural failure had come to pass, but rushed to Goura Street, finally seven months pregnant after many miscarriages and leaving her husband despite his pleas to her to simply call her mother on the phone. They lived then at the base of Kolonaki near the university where he was a law student, so it took her a quarter hour of fast trotting to arrive, and when she did, she found the street full of bystanders and the car alarms still wailing and the family home sending a cloud of plaster dust out of its shattered windows as if it had landed just then from a great height. Across the façade of the house a fine crack ran from lower right to upper left. She began calling for her mother, who she knew was home that day awaiting the arrival of three friends for their regular game of pinochle. Her father was at his office and she had not reached him when she called from her phone as she ran. She shouted again for her mother and for the three friends and asked if anyone had seen the four women who were in the house. No one had, and the shaking heads of all the bystanders sent Marianna into a panic for her mother, exacerbated by the thought that she herself would be a mother soon. She ran up the steps and before anyone realized what she was doing, she scrabbled with her key and unlocked the front door and rushed inside. Again, she shouted and there was no response save from the bystanders who now called to her to get out and come back and then a loud crack and a scream—her own scream too—and the crash of a vase falling from its shelf that had just toppled. She was in a sinking ship and its hull was groaning and shuddering around her, but she stepped farther in, still calling her mother's name. Then she heard her own name, in her mother's voice, calling her from outside.

"She wasn't in there," Marianna said. "She hadn't been there when it happened. She was safe." She said the word with loathing. "I had gone into the falling-down house to save my mother. And she was across Athens screwing the man she saw every Tuesday when she told my father she was playing cards." Marianna waited. "I could have died that day. I could have lost my son. So don't come here and tell me to be nice to my mother, and listen to me when I tell you to get out while you still can. She blew it all up, didn't you, Irini?"

Irini had no answer.

"There was no money to fix the place," Marianna went on, "but, hey, it's mine now. I should be glad she convinced the priest to take her in so I don't have to try to cover that."

"I wouldn't ask you to," Irini said, and this was true for it was her sense of responsibility for all the damage she had caused that had led Irini to the new priest four years ago with her tale of poverty. And she had only done this after the government had cut her widow's pension fully in half and she had not been able to pay the rent on her one-bedroom on another Plaka street.

"But how long ago was all that?" Anna said.

"Nineteen years," Irini said.

"Nineteen years! To hold a grudge?"

"You think that's what this is," Marianna said. Anna was not sure. Did she? "What my mother did that day is only part of it. I think you can imagine the rest."

Anna was not certain that she could. Nor could she imagine strained ties with her own mother for nineteen years—almost her entire life—and the thought made her breath snag. She did not know what to say. She was mindful of the pain that had come back for her after the first distracted flush of the argument. She tried to tell herself the true story but could only add up a list of Irini's lies. The daughter in Australia and the grandson too busy to write or call, and the husband dead and the Mozart and the cinema owner's affair and the travel to Paris and the Aznavour. Somehow, it was the memory of the singer's name with its unusual sounds and its blend of languages and cultures and the man's sad eyes in the film she had taken Irini to see that sparked the bonfire destroying all Anna's joy and pride in her friendship. She had been taken in. By an old woman. She had allowed herself to become entangled in this hor-rible pair of mother and daughter—the thought suddenly crossed her mind that Marianna's indignation, too, could be part of a long con—and she had fallen from a height of ten feet onto a hard floor—a thought which, for years afterward, made her newly and powerfully afraid every time she remembered it. She looked at Irini who stood with surprising composure at her daughter's door, and Marianna—was that even her real name? it seemed so suspiciously like Anna's own—who seethed even now with anger, and she took as deep a breath as she could, considering the cracks in her ribs.

"You two are truly fucked up, you know that?"

"Anna, wait," Irini said, as Anna walked away. Anna did not turn around—it would have hurt her ribs to do so—but shook her head slowly and kept on walking.

Her silent departure looked like toughness to both the women who watched her disappear around the corner. In fact, Anna's eyes welled up with tears—she had been crying often lately and should have taken this as the sign it was—and she did not really know where to go or what to do. So, while Marianna stepped back inside her house and Irini sat neatly on the steps hoping her daughter would reemerge, Anna found her way to the little church with the stubby nave. Father Emmanouil was not there, but she found him in the vestry.

"Dear girl," he said. "Here. Please sit." He pulled the chair out from his desk and sat her down before framed photographs of his sons and of Nefeli and a photo of men in gold-and-black soccer uniforms all standing in a goal.

"I am so sorry this has befallen you." His concern for her had made him formal. "What can I do to help you? Shall we pray together?"

"I'm not really in a praying mood. But I don't know what to do, Father E."

"You need to rest. You will still be able to come to Patmos, I'm sure. But you need to rest." She was shaking her head vigorously. She had remembered she was to share a room with Irini.

"Not that," she said. "I don't even know what to say."

"Go on, my child. I can hear your confession anytime."

She laughed and this surprised the priest, who knew from more than one of his teammates how painful it was to laugh with cracked ribs.

"It's Irini," she said, able finally to formulate only this simplest of statements.

"Is she all right?"

"She's lying." She looked him straight in the eyes with the mustered courage of a hero—and in fact she had only convinced herself to speak out of a sense of heroism for her truth. She expected him to be shocked but instead he seemed to be gathering himself quietly as if against attack.

"She's lying, Father E. Her daughter. I just saw her daughter. She lives around the corner practically and the whole thing about the house is one big lie. She was cheating on her husband. She's been lying to me about everything, and she's lied to you, too. To the church! She wouldn't need an apartment at all if she hadn't wrecked everything in her family."

"Sit down," the priest said, for Anna had pushed herself up and now leaned toward him across his desk.

"I'm fine," she said. "It doesn't hurt so much."

"I'm not talking about your arm. You need to listen to me."

She saw for the first time since she had come into the vestry that he appeared neither shocked nor upset at what she had to tell him.

"The thing is, Anna," he began, and then he caught himself and sat heavily in one of the chairs usually occupied by congregants and last used by the two widows when they came to explain why they were abandoning his church in favor of the one in Monastiraki. As he gathered himself to explain everything to Anna now, he considered that the widows had seen through to a deeper truth about his own vocation, though he wanted to believe that he was right and priestly in what he had done four years ago. He began to explain all this to Anna with the most bland and universal of universalities.

"Life is a nuanced thing, Anna. We like to speak in the church of good and evil as absolutes but in reality, my girl, they are nuanced and quite complicated. I ask you to keep this in mind when I tell you," and here he shrugged emphatically, "that what you have told me about Irini I already knew."

"You knew?"

"Yes."

"About the daughter and the money? About the affair?"

"I did."

"How?"

And because he was hopeful he could return from here to the larger ideas of good and evil, he answered with the facts of how he had come to hear the true story from the priest before him who had heard it from the priest before him and before him. The great gift of Irini's unusual devotion was that no one she knew attended church except at midnight mass on Easter or for weddings, funerals, and baptisms, and none of her friends had a connection to a priest or congregation who would have revealed to them—perhaps—the difference between what they knew about Irini's life in Plaka and what was known about her in the church.

But even Father Emmanouil didn't know that Irini's estrangement from her daughter had truly begun much earlier than the day of the earthquake and the daughter's discovery of the mother's lies. More than a decade before that, Marianna had brought home a young man to meet her mother, despite her suspicions that Irini would disdain this Germany-raised son of Greek guest workers. The young man was lower class, and in those years Irini was still the longtime resident and owner of a grand neoclassical home in Athens' ancient core. No amount of leaning on Irini's progressive tendencies—tendencies she declared with every art film she went to see at the rooftop cinema and every modern French novel she read in the original and every pretended embrace of the very jazz with which her husband was driving her mad—no amount of Marianna's reminders of her mother's supposed liberal heart could sway Irini into acceptance of the young man. Marianna left. For five weeks, she disappeared and left behind no details, and Irini had not even the young man's last name with which she could try to trace them. When Marianna returned to Goura Street more than a month after her departure, angry and ashamed, because the almost-elopement had soured under the strain of its forbidden nature, Irini had had a choice to make. She could have welcomed the girl home and asked the housekeeper from Hydra to cook up Marianna's favorite soup. She could have offered wise solace about the travails of the loving heart. Considering that she had just embarked on the affair she would sustain for the next eleven years, she could well have given Marianna advice on heartbreak. Instead, she uttered the words whose simple facts became daggers when repeated: I told you so.

Father Emmanouil knew none of this, but was aware only that Irini's daughter had discovered her affair the very instant she had gone looking for her mother in the destroyed Plaka home. Marianna's marriage to a caddish son of Plaka's high social class had quickly ended in divorce, and she had been living for many years just a few hundred yards away in Koukaki.

"No." Anna shook her head. "How could you just let her? How could you let *me* believe it was all true?"

He pursed his lips in the way Irini had with the lemonade whose sugar fell to the bottom of her glass.

"Irini is an old woman who has made at least one grave error in her life and who has suffered many losses."

"That doesn't make her special. Not here. Not for someone her age."

"No, it doesn't. But I would ask you to consider the benefit of correcting her wanderings from the truth—"

"They're not wanderings, Father. They're deliberate. She's fabricated a whole life and she and you—and Nefeli?" Anna asked this last with a new shame and sadness. "You both knew and you let her lie to me. And you lied to me too."

Father Emmanouil saw the girl beginning to lose her breath from the twin pains of the body and the soul and rushed for the little half-bath attached to the vestry and filled the plastic cup he kept there to hold a toothbrush for the moments when he snuck a cigarette. He handed it to her but she would not take it from him so he set it on the desk and returned to his folding chair.

"I can't believe this," Anna said when she had recovered her breathing. "If *you* can't be honest, then why should anybody else be?"

"What would you have done?" he said. "No, really, what would you have done? An old woman comes to you needing a place to live and says her daughter is in Australia and can't help. Do you tell the woman she's a liar because you know the daughter lives a few blocks away?"

"Yes. I don't see why that's so awful."

"My point is this. It is not up to us to judge these things like who will be considered worthy and who unworthy."

"It is exactly your job."

"Not mine, but God's."

"And lawyers and police and courts." Anna sprang from the chair. "This is ridiculous. You're saying actually nothing matters at all until we're dead and that's bullshit, pardon me, Father."

"That is not what I'm saying." He spread his arms wide in the ecclesiastical gesture she had seen him do at the altar when it indicated supplication. Now he meant to remind her of his priestly authority as well as to keep her in the little room.

"I am saying that what matters is to count the kindness. That is where grace comes from, my girl. From learning when to exercise judgment and when to be kind."

"Maybe I'm not kind, then."

"I think that you are hurt because Irini did lie to you."

"I'm hurt because *you* lied to me," she said, though the priest was right.

"And your arm is broken," he went on, "and your ribs, and this is very frightening indeed. I do not like to think of what could have happened to you in that fall, and I have prayed thanks to God that you have suffered only this. And this"—he smiled sadly—"is plenty."

He had indeed prayed copiously and crossed himself repeatedly since Anna had followed Irini from the church. He had called Nefeli to tell her he would not be coming home in the middle of the day for lunch or lovemaking because Anna had learned the true story of Irini. He had been waiting for her in the vestry since then. Anna took up the cup of water from his desk and turned it to see its decoration before taking a long drink. She made sure he saw her scoff at the pink heart-shaped frame around collaged photos of his older son as a toddler. The cup had been given to the priest and his wife by the sweet-shop owner who had prepared the pastel-colored Jordan almonds for the son's third name-day.

"But I would encourage you to be kind and I would encourage you to forgive an old woman her small errors."

"Her lies are much more than small errors."

"I would encourage you," he said again slowly, "to forgive her."

Anna understood that he had nothing more to say—that his faith returned to and rested on this essential notion and that, as with all elements of faith, there was no reasoning around them. She could try all day to make him see how wrong it was that Irini had lied and that he had let Irini do it, but he would never waver from this single fact of forgiveness. She set the cup down on his desk and turned it slowly on its base. She saw what the priest and her faith were calling upon her to do and she did not know whether she could manage it. All summer she had thought herself good and so generous for spending time and money with her new elderly friend. Now when she was asked to exercise the deepest kindness of an expansive church, she balked. She did not know whether this should make her ashamed or proud. She looked up at Father Emmanouil, Father E. as she had taken to calling him in deep affection, and squinted as if to discern the answer in his round face and round brown eyes. She had seen enough icons in her life and studied Byzantium in her art classes and knew the Fayum portraits with their eyes wide as if to the eternities of life and afterlife that only they could see. Father Emmanouil's eyes reminded her of all those ancient visages and she thought of how much she wanted to follow him where he would lead her.

"For you, Father," she said. "I'll try."

"Please, no, Anna. Not for me but for God."

On her way home to Anafiotika, Anna was exhausted enough to laugh at the recollection of the priest's parting words. Not for me but for God. In another life she would have chuckled with Irini over the accidental grandiosity of the line. Irini would have pointed out that this was precisely what made religion such a vexing thing—the way its sincerity came so very close to melodrama. Of course, what Anna did not realize was that in these very suppositions, she revealed how much her friendship with Irini had changed her. The old woman's cast of thought was already and would forever be a part of Anna's mind. Even as she reckoned with the dilemma of what to do now that she knew the truth, she performed the same bargaining that Irini did with her God. Even as, in later years, she rebuked what Irini had done, she could not escape the fastidious judgment of the old woman's thinking.

PART
FOUR

All over the city, people had returned from their summer holidays and were getting back to work and school with the determination of a new year. This migration included Anna's friends whose camping trip had ended and whose text messages began again to agitate her phone. Her friends had, if not forgotten her, lost track of her as the camping trip had progressed. She had become less and less relevant to the jokes and dramas of their days under the pine trees. With their return to the city, their usual friendships and connections came back into view and so they messaged her. *Tonite bar reunion? how R u?* Anna did not jump to accept, for her world had shifted so much beneath her that she felt her friends to be as irrelevant to her as she had become to them. What could she say to them in answer to their tales of sunburn and sex? That she had come face-to-face with moral questions and had endured a challenge to her very faith? Her life had become melodrama at the very least, perhaps tragedy, she told herself—not without self-pity—and theirs was bound to reveal itself as farce. She was at the point of rising into self-importance but replied in time to save herself from pomposity with a message in acronyms and emojis. She would meet at the birdcage bar at ten.

When she arrived at the bar, it was easy to explain the presence of a cast and the absence of the motorbike by telling the story someone had suggested when she had arrived last Sunday at the church. A motorbike crash. A car that had cut her off when she was driving down to the new cultural center on the large boulevard that passed the brewery now turned into a museum. Again, she burdened her tale with too much detail, but her parea did not notice for they were overtaken with alarm that their friend had had this accident while they had been having fun. Anna paid for nothing that night—and because she did not have the bike and was no longer taking painkillers, she drank each of the several beers that she was given as the night wore on. She let something slip once, as she raised the bottle to her lips and spotted the birdcage with its evening drape. She muttered darkly about free beers and cons, but then someone sang a phrase of *Chandelier* in Greek-accented falsetto and everyone laughed at the attempt and she remembered she was young and it was better after all not to be tied backward and forward like some Gulliver of time but to be living now, now, and again now, with every moment its own flash of light.

They stayed at the birdcage bar until well into the new day, though it was Wednesday and they would all be staggering to work in just a few more hours. They called for photos, to include Anna, Anna, their wounded warrior who had survived the city's time of heat, and they gathered with arms around one another's shoulders and Mel handed their phones one by one—she insisted in her drunkenness that it would not count unless each phone preserved the moment—to the indifferent waiter. Anna was herself too drunk to see Mel open Anna's phone to the photo she had taken of the mural at Goura Street and glance and swipe away. She would have hoped, had she known, that Mel would at least be arrested by the artwork that had cost Anna so much to make.

Her friends' days at the Ionian coast had made them strangely hungry for each other's company in their city haunts, as if they had been with different people while they had been away. They were hungry for Anna too, now that they were back, though by the Thursday of that first week Mel and Sophia wondered where Anna's willing participation had been all August. Now that she was solidly in the parea again, they resented the time when she had drifted out.

"What happened to that friend of yours?" Mel said that night as they left a cinema complex in the large mall outside the city center. They had seen a brand-new film, and there had been previews and advertisements, and Anna had laughed overmuch at the jokes to keep from thinking of the rooftop and the moon.

"What friend?" she said, though she knew Mel meant Irini and as Mel answered she tried to formulate her own reply.

"That old lady with the house."

"Did she die?" Sophia said darkly.

"No!" Anna exclaimed with the emotion of what she thought of simply as *before*—though it was merely five days ago—as if Irini were still her wonderful old friend whose death would be a shock and a great sorrow. "She's away," she said. "She's sick, actually." And then to meet Mel's and Sophia's looks of polite concern, she added a line that only she could value for the stab it was. "She's staying with her daughter."

She didn't care if Mel and Sophia remembered Anna's earlier tales of a daughter thousands of miles away and an old woman lonely and alone.

"Well, it's nice to have you back," Mel said. "Can you tag with your other hand?"

"Yes," she said, though she neither knew nor cared if this was true.

"Awesome. I've got another wall for you."

Mel possessed a string of ex-boyfriends, none of whom remained in the parea after Mel's dramatic breakups, and she claimed that it was nothing more than coincidence that each of these young men lived near a blank wall suitable for painting, where even an artistic mural would rile the parents.

Anna did not know it but her answer to Mel's question about Irini was not entirely incorrect. No, Irini was not sick, but she was staying, every day, on her daughter's front steps. She arrived in the afternoons when Marianna was home from her job at a health-food store and, tucking her skirt neatly around her and twisting to hold the sun off her face until it moved behind a building, remained there until the streetlights came on. This was Irini's version of the women who crawled on their padded knees up from Tinos harbor to the church of Mary. She had a penance to pay just as they did, and all her life, having watched these pilgrims on the ship to Siros with horrified fascination as they prepared for the next stop, she now understood their suffering as a kind of courtship. To crawl up a hill some seven hundred meters long to reach the church of Mary, to sit day by day at your daughter's front step in hope she would open the door, was to demonstrate persistent and unwavering love. Irini felt a fool for having chosen all these years to show her love through an obedience that suited her far better than her daughter. Her daughter had wanted her to stay away. And, for the most part, she had, with the exception of certain milestones she had been permitted to attend—her grandson's passage from elementary school to secondary education, particular important birthdays, his decoration with a special honor in the Scouts. It had been in many ways much easier to fashion her life entirely on her own.

The truth was that she would not have done anything differently. Her embrace of Marianna's punishment had turned to a resentment that, for several years, convinced Irini it was she herself who had been wronged. Even if Marianna had set her free, she would have refused her liberation. She would have said then that Marianna had made the situation worse by insisting on the estrangement. The fact that Marianna kept it up, even in the face of Irini's advancing age, revealed a cruelty in Marianna that far exceeded the harm of Irini's infidelity. Even when she added to her calculus the fear the daughter had felt at her narrow escape from the deadly house, Irini's equation had placed her on the side of right. So, it was only now, as she sat on the front step listening for the sounds of the latch lifting—sounds that never came—that Irini knew she had been wrong to give up on her daughter.

Marianna's son was on holiday with his father and so she watched her mother alone from inside the house, pinned there by the presence of the trim figure with her knees drawn up together and her hands shielding her eyes from the sun or, later in the day, in her lap. She could not be expected to undo decades of anger and hurt in one moment. She could not be expected to change the fundamental shape of her life—the divorce, the inheritance, the legal and economic millstone of the damaged house around her neck—because a young woman had trespassed on Marianna's property and been badly hurt. And yet each night she watched her mother just a few minutes more, in part to see if she was secretly breaking her strange martyrdom by resting on a pillow or receiving refreshments delivered by a nearby kiosk, and in part because she worried for her mother's health. Her father's death had come from nowhere. What if her mother perished right there on Marianna's steps from the stress of sitting every day on the cold masonry? Marianna did not share her countrymen's belief that all manner of internal illnesses came from sitting on cold stone. But she knew about stress and age and hearts. By Thursday she considered whether she could abide by her own rules and still bring her mother a cup of tea and perhaps a little stool.

There was more to Marianna's watch over her mother. She was impressed. She had always known her mother to be determined and demanding, and now she saw that these evenings on her doorstep were in fact an achievement of great strength. She almost felt that to interrupt her mother's vigil would be to rob her of a triumph. It was a measure of her own yielding to the steady pressure of her mother's penance that she could see it this way.

All week Anna had been ignoring text messages from the priest, whose messages read more like letters than texts, with proper punctuation and orthography and a mounting concern about Anna's participation in the Patmos trip. She had missed a discussion of Revelation and he needed to know whether to rearrange the accommodations. If necessary, he would bunk with Oumer and Tamrat and leave Nefeli to share with Irini. He did not add that this would be a great disappointment. He and Nefeli had been looking forward to the privacy of separation from their sons and to the romance of sea air. Patmos was, for Father Emmanouil, more than just a pilgrimage to the source of John's apocalyptic vision, if one could imagine holding both apocalypse and romance in the mind at once—and had not the priest's entire vocation come from the ability to do just that? By Thursday, he had become worried about the entire enterprise of the trip, for neither Anna nor Irini had attended an important briefing—as he liked to think of his meetings—and Oumer and Tamrat were visibly annoyed that they had rearranged their days in order to attend.

"Are we still doing this?" Tamrat said. "Because if not, I'm going to take a deadline for next week."

"Of course we are."

"These two"—by whom Tamrat meant Irini and Anna because he did not know about the lying—"can't skip meetings if we have to come."

Worried that Anna's absence would cascade into the withdrawal of the rest of the pilgrims from the trip, the priest dispatched Nefeli to secure assurances that Anna would travel with them to the island. Remind her about forgiveness, he told his wife.

Nefeli found Anna at the gallery where she was now well enough to return. In fact, she could have stayed away until early September and the gallery owner would have never known, as he was extending his holiday with a buying trip to Basel. Anna sat behind the desk checking Instagram for signs her mural had been caught and hash-tagged. Her work there and on the retaining wall had been noticed only by passersby who registered simply the presence of new paint and not the signs—or lack thereof—of artistic merit.

"My dear girl," Nefeli said, in the Greek habit of using possession as endearment. Father Emmanouil used this phrasing for Anna too, and she had liked the feeling of belonging that his words in particular conferred. Now, though, Anna sensed an agenda behind the appearance of Nefeli who had not been to the gallery before—her preferred art form was theater not paintings—and now looked about the nearly empty space with only passing interest. Anna remained behind the desk.

"Not much here, is there?" Nefeli said.

"Just these." Anna waved at the only art currently hanging on the wall: eight large canvases in blocks of color reminiscent of Rothko but without the hum of mystery. Nefeli was wearing leather sandals to go with a shift dress and T-shirt that made her look like something from the sixties. Her sandals clicked on the marble floor as she drifted from one canvas to the next.

"Come on, Nefeli," Anna said. "Why are you here?"

"I can't come see how you're doing with your arm?"

"Hello? My arm is over here and it's fine."

Nefeli came to Anna and saw the decorations her parea had made on her cast one night at the bar.

"Nice to have artist friends," she said. "What's this?" Nefeli peered over the mesh of the cast at a blotch of lettering.

"That's where one guy made the anarchist A and I tried to turn it into something else with my left hand."

"Don't need to be going around town looking like an anarchist with a broken arm. Or maybe you do."

"No." Anna shook her head. "Nefeli, what?"

"My girl," she began, lowering herself onto the corner of the desk. "Father wants to be sure you will be coming to Patmos with us."

Anna still found it strange that Nefeli called her husband Father in this way and wondered what she called him when they were alone. If there were rules, Anna did not know them.

"But mostly, Anna, he wants to remind you of forgiveness. You're not answering his texts and he wants to talk with you some more. He wants to pray with you."

What Nefeli did not know was that in the days when Father Emmanouil had been texting her, she had not answered him precisely because she was trying very hard to embrace the spirit of forgiveness. It was only by coming to it on her own that she could come to it at all. To return the priest's texts and to speak with him again about it would be to complete an assignment, to perform a task, little different from cataloging the few canvases that came and went into and out of the gallery. Anna believed that to reach forgiveness she would have to arrive at it almost by accident and not because somebody—even a priest—had told her to do it. Rather than explain all this to Nefeli, which would have amounted to the very thing she wished to avoid, she said merely, "I'm good."

"Which means what?"

"I'm sitting with it." She translated the English phrase she heard some of her friends in America use, though in Greek it did not convey the proper meaning. "And I'm going to do the right thing."

Nefeli waited for an explanation, but Anna offered none. She was not trying to be mysterious or unkind, but she was trying to preserve a mental space for herself, an autonomy. The spirit she craved was somewhere nearby and she felt a too-quick movement or too-loud voice would send it away. What she meant by the right thing was beginning to be clear to her—though Nefeli felt it was deliberately vague—as the forgiveness she knew could return everything to the way it had been before. Or, rather, to the way it had seemed, with Irini as her friend and Father Emmanouil as her conduit to the live current of faith and heritage that Anna so desired to seize hold of. For Nefeli's part, she was not clear but understood Anna would give her no more information. She said all right and gave Anna kisses on her cheeks and wished her swift healing for her arm and ribs. On her way home, she allowed herself to be irritated at the primacy the girl's feelings had taken in her household. Anna was just a lost girl who had come face-to-face with something difficult for the first time in her life—Nefeli did not know this to be true—and they did not all need to hang on the question of her faith as if she were a saint or martyr. Here she differed with her husband, for where he saw every person as a soul to be embraced in faith, she would have been content to leave some souls behind. She was beginning to feel it would have been all right to leave Anna and Irini both behind and take Oumer and Tamrat to Patmos and sit in the cafés with them and speak of all manner of things besides the Book of Revelation, which she happened to find shrill.

⁂

That same day, Irini was on her fourth afternoon at her daughter's doorstep and though she showed no signs of fatigue, Marianna had grown weary of her mother's stoicism. It impressed her, yes, but her admiration had more to do with the abstract idea of her mother's unwavering patience and less to do with the reality, day after day, of an old woman sitting for hours on the ground. The day before, when she had left for work and before Irini arrived to take up her post, she had laid a flat pad she used sometimes for yoga on the top step in place of the doormat with its coir bristles. Then Thursday, on her way out for the day, she added a cushion to the step. And when she came home from work, rather than circle the house to enter from the old service door as she had been doing since Sunday, she walked directly to the front where Irini sat, her head tipped back against the door and her eyes closed to the sun that was, in September, suddenly welcome rather than unwanted.

"Day four," Marianna said, and saw that though Irini's eyes remained closed, she was alert to her daughter's presence. "Please tell me this isn't some religious thing and you're not going for forty."

Irini tipped her head forward and took her daughter in. She saw in Marianna's face what could be best described as a simplicity of expression. In truth, it had been so long since she had seen Marianna before last Sunday—not since the appendicitis of the grandson two years ago and Marianna's dutiful call to inform her he was in hospital—that the face in its middle age surprised her. There was much in her daughter's face she did not, could not, recognize—two bold lines like an eleven between her brows, and the auburn color of the hair that had been dark brown before. There was also the absence of anger or anxiety or shame. The expression on her face was one of simple interest with no agenda or motive, save perhaps the slightest hint of an affection.

"I don't think I could last that long," Irini said.

They remained in their positions for long enough that a woman pushing her five-year-old son in a stroller saw them and halted, believing the street to be under the injunction of a filmmaker or photographer to pose for an unseen camera.

"Good thing, then, you won't have to."

Marianna reached a hand out to lift her mother from the top step of the house and Irini took it, being sure to place in it only some of her weight so as not to seem too weak.

"Are you going to say something?" Marianna said.

Irini breathed deeply.

"Marianna," she said, "I am sorry."

It didn't matter that neither woman knew exactly what Irini was sorry for—the rejection of the first young man, or the affair, or the lies, or the way she had enmeshed this latest young woman Anna in the drama of her life. In the strange way of reconciliations, the solution was so easy and so sudden that it made the estrangement and the strife seem either to have been trivial all along or to remain unresolved. How could, after all, an estrangement lasting over two decades be overcome in less than a minute? And yet it could and it could not. It had taken Irini and Marianna far longer than a minute to arrive at the thinking that brought them together now. And it had taken but an instant for the switch to flip, closed to open, off to on, once it was discovered that there was a switch to flip. Later, when the first flush of closeness had subsided between Irini and Marianna, they would argue about the causes of the affair and about the entrenchment of Marianna's rejection as they sat at Marianna's kitchen table. Marianna would try to make her mother see how much might have been different if the relationship with the son of the guest workers had been allowed to bloom. When Irini died two years later, Marianna's self-recriminations came back through the very door she thought that she had closed for good. But on that Thursday at the very beginning of September, Marianna and Irini were, to use Anna's word to Nefeli—and to use it with more sincerity than Anna had possessed—*good*.

*

Was Anna still good, by Thursday evening when Marianna brought Irini inside the house? Had she been good, when she had announced it to Nefeli in the gallery? She was not certain. She wanted very much to be settled in her mind. It seemed to her that the right thing to do—though *do* suggested action when the only steps she could take were internal—was to forgive. She should turn the other cheek, she should be tolerant and kind. How odd that in kindness she would be tolerating dishonesty. How odd that she would turn the other cheek to a blow of betrayal struck by none other than her priest. She left the gallery as the city was bathing in the golden light of the hours before sunset. She walked around what she thought of as the bottom edge of the Acropolis, along the pedestrian boulevard Irini had told her had once teemed with cars, and toward the open spaces of the Thisseio where those who had jobs were strolling together after work and those who didn't sat at cafés nursing single coffees and then single beers. The sun stretched the shadows and caught the highlights in the women's hair. She wanted very much to be a part of this. She was a part of it. She had her apartment and her job and her parea, and she was just about to arrive at that experience that proved to all exiles or wanderers that they had made a home: the repetition of a specific month. It was September now and that meant in only sixteen weeks she would arrive at the anniversary of her arrival, and her social media feeds would show her again the photos she had taken on that January day: the bleak landscape near the airport with a tagged billboard on tall posts above brown grass, the red-tiled roof across the street from her balcony, and a selfie she had taken somewhere in Plaka with the Parthenon and its Greek flag in the background. Moments from past time flung up at her in the present and, on the face of it, unchanged despite the passage of a year. So, she expected it to be in sixteen weeks. In truth, a great deal had changed and would change between this Thursday at golden hour and the fourth of January in the coming year, and it would be—was already—a different Anna who would look back on these photos from a different place.

But. She wanted to be part of this world where she had stayed almost a year, and to do that she would have to lower her standards. It came as a shock as this occurred to her. She sat down on a bollard near a vendor whose roasting corn made her hungry. Was she saying she had stricter morals, higher standards, than her priest? Did she really think she would be stooping if she followed his advice? If this was the instruction of her priest—to forgive—then surely it could not be wrong and she could be on the right side of her God if she obeyed it. She could be good.

She watched the corn vendor roll each of his cobs with long tongs so that new rows of kernels met the brazier's heat. He performed this task according to a rhythm learned years ago, turning the scorched kernels from the coals little by little so the cobs burned to an even char. Anna did not understand it this way, but she was looking for a task like that, delicate and precise, something to mark her devotion as the Catholics marked it with a rosary, to express her faith in the small, mundane acts of living. She pulled her phone from her jeans and found the thread of texts from Father Emmanouil. *What time is the boat on Saturday*, she wrote. His reply came within a minute—she had found him chopping onions by Nefeli's side in the kitchen. *Three in the afternoon*, he answered.

Having not prepared yet for the journey, Anna had laundry to do in the little washer that fit into the kitchen sink. She hung her underpants and T-shirts up without the help of her good hand on the line she strung across the balcony. She had to pack and, on the Friday, purchase toothpaste and shampoo. She stuffed her things into her backpack, brought into the hospital by the paramedics and emptied there of its cans of spray paint. The admitting staff had looked the other way and not summoned police to charge her with vandalism and trespass, for they felt, correctly, that her fall had been punishment enough. The information of the cans had never reached the treating staff who had then formed their own story of how she had come to fall through a floor. With that, Anna's risk of ever being charged vanished to zero, for she did not pick up a can for the remainder of her time in Athens.

On Friday evening, when she would catch her mother at her lunch break in the office where she worked as a paralegal and where the Wi-Fi was robust, she placed a Skype call to let her know she would be sailing for Patmos the next day. When her mother commented on the second boat ride in as many weeks, Anna was puzzled for an instant before recalling her fabrication of the boat trip in the Ionian with her parea. Her mother did not fully appreciate the magnitude of Patmos and its Cave of the Apocalypse—that was what it was called—but she mistook Anna's hesitation for deep emotion and so was happy for the opportunity she was about to have. Anna told her mother that she loved her and her mother said she loved her too. Call me if you need me, Anna said, because journeys always made her worry about the dangers she might leave behind. I'll be back a week from tomorrow and I'll be with the church so it will all be very tame. Not like the camping, her mother said, and Anna wondered was her mother testing her. She had worked hard to keep her casted arm out of the frame. Not like the camping, she repeated, and she laughed.

❦

The boat to Patmos left Piraeus and would follow the shore along the entire coast surrounding Athens before entering the eastern Aegean to head north. Irini had already observed, when Father Emmanouil first described the itinerary, that the island would be better served with ships running from Lavrio or Rafina on the eastern side of the city's sprawl. But this was not an option, and so the journey to the island of Patmos a few miles off the Turkish coast began with a drive west down the city's widest boulevard where cars reached highway speeds between the frequent traffic lights. Anna had made Father Emmanouil and Nefeli happy in making up her mind to come. Oumer was pleased at the thought that Anna might watch some of his parkour runs on the island. Tamrat mostly hoped that Anna would not prolong every theological discussion with her eager questions. The priest had told Anna that Irini was pleased at the news of her participation, but that she had news of her own—news he proceeded to tell Anna himself. She and her daughter had reconciled and he could credit Anna for bringing about the end of their estrangement. He described all this on the phone when he called his congregants one by one on Saturday morning to remind them of the departure time that afternoon, so he could not see the frown on Anna's face when he told her—or so it seemed to her—her accident had been worth the pain because it had brought happiness to other people's lives. Now as Anna's taxi passed the orderly olive groves of the new cultural center and turned to run along the sea—the Metro required two changes and would have taken too long—she tried to fight the feeling she had been replaced. She feared that after days spent wondering whether to fit into Father Emmanouil's moral vision, she might reach the harbor to find her berth had been filled by someone else. She tried not to be petulant in her thinking. She tried to let go of the growing sense that she had been losing all along at a game whose rules she had never really learned.

For a time, the taxi matched the speed of the seaside tram, and Anna watched its heavily graffitied cars pull slightly ahead and then fall slightly back. The tram line was not afforded the protections of the Metro, so its cars were fully and thoroughly covered with tags and murals. Inside the car nearest the taxi, a young Roma boy with an accordion strolled down the aisle playing a folk tune whose melody Anna could hear through the car's open windows. The boy's walk against the movement of the tram kept him in view for a few seconds as the taxi halted at a light, and then he and the tram went on, the boy still walking backward while the tram bore him ahead. Soon after, the taxi dropped Anna on the vast apron of the ship terminal. The asphalt was spongy from the sun, and Anna squinted through the heat mirages until she spotted Father Emmanouil in his cassock, a black triangle against the haze. He was the tallest of them—taller even than Oumer who stood beside Tamrat, along with Irini and Nefeli too, and the boys at some distance away. The others wore bright colors—stripes for Nefeli, blocks for the boys, and florals for both Irini and the men. They hardly seemed steeped in the dire warnings of Revelation. Anna alone had dressed in somber tones, in one of the black shirts she had set aside early in her sojourn in the city and that she wore now in deference to the seriousness of the Patmos mission.

Father Emmanouil saw her and raised his arm overhead and waved. The rest joined him and Anna had to answer with a wave of her own, though she did so slowly to protect her ribs. But she did not go toward them. They continued waving, and she heard Father Emmanouil call her name and move a step toward her. And then Irini's arm went down to her side because the old woman understood before Anna even understood it for herself: Anna would not go to Patmos. She could not. She hitched her backpack up onto her shoulder with care—it kept sliding off—and watched as even Father Emmanouil stood silent and immobile.

The ship horn boomed and Anna saw Irini check the time—a gesture that required two hands to hold her husband's overlarge watch in place. Anna wondered now was the watch the husband's or the lover's? The little group began to shuffle toward the queue waiting to embark. Nefeli turned around and held Anna in a gaze for a brief moment. Anna shook her head, though Nefeli could not see the signal. Anna could not go with them, for she could not do what the priest had asked. She had been asked to forgive a woman's life of falsehoods and she had failed. There was no pride in this, no honor. It was not Father and his church who were on the wrong side of good. It was Anna. If she had been a better person, she told herself now, she would have tolerated the failings of others. The ship's horn sounded again, twice this time, and Anna watched the group walk up the gangplank. She thought this was likely the last time she would see them, and she was right.

The group went to Patmos and sat silently in Saint John's cave, and they prayed at his church and in his monastery. They ventured once to the beach at Kambos where the cold of the water took their breaths away, and where they grew sheepish to be confronted with each other's bodies in so secular a fashion. They kept the lights on in their hostel rooms late into the evenings as they read and contemplated the ends of their particular days.

And Anna? By the time they returned from Patmos, she was gone. She never passed again through the little square with the rooftop cinema and never saw the three-wheeled motorbike with its miniature truck-bed loaded with Irini's suitcases and books and photographs in frames when she moved in with Marianna. She never went to Goura Street and never saw the house with its padlock chain pulled tight and new engineers' warning symbols spray-painted across the door. Sometimes as she plucked withered leaves from her father's tomato plants, she thought of her parea and the church with the stubby nave and the plastic cup with the heart-shaped photo of the priest's oldest boy from which she had once drunk thirstily. Sometimes she thought of the little congregation that had set sail for Patmos and for an understanding of the way things end. She imagined the Revelator's cave and its stalagmites and stalactites damp with the groundwater of the living rock, and she wept for all that she had lost.